# FALLING PREY

**M.C. NORRIS**

SEVERED PRESS
HOBART TASMANIA

# FALLING PREY

This book is dedicated to my fantastic fans!

You're all invited to connect with me on Facebook and Twitter @mcnorrisauthor.

For news, updates, "Impossible Blog" posts, and links to my other works of strange fiction, visit the online lair of M.C. Norris, at www.mcnorrisauthor.com

Deep Devotion (2014, Severed Press)

Krengel & the Krampusz (2014, Severed Press)

The Dread Owba Coo-Coo (2014, Severed Press)

God of the Dead (2015, Severed Press)


Sincere thanks for your ongoing support,

- Mike

# CHAPTER ONE

28-D

"Ladies and gentlemen, good morning. This is your captain speaking. Welcome aboard Trans World Airlines, flight 613. This will be a transcontinental flight with an estimated flight time of five hours and fifty-three minutes. Our time of arrival in sunny San Francisco will be approximately eleven-thirty a.m., Pacific Time. Looks like we've got a little fog hanging over Baltimore this morning, but the weather along our route is looking pretty clear. We'll be taking off shortly, following some non-routine procedures by federal authorities. We apologize for the short delay, but if you would kindly take your seats, and have your boarding passes in hand, we'll taxi out to the runway here in just a few minutes. Feel free to smoke 'em if you got 'em, and thank you for flying Trans World Air. Up, up and away, with TWA."

There they were, same as always. The cast of characters seldom changed on a jumbo jet loaded to capacity for a coast-to-coast flight. Row after row of swindled fortunes and piratical ambitions all marinating in a haze of tobacco smoke, body odor, stale booze, and plenty of that noxious, spiced cologne. Up front, it was always a big shootout between the biggest mouths. Egos were drawn from their holsters, waving in faces, ready to fire at anything that moved. White collar gangsters, they never failed to exhaust the quiet ones trying their hardest to remain invisible behind their newspapers, magazines, and sprung briefcase lids. All round them, the competition touted affiliations, referenced accolades, puffing up their chests so much that they were squashing the other sardines in their can. Funny, no matter how big of a fish each one fancied himself to be, whenever one of them glanced up to find Hart looming in the center aisle, they shrank right down to a little minnow.

It was his size, his swaggering gait, but most of all it was his scars. Hart's face had a shriveling effect on people. Since he wasn't born with them, he was aware of their intimidating effect, and he was also aware that if he felt like it, he could offset his startling appearance by making an extra effort to be friendly and approachable. Winks, smiles and nods … they were all steps to the old dance that he'd sometimes perform to reassure women and children that he wasn't going to eat them, but it wasn't a dance that he always chose to do, and he never performed it for other men. He saw no reason to make some sort of an obligatory apology for the way he looked. The truth was that he secretly enjoyed taking other guys down a notch, especially bawdy showboats like the jabbering heads on either side of the aisle. It pleased him to observe how much quieter the ambiance became with every row that he hushed into silence, as though he was a harrier of quietude that dropped the volume all around him with every step that he took along his life's violent path.

Hart liked quiet places, and he liked his scars. He liked scars in general. It was satisfying to stand before a mirror and admire his impressive collection. When folks stared, he had his own conception of what they were seeing, and it pleased him. Ever since he was a kid, his attention was always drawn to those healed injuries on the bodies of older men. Beneath every scar, he learned, was a darned good story waiting to be told. Whether they were funny, scary, or astonishing, those stories evidenced the better qualities of men. Each scar was a badge for taking a direct hit by life, and having the stones to stand back up again.

Guys like these didn't have any scars. Not the kind with good stories beneath them. Couple of paper cuts maybe, chunk of graphite from a pencil lead, but nothing like his. When one of these poofs stole a peek at his collection, they had to realize that Hart's life experience was something entirely beyond theirs, something they lacked the background to comprehend, or the guts to appreciate. One good look at his face silenced their bragging. Hart didn't have to brag. He wore his accolades, every damned one of them. He wore them all over his face, his neck, and across the knuckles of his sledgehammer hands. Plenty more were hidden beneath the layer of skintight denim.

The line came to a halt. Center aisle was clogged. Looked like a problem up ahead, where an older gentleman with a pipe clenched between yellowed teeth swapped seats with a ponytailed hippy in an apparent effort to quell some confrontation with a homecoming Marine. These days, that conflict was flaring up everywhere you turned. Hart didn't keep a dog in that fight. The war in Vietnam didn't really interest him. He guessed he'd have gone overseas without much of a fuss if they'd called him, but his age was just north of the cutoff. So, he'd just continued living his same life uninterrupted, cheating death from one side of the globe to another.

"Baby killer! Ain't sitting next to no damn baby k—"

Hart swaggered past the bellyaching protester, and glanced at his boarding pass. He'd already checked it twenty times, but he still needed the reassurance that nothing had changed. 28-F was his seat. He refused to sit anywhere else, so he always booked his special seat well in advance. It was familiar and comfortable. Nice window seat near the restroom, all the way at the back of the plane. That was where Hart liked it. Right up until he'd dropped out of school, and laid tracks of burning rubber down a new path in life, the back of the classroom was where he preferred to sit. The same went for subway cars, restaurants, and church, on those rare occasions when he'd attended a wedding or a funeral. At the back of a room, he could see everyone, but no one could see him glowering like a surly gargoyle with his eyes on the backs of all their heads.

A man with tanned skin and crinkled eyes lowered his copy of *Skin Diver* magazine. His eyes narrowed as he examined Hart with the measured interest of a physician. Fear and loathing Hart could handle, but scientific scrutiny made him feel a little uncomfortable. He didn't enjoy feeling like a freak of nature. The tanned man's murmuring wife gave a moment's pause, following her husband's gaze with a visage of pity. Hart didn't care for that sort of reaction, either. His skin began to crawl, and he sped up his pace. He was ready to disappear into the privacy of his favorite seat.

"So, she was the tenth caller, and we never win anything! Can you believe that?" A couple of sports fans wearing matching blaze-orange jerseys waved their tickets in the air. They grinned maniacally across the aisle at a man also wearing an Oriole's baseball cap, who just nodded and smiled. "Oak-town, here we come, baby! Game three, for the sweep." The man in the orange jersey kissed his wife, and squeezed her in close for a ferocious hug. "I told her, we ought'er pick up a couple of brooms when we get to Oakland, right sweetie? We ought'er take a couple of brooms into the Coliseum—for the sweep, you know? Get it?"

The sports fans didn't seem to notice Hart. They didn't even look up. Without breaking their conversation, or their embrace, they exchanged happy kisses as Hart lumbered by.

A teenager popped-up over the back of his seat. With an impish grin, he zinged a wad of paper at the head of another boy, three rows behind him, and then dropped back down into his hole like an ornery gopher. There were a bunch of kids on this flight. That was strange. All teens. Noisy, dramatic, ramped-up on caffeine, sugar, and who knew what else, they lurched over the backs of their seats to communicate with scattered friends throughout the plane with raised voices and exaggerated gestures. They shouted the same names over and over. Their faces were all aglow with excitement. Probably their first time on a plane. Some sort of a school trip, it looked like, but they didn't appear to be athletes. Maybe band members, debate team, or any one of those youth clubs that Hart had always been too intimidated to join. Hart never fit in. All his life, he'd never really had a friend. The truth was that people scared him. That was kind of his dirty, little secret.

"... she thinks I've got a meeting in San Francisco," an executive in the next row murmured, winking at the man seated next to him. "Truth is, she doesn't even bother to ask where I'm going anymore."

Every row provided a snapshot into another life, another world, a fleeting glimpse into the mind of another human being. Whenever he boarded a plane, those snippets passed like frames of film falling to the cutting room floor. His little game was to fill in the blanks, to imagine the rest of the story, and then, to wonder for hours on end if the imaginary lives that he backfilled were normal or not. He didn't know, having lived his whole life in a vacuum.

" ... spit it. You're not supposed to drink it."

" ... sitting at three-and-a-quarter, so I bought a hundred shares ..."

" ... procedures by authorities? Far out! Maybe the girls will get strip searched ..."

"... a maple sugar glaze, and Keith's sister always brings a ..."

" ... saw a couple of secret servicemen back there in the terminal ..."

" ... had no choice but to cut him loose, you know ..."

"... new agent is a godsend. I couldn't function without Brad ..."

" ... nine hijackings in the last year alone. What is wrong with..."

Hart passed the last block of rows ahead of the restrooms and galley, and he came to a halt at row twenty-eight. Uh-oh. There was about to be a big problem. He glowered down at the young mother and the boy, who'd not yet noticed him towering over them. She was leaned across an empty middle seat, wiping something brownish from the corners of the kid's mouth. Hart glanced down at his usual window seat assignment that was clearly printed on his boarding pass, and he scowled.

"He's in my seat," Hart said.

"Excuse me?" The young mother peered over her shoulder.

Hart flipped his boarding pass around, and held it level with the woman's face. "28-F. That's my seat. He's in it."

"Oh, I'm sorry. It's his first time ever on a plane," she stammered, smiling hopefully. "He really wanted to look out the window during takeoff. I told him he could have the window seat if no one else was sitting there, but it's no big deal. He can move. Honey?" The woman reached across the empty middle seat, and tapped the boy on his leg. A black crescent of stitches grinned from his kneecap.

Hart stared at the boy's healing wound, and something wound tightly at his core suddenly began to relax. "Never mind. It's cool," he said.

"Hmm?"

She was attractive in a natural sort of way. Dark sheaves of hair fell from a perfect part to frame her pixie face. As Hart found himself reflected on the surface of her innocent eyes, and detected no trace of fear in them, his stony exterior softened. "Don't worry about it." Hart stuffed his leather satchel into the overhead compartment.

"You sure?"

"If you don't mind me sitting in between you two."

"No, of course not."

The woman swiveled her knees toward the middle seat, allowing him access to the center. As she did so, her tweed skirt slid partway up her thigh. Hart pretended not to notice, but only a blind man would've missed it. His wallet chain clattered against the back of the chair ahead of him as he attempted to squeeze past her into his tight, new quarters. He hesitated. There was no way he was going to fit. It wasn't happening.

"How about I just hop over one," she said, "and you can sit right here in the aisle seat."

"Thank you." Hart collapsed into 28-D with a sigh. His right leg began to bounce almost immediately. People made him anxious, but flying was a true terror. Waiting for the take-off was pure torture, all smashed into a little nook with strangers. He stared across the woman at the young boy, who was probably around the age of nine. The kid hadn't yet bothered to glance up from his comic book, transfixed by the lurid panels of roaring dinosaurs that snatched screaming natives from tangles of jungle vines.

"What'cha reading?"

The boy gawped up at the sound of his gravelly voice. His eyes seemed to gradually clear, as the epic fantasy that had so recently enraptured his mind dissolved before an even stranger reality. He blinked, studying Hart's face with a stunned expression that Hart had encountered more than a few times.

"He asked what you're reading, honey."

The kid swallowed. He glanced down at his comic book, and then flipped the pages back to reveal the cover. There, a shirtless man with a dagger clenched between his teeth pried at the maw of some gigantic reptile with his bare hands.

"Tarzan, huh?"

The boy nodded.

"Any good?"

The boy shrugged.

"What happened to your knee?"

Frowning, the boy lifted the comic book to inspect his leg, as though he'd forgotten all about the injury. He extended his leg, studying the injury. "Crashed my bike," he said, clearing his throat.

"Yeah?"

The kid nodded vigorously.

"Did it hurt?"

The boy lowered his leg. "I jumped two whole trashcans, almost three."

"Playing Evel Knievel, weren't you?"

"Oh, God," his mother whispered.

The boy eyed her contemptuously, and then managed a wry grin.

"Did you see his last jump? Over all them Pepsi trucks?"

The boy nodded, grinning a little wider.

"Might not ever jump a bike again after that one. That's what all the doctors on the news keep saying."

"Bet he will," the kid said.

"Think?"

The boy nodded, extending his wounded leg again. He pressed the pad of his thumb against the stitches. The inflamed flesh flashed white, then slowly reignited again. "I know he will."

"What's your name?"

"Lonny."

"Hart Perkins."

"Well, shake his hand." The woman leaned back in her seat. "Say, pleased to meet you, Mr. Perkins."

"Pleased to meet you, Mr. Perkins."

"Once them stitches come out, you'll have a good scar, and a good story to go with it."

The boy looked up, squinting at Hart through one eye. "What happened to your face?"

"Lonny! That was rude."

"No. I asked him about his scar, so he asked me about mine. That's what you're supposed to do."

"Well, I don't think that it came out quite right."

Hart raised his right hand, and he stroked his fingertips down the path of destruction that rumpled the skin beneath his right eye to his crooked jawline. He liked the feel of it. Pebbly, yet softer than all of the other skin around it. Like a newborn baby's skin. "Got this from being dragged through Rome behind a sixty-five Triumph Bonneville." His fingertips slid up to a wide gash above his right eyebrow. It felt like a slot for inserting coins. "Switchblade got me here." Tracing the disjointed bridge of his nose, he dabbed at a cleft in his lip that swept upward to meet the flare of his nostril. "Handlebars of a Ducati Scrambler, and a little bit of sixty-eight Mustang."

Hart's fingertips crept over his battered face, exploring every ridge and valley. He browsed through the volumes of permanent records from a hard and violent life, as if each glyph encoded portents that he alone discerned. Hart could lose himself in his scars sometimes, just as one could become lost in an old photo album. Severed nerve endings left whole patches forever numbed. It was strange. He could feel the contours beneath his fingertips, but never their caress upon his deadened face. "But the worst one of all," Hart said, lowering his voice to a whisper, "the one that hurt the very most," he reached down to shuck up a pant leg, revealing a small crescent on his kneecap, "is the one I got trying to jump my bike over a bunch of trashcans when I was nine."

The kid stared. "Are you like—Evel Knievel?"

"Yeah. Something like that."

The plane lurched. There was that queasy feeling in the pit of Hart's stomach caused by motion felt, but not observed. They were moving. His leg began to bounce again.

"I'm a stuntman."

"Like, in movies?"

"And TV shows."

"Whoa." The kids face lit up. "Did you hear that, Mom? This guy's a movie stuntman."

"I heard. Wow. You can tell your dad that you met a real stuntman once we get to California. He'll probably think that's really neat-o."

Hart glanced down at the woman's lap, where her hands were casually folded. He hadn't noticed any rings on her fingers. There weren't any.

"I'm Heather."

Turning back to her, he took her offered fingers into his own. They were soft and warm. When their eyes reconnected, a current of funny energy buzzed right up from their hands, through his chest, and into his brain, switching things on like a bunch of Christmas lights out of season. It was an emotion that he'd never really learned quite how to process, because it made him feel out of control, and losing control made him feel anxious. Releasing her fingers, he gave a sullen nod.

Her smile fell, just a little. She cleared her throat. "Lonny's dad is something of a screenwriter, aspiring actor ... all sorts of those Hollywood kinds of things." She nodded, biting her lip, and shrugged. "To be honest, I'm not sure what he does, really. Lonny hasn't seen him in two years. That's why we're—"

"Ladies and Gentlemen, this is your captain speaking. We're next in line for take-off. Please fasten your seatbelts, and please remain seated until you've been notified that we've reached cruising altitude. Thank you, and enjoy your flight."

Lonny reared up on his knees to peer over the seat in front of him.

"Weren't you paying attention?" the woman said. "Sit down, and fasten your seatbelt."

"Those guys up there aren't sitting down," the kid grumbled, dropping back into his chair. His Tarzan comic slid down onto the floor as he groped for an elusive buckle.

The first beads of sweat welled up on Hart's brow. He was quick to wipe them away. Once a plane reached altitude, he was able to relax a little bit. It was getting up there that bothered him.

His height provided him with an unobstructed view over the tops of twenty-eight rows of oscillating heads crowned with variously styled hair. From this angle, they looked like a bunch of motorized androids programmed to swivel back and forth.

Invariably, some kid was bound to peer up over the back of his seat, and try to make a game of staring at him. Hart hated that. He hated being stared at when he was feeling anxious, out of control, and just trying to avoid the spotlight. Mean-mugging a staring kid by making a scary face was a temptation, but it almost always resulted in a backfire. It only increased their fascination with him, or worse, would prompt them to tattle.

Hart narrowed his eyes at a dark recess near the forward boarding hatch, where three, new men appeared. They turned, and began to walk single-file down the aisle. They had an official look about them. The first and the last wore matching suits, sunglasses, and black hats. The figure shuffling in between was less distinct. Slumped forward at the waist, he tottered side to side with every abbreviated step. As he swayed in and out of visibility, Hart noticed that he had a jacket draped over his clasped hands.

Hart's brow furrowed. His gaze flicked from the strange trio to the three, empty seats in the half-row across the aisle, and slightly behind him. Row twenty-nine was always kept empty, reserved for use by the stewardesses during times of turbulence. However, there was no question in Hart's mind where these goons were headed. They'd remained out of sight until just seconds before take-off, when there was no chance of turning the plane around.

"They said something earlier about non-routine procedures, and federal authorities," Heather muttered, rifling through her purse. "I've only flown one other time, and they didn't check our boarding passes once we'd gotten on the plane. Oh, my gosh. Here they are. I'm so glad I didn't throw them away."

"Hello." A stewardess materialized beside him, causing Hart to jump involuntarily. "Would you care for any refreshments?"

"Coors." Hart dropped the pad of his index finger to the armrest, as if there was an invisible button there that made cans of Coors appear.

The fixed, professional smile of the airline stewardess wavered, struggling to maintain perfect form as Hart revealed his imperfect face. He doubted that it would've much mattered what he ordered, or how politely he ordered it. She was the sort of person who was revolted by his appearance, and was unable to mask it.

Snapping out of her momentary shock, the phony smile was reactivated. "For you, ma'am?"

"Tab, thank you. Lonny?"

"What's a Coors?"

"He'll have a Tab, too."

"Two Tabs and a Coors, right away."

The turbines began to whine. Jet engines ramped up to a deafening roar. Forces gathered upon his chest, and began to press down. Skeins of Baltimore fog and ghostly airfield imagery rushed past Lonny's window. Hart gritted his teeth, scowling over the top of the seat at the wooden face with dark glasses that showed every intent to invade Hart's personal sanctum at the back of the plane. A white cord dangled against the side of the man's neck. It stretched from beneath his collar to his ear. Above the howling turbines, Hart could hear the ring of what sounded like chains against metal shackles.

"Unbelievable," he whispered.

They'd pulled a fast one. A real dirty trick. Kept them stowed in the cabin until the point of no return to avoid a big fuss from the passengers. U.S. Marshals, FBI, CIA, or worse, whoever these G-men were, their exact affiliation was of less concern to Hart than whatever atrocities the man in their custody might've committed that required him to be transported across the country on a commercial airliner.

Hart glanced over at Heather and Lonny. Both of their smiling faces were pressed to the small window, awing over the terrifying speeds at which ordinary scenery could rocket by. Hart's gaze fell to the dark crescent on the boy's knee, and he felt strangely ill. During take-off, the same injury that had intrigued him just minutes ago was now a stark reminder that human beings were fragile creatures. Flesh tore. Blood sprayed. Bodies at high speeds flew right to pieces.

Fear of injury and death was not an unfamiliar sensation. Hart embraced those purest of emotions on a pretty regular basis. Although stunts could sometimes go awry, there was always that illusion of control, because the inherent danger was carefully planned. Control was key. Fear could be just as manageable as a predetermined rate of speed, an angle of approach, the timing of a charge placed in a precise location. He supposed that his obsession to control utter chaos was what compelled him to become an emotional masochist, forever diddling with that entropy he feared. However, on a plane there was no control.

As the trio shuffled by, Hart kept his eyes locked forward. Assuming a sort of trance during take-offs and landings was one of his techniques. He would focus his eyes on the most distant part of the plane until the nauseating hot flashes passed over him. Dozens of heads swiveled around in their seats to stare at the newcomers while the feds secured their prisoner between them in the middle seat. Hart could hear them rustling around, but he didn't turn his head. He just closed his eyes. It felt like the whole planeload was staring back at him. Beads of sweat cut cold trails down Hart's ribcage. He just breathed in and out until a familiar numbing sensation displaced the nausea, leaving his skin chilled, and his lips tingling. The airsickness released its terrible hold, for the time being. Sometimes, it was just one wave of nausea, and other times it was two or three, depending on the severity of the turbulence. Alcohol, when available, really helped to take the edge off. Where was that Coors?

With a jolting bump, tires left pavement. The nose of the Boeing 707 lilted skyward, and they were off. The plane wavered in the new stream of air, climbing steadily, as landing gears groaned into retraction. He hated this part so much. Always felt like the slightest puff of air could tip a wing to some disastrous angle, swatting an airliner right out of the sky, and back down to earth like a hawk-struck pigeon.

Another hot flash swept over him, soaking his skin with perspiration. Don't get sick. Please don't get sick. Hart squeezed his eyes shut, trying not to dwell on the fact that he was no longer in control of a single thing in his world. He tried to ignore the rasp of chains through steel manacles, the snap of locks, the grumbling of federal goons an arm's reach back and to his left. Even when everything went smoothly, flying was a horrible experience. The added stress of the unusual situation behind him was about enough to send him over the edge.

"Mom, look how tiny everything is down there."

"Say, bye-bye, Baltimore."

"Bye, Baltimore."

Hart's eyes flicked open. Both of his hands were clamped like a couple of crocodiles onto the ends of the armrests. He forced himself to relax his grip, to lift one quavering arm to wipe what felt like about a pint of sweat off his face against his denim sleeve. He exhaled through pursed lips, and blinked his eyes.

"Sir?"

Hart cranked his head around in the direction of the female voice emanating from the galley. His hand was already cupped in a receptive gesture, ready to receive his cold beer. The flight attendant stepped forward, pointing her finger in the direction of someone further up the aisle.

"Sir, you need to take your seat," she said.

No beer.

While his head was turned in that direction, Hart stole a quick peek at the occupants of row twenty-nine. Flanked on either side by his handlers, the shackled man was slumped facedown over his knees. The position was not one he'd assumed by choice. The feds each held fistfuls of his collar. They were stiff-arming his head down into the well. Looked pretty uncomfortable. Hart could hear the man's labored breaths, the phlegm bubbling inside his lungs. Nylon straps were cinched around the back of the prisoner's shaved head, securing some strange device to his face. That's when Hart noticed the worst scar that he'd ever seen.

A deep channel haloed the captive's crown. Crimped at regular intervals with surgical staples, it looked like a hot zipper of red flesh hewn above his ears and eyebrows, encircling the circumference of his head. The wound burned an indignant shade of crimson, and it glistened with antiseptic ointment. It looked pretty fresh. The rude path of the incision gave the impression that the top of his head had hastily been removed, as one might pop the lid off a cookie jar, and had been stapled back into place.

"Sir. Please take your seat!"

Emitting a boar-like grunt, the shackled man reared back his head. Glowering over the seal of a rubber respirator mask, the whites of his feral eyes were stained red with blood. He lurched back, inadvertently hoisting the front of his shirt to reveal another incision hemmed into his belly. The man released a gurgling cry as his handlers grappled him, and forced his head back down between his knees. Jackknifed at the midsection, his back heaved with every strained breath, yet he managed to twist his head back to the side. Bloody eyes shimmering with a nameless emotion, he appeared to plead to Hart for something for which he was unable to ask. A thread of drool dropped from the chin of his mask, and whipped languidly over the tops of his slippers.

"Sir!" The stewardess marched out of the galley. "If you do not take your seat, I'm going to have to—"

Her sentence was cut short by a thunderous explosion, and some screams. Hatless, the nearest fed toppled over into the aisle. His body quivered with reflexive palsies. Gobbets of brain matter drizzled down the galley wall.

Four wolves arose from amidst the sheep, and they stepped out into the aisle. With the exception of the revolvers in their hands, the black bandanas covering the lower halves of their faces, they didn't appear to be dressed to any uniform congruity. Two, clothed in suits, blended seamlessly into the predominant business culture. A third wore a tee-shirt and jeans. The nearest, who'd fired the fatal shot, was the man wearing the Baltimore Orioles cap. Pistols leveled, they pressed their way down the center aisle toward the rear of the plane.

"We're here for the prisoner," Oriole shouted, aiming his revolver in the direction of row twenty-nine. "Hand him over, and no one else gets shot!"

A backpedaling stewardess tripped over the brainless corpse. She landed on her rump in a pool of gore. Smearing her hands on the hips of her skirt, she crab-walked back into the galley, whimpering with every breath. The surviving fed was humped protectively over his captive, keeping low behind the seats. A revolver was clenched in his hand.

"We're not playing games," Oriole shouted. "Let him go! Now!"

The plane was still gaining altitude. It was tilted at a precarious pitch. The hijackers clung to headrests, sliding their feet as they edged their way down the sloped aisle. Lights flickered along the roof of the fuselage, suggesting that something electrical might have sustained some damage. With a static pop, all the lights went out. A collective cry arose in the sudden gloom.

Hart glanced over his shoulder in response to a whisper. It was the federal agent. The man snatched off his dark glasses to reveal his wild eyes. He jabbed a finger in the vicinity of Hart's feet.

Shifting his knees to the right, Hart peered down into the shadows of his foot well. His eyes widened. There was a dropped revolver resting right beside his foot. Just inches away from the corpse's twitching fingers, it had somehow tumbled beneath the chair.

The fed emitted an insistent grunt, stabbing the air repeatedly with his index finger. There was no way. There was no way in hell that he could contort his oversized body into a position that would enable him to reach that weapon without the hijackers taking notice. They'd kill him if he went for the gun, no question. They were only about twelve rows away, and closing in fast. Hart slid his boot over the chunk of steel. Keeping his eyes locked on the four hijackers, he scooted the weapon beneath his foot until it was within Heather's reach. She was flattened behind the seats with her son. Once he was certain that her eyes were fixed on the suspicious movement of his foot, he lifted his boot, and gave her a quick glimpse of the hidden revolver. The rapid cadence of her breathing stopped. She'd seen it. She understood what he needed her to do.

"Put your hands in the air, and get up from behind the seat!" Oriole halted his advance, a few rows away. "I'm going to count to three, and then I'm going to put a few hot ones through those chairs!"

Trembling, Heather's hand descended.

"One ..."

Blood chugged up the sides of Hart's throat, pulsing wildly inside of his ears. His mouth went dry. He could feel the color draining from his face.

"Two ..."

Her fingers curled soundlessly around the weapon. Lifting it from the floor, she passed it right up to Hart in one smooth motion. Before he was ready to receive such a terrible thing, he felt the weight of cold steel drop right into the palm of his hand. It was his turn.

"You idiots have no idea what you're dealing with." The voice of the federal agent growled up from behind the seats, better resembling the warning sounds of a cornered animal than the words of a human being. "I don't know who you are, or who you're working for, but they're lying to you. This prisoner is a living, breathing—*weapon*."

Oriole popped his neck one way, and then the other. His fingers tightened around the grip of his revolver. "Just let him go."

"I'll kill him before I hand him over to you."

The plane bucked, canted, throwing the hijackers momentarily off-balance. They swiveled their heads, gawping around, as surprised as everyone else by the gaps of silence that interrupted the droning engines. Something was wrong. The grinding staccato of failing turbines gave way to the terrifying stillness of rushing air. An unmistakable stench permeated the gloomy fuselage. It was the reek of hot wires, melting plastic, overheated electrical components. Vibrations coursed through the fuselage, rattling unseen sheets of metal against their rivets. A flash of greenish light through the starboard windows wrought a collective scream.

The furthest hijacker broke rank. He began wrestling some duffle bags out of the overhead compartments. As each identical piece of luggage was freed of its trappings, it was tossed through the air. The other hijackers caught these bags, cinched straps around their shoulders, and snapped tactical clips to metal grommets on the hips of their belts.

"Have it your way," Oriole said, snatching a thrown duffle from the air. "They never specified whether or not we needed to bring him back alive—not when all they want is that junk sewed up inside of him."

Hart erupted from his seat. A piercing screech unlike any sound he'd ever produced erupted from his throat as he squeezed the trigger again, and again. Hijackers toppled and writhed before the snapping hammer, deafening concussions, flashes of burning cordite. A couple of them rose, and returned fire. Windows detonated, sucking paperwork and litter from the rows into a howling vortex. Screams filled an airplane that seemed devolved to a canopy of apes alerted to the predators in their midst. Hart's eyes widened as bullets ripped hot tunnels through his flesh.

Blinded by a spray of his own blood, he felt the revolver tumble from his hands. He was done, retired. His last and greatest stunt was complete.

Hart crumpled behind the seats, landing face-down on a Tarzan comic. He moaned in the roaring current of air. Pages of the comic flapped wetly against his cheek, painting his skin in the feast of blood slaked by hordes of illustrated dinosaurs.

Rending metal delivered the brightest light he'd ever known, peeling back the walls of reality, and scattering its remnants across the zenith. It was all air, out there. A vast openness received him, where flesh and metal enmeshed, where ruby droplets pelted blizzards of paperwork in a plummeting cloud of debris that dreamt it was once a plane, before being rudely awakened.

Flying, dying, beaming up at the infernal sun, Hart sailed through waves of profound gratitude known only to those souls with seconds to live. For the first time in his life, he felt at peace. Death was something beautiful to behold, even as the heavenly effervescence was eclipsed by a passing shadow. Hart blinked. A man came gliding by. Pumping his cuffed limbs through the wailing airstream, he cocked his malformed head to regard Hart through a blood drop eye. An infantile smile crept over Hart's face. Like a strange bird sprung from the trappings of its cage, the shackled man soared off through littered skies, delivered from peril into paradise.

# CHAPTER TWO

28-E

She plunged from one element into another. It was a jarring transition that struck with such terrible force that she felt no specific pain beyond one overwhelming jolt that left her hanging in a blue abyss, wondering how she could be looking at the bottom of her own foot. Agony came when she attempted to thrust herself toward the surface with a kick from pulverized legs, and didn't move.

A garbled scream spewed from her mouth in a torrent of shimmering spheres. Her nostrils burned with the saline fluid that surged down the back of her throat. Choking. Retching. Must go up. She scooped at the ocean with great heaves of her arms, grimacing at the sound of popping bones in the useless legs she dragged behind. Swallowing great gulps of seawater, she clawed at the suffocating layers that enveloped her, denying her the desperate reunion with her lost surface world.

She couldn't make it. Too far out of reach. Her shattered legs were deadly anchors. The yearning for air seared her chest, her skull, turning each sweep of her arms to a spastic flail. Done. Toxic gases egressed her lungs in an involuntary burst. It was with the starkest realization, not submission or acceptance, that Heather met her death screaming his name in the blue. *Lonny*. Bucking, seizing, her bowels released as her throat gaped wide to admit the awful torrent of brine.

### 

25-A

"Help me!"

A swell rolled beneath him. He kicked loose his remaining shoe, floundering hard in the gooey folds of his suit. With every kick, he felt his socks flapping awkwardly from the ends of his feet. It was decades since he'd last been swimming, down in a sexy Hampton grotto by the glow of Tiki torches, in the aftermath of a property management convention. He was a younger man, back then, in the days when swimming was something effortless, and relaxing. Not anymore. These days, swimming was terrifying.

He wailed, grabbing for his toes as a cramp jerked his calf into a knot. He went under, sputtering to the surface once again. With every passing second, it became more difficult to keep his face above water, and the shore was so far away. He wasn't going to make it. Waving an arm back and forth, he dipped beneath the waves once again. The others could see him. They were looking right at him, but they weren't swimming back. They weren't slowing down. He hailed to them frantically, crying out with a wordless bleat, but no one acknowledged him. They were younger, stronger, the way he used to be, and they were leaving him behind to die.

A breaker thundered over him, tumbling him beneath its oceanic might. This was it. He might not be coming back up from this one. Slipping his thumbs beneath his waistband, he wriggled out of his pants, kicking them to the wayside. Being naked from the waist down felt a little strange, but it helped. He could thresh the water more easily. The shirt and jacket would have to come off as well, after he stole another breath. A few frog kicks returned him to the surface, where he found himself entwined in a mass of kelp. It bogged him down like a heavy net.

Choking, sputtering, he began to panic before seizing an armload of the weird vines and bladders, and he was relieved to find them buoyant. Slurping a breath from the surface, he raked his arms wider until he'd amassed a small fortune in seaweed. He hugged it to his chest, and he found himself breathing more easily. God, his legs felt so weak, so atrophied from all those years behind a desk. He had no idea just how terribly out of shape he'd become. He winced as another cramp bit down into his pasty muscles. Once he was out of this mess, he decided, it was time to hit the treadmill. A couple of the partners had regular gym memberships. Whenever they talked about their morning workouts, he never had much of anything to contribute to the conversation, and it always felt a little awkward. Sometimes, he'd joke about the donuts he'd enjoyed for breakfast, or how much later he'd slept than them. It didn't seem so humorous now. This week, all of that was going to change. Once he'd regained his wind, he began to kick.

It wasn't easygoing to fight through the waves with a tenuous bundle of weeds in his arms, but at least he was sure that he wasn't going to drown. He grunted, spitting the vile salt from his lips, and kept kicking. Some vague boyhood memory settled upon him, in which he'd once clung to a colorful buoy, and kicked his way across a shallow swimming pool. How old would he have been? Five or six? This absurd recollection, and its utter irrelevance to the moment at hand, inspired a smile.

The seas folded over him. Two colliding plates of foam slammed across his midsection with bone-crushing force. Before he was fully aware that his own innards were ballooning from his mouth, he was rolling beneath the blue seas through a crimson cloud. Twirling in a gorgon's skirt of ensnarled kelp and intestines, he slapped his palms repeatedly against the smooth solidity of the massive head. The seas were whipped to foam, and his body was thrashed into a slurry.

### 

22-D

"Did you see that?"

Nate stopped swimming. He'd heard Dawn's question, but he couldn't formulate a response. Yeah, he'd seen it. He'd sure as hell seen something, but he couldn't make any sense out of what he'd just beheld.

"Was that a shark?"

If there was one thing of which he was certain, it was that the creature that had just breached the surface to snatch a human being out of the kelp was not a shark. It was jet black. Orca black. However, it lacked the telltale, dichromatic color patterns of a killer whale. He'd seen a flipper pretty clearly when it rolled. It was long and lancet as a scythe, and he'd also seen what appeared to be a second set of flippers ten meters behind the first. That was a big problem for him. Nothing in the ocean had two sets of parallel flippers. It had to have been more than one creature.

"It might've been a couple of pilot whales," he lied, trying to forget that he'd also seen an elongated set of crocodilian jaws owned by no living animal in the seven seas. Dawn was having the same problem, Nate intuited. She knew every species of marine life on the planet on a pretty intimate level, but she wasn't arguing with him. She was just quietly treading water, staring at the spot where the swimmer was taken down for a death roll. Nate guessed that it didn't make a whole heap of difference what the creature was when an immeasurably bigger question loomed that hadn't been voiced by either of them.

"We need to try and keep up with those kids," Dawn said, thrusting off into a sidestroke. "Don't want to get too far behind."

It was their location. That was the biggest problem. The water was warm, and sapphire blue. A kilometer to the east rose verdant hillocks of palm trees from what appeared to be a tropical coastline. It sure as hell wasn't Baltimore. The clues offered nothing but mind-bending, sickening impossibilities.

"Wait up," Nate said, tightening his elbow beneath the chin of his patient, and resuming his scissor kick. Those unfathomable depths beneath his jerking legs seemed to be suddenly watchful, and hungry. Being devoured by some Kraken of the deep didn't rank highly on his list of wishful thoughts, but the conundrum of their location weighed more heavily on his mind than the threat of predators.

The human mind was a fragile instrument. The invisible thread on which sanity dangled was never something perceived until the moment that it was threatened. Fundamentally insecure, the unconscious mind required a steady flow of reassurance that it was functioning properly. Minute to minute, it was constantly collecting evidence as a sort of quality control, evidence meant to ensure that its perception of the living world was accurate. Recognition of the ordinary, time's linearity, even the hues of the color pallet were all critical parameters in the reassurance of sanity. When all empirical evidence suggested their geographical location was a few degrees south of the Tropic of Cancer, the incongruity threatened to shake Nate's reality to its foundation.

"Those hijackers," Dawn said, spitting brine, frowning at the distant coastline, "they must have diverted the flight somewhere south."

"But we weren't in the air for five minutes." Nate heard a twinge of desperation in his voice, which had taken an almost accusatory tone, as if his wife had any fault in their situation. He watched her stricken expression become almost fearful as she searched the horizon for any sign of familiarity. But, there wasn't any.

"We were higher," Dawn said, her voice trembling.

"What?"

"We'd almost reached cruising altitude. We were above the clouds. I was looking out the window right before—everything happened." She shook her head, biting her bottom lip. "Nobody should've survived. Not at that altitude, but when our plane came apart, we were right above the water."

"I don't know."

No explanation could account for their whereabouts. Even the sun's position was wrong. It was early morning when they'd boarded the plane, but the baking equatorial sun was directly overhead. Whole hours had been lost. Thousands of missing miles. It sent the mind adrift, grasping for answers from tales of the Bermuda Triangle, where ships and planes allegedly winked right out of existence. The problem with that stretch of the imagination was that they weren't anywhere near the Bermuda Triangle.

"There was a flash. A flash of green light. Right about when all the power went out," Dawn said. "Did you see that?"

Nate shook his head.

"You didn't see that flash?"

"No."

The whole experience seemed so damned surreal. The memory was blurred by the rush of adrenaline and terror. His recollection of the penultimate moment was vivid, when those masked men rose up from their seats, and withdrew revolvers from inside their jackets. That was perhaps the most terrifying moment that Nate had ever experienced in his life. After that, everything kind of went fuzzy. Gunshots, screaming, rushing wind, the smell of burning plastic … it was all a blur.

"It was a bright flash of greenish light."

"I said I didn't see it."

"It came from outside the plane."

He shook his head.

"I think something happened, right at that moment."

Nate adjusted his grip around the neck of the federal agent. The man was slipping in and out of consciousness. He was groaning, murmuring unintelligible words. If his life could be saved, then there might be at least a shred of hope that some answers could be obtained. He was the key. No one else but the hijackers, and possibly this man, could provide some explanation as to what exactly that fight was all about up there. Nate recalled the agent saying something about the man in his custody, something strange. He'd referred to his prisoner as—*a living weapon*?

"It was a bright, blinding flash of greenish light, and then the plane came apart."

"Honey, I get it, alright. I don't know what you saw. All I know is that it's important we get this guy to shore, and maybe then we can start to get things sorted out."

It was not an easy swim. Even without the extra burden of an unconscious human being, it would have been pretty tough going. He could see that Dawn was straining, and she was one of the strongest swimmers he'd ever known, a true mermaid. When they lost the *Calypso's* engine in the Sea of Cortez, it was Dawn who'd made it to shore. It was she who'd returned an hour later, smiling over the gunwales of a squid fisherman's skiff when they'd hauled his puny carcass out of the drink. They never did get any footage of swimming with a whale shark that day, but they'd certainly gotten their fill of swimming.

"He's bleeding."

Dawn's words snapped his mind back to the situation at hand. Sure enough, crimson plumes billowed from the man's abdomen. Not good. If he'd taken a bullet to the gut, then his life was going to depend on receiving prompt medical attention. By the uncivilized appearance of the island, there would be no guarantees in that regard. There was no doubt in Nate's mind that they'd find some help eventually. No place on earth was uninhabited, untouched in some way by humankind. There was probably a fancy beach resort within a mile, but if they were approaching the wild side of an island, a nature preserve, then it could be a long while before their patient received treatment. Hard telling how much time the guy had left in him.

"I'm afraid he's going to draw in sharks."

Nate hissed through his teeth, as he gave an extra boost of power to a kick. Dawn's comment irritated him. She was right, of course. They'd just watched someone else get taken down. All of the blood and floating debris scattered throughout the area were going to excite the worst instincts in the local marine life, thereby creating a great potential for a feeding frenzy, but he didn't like where his wife's train of thought was headed. "Well, what the heck do you suggest that I do? Just let him drown?" Again, Nate caught himself sounding accusatory.

Dawn didn't reply. She just kept kicking, squinting up at the blazing sun.

Nate grunted with every snap of his legs. He was starting to have real trouble keeping up with her. His arm was going numb, hamstrings screaming, threatening to cramp. Dawn's strong legs kept rhythmically churning, rafting her smoothly over the swells, broadening the distance between them. She was the skin diver, the scientific celebrity whose acclaimed research was little more than just an excuse to stay wet. Nate wasn't a swimmer. He loved the ocean as much as Dawn, but he preferred to be floating atop it. He was more of her muse, just a pilot whose lot in life was forever returning his mermaid to her home in the sea.

He was losing her. Eyes rolling crazily, Nate grimaced in the direction of Dawn's shrinking form. Maybe it was just paranoia, but it almost felt as though she was distancing herself from him intentionally.

"Hey," he shouted, looking back over his shoulder.

Right there. Just like that. That's how Nate would always remember her. To know with dread certainty that this was his last glimpse of Dawn was of course an impossibility, but to rightly intuit the moment of her demise was a vision to haunt him to the end of his days. With her pretty face pinched in a sunny frown, tilted perfectly on the point of her chin, she vanished with the monster's breech and roll. Just like that, his mermaid was gone.

### 

21-A

Foliage slapped at his face. Thorns clawed at his chest and shoulders. The jungle was an unforgiving bitch. Estranged just three days, and already she'd flown into a jealous rage over where he'd been, where he thought he was going, and who was that other woman on the other side of the world? He should've known better than to believe that there would ever be a chance of escaping her warm, wet embrace. She owned him. Alonzo understood that now. He was supposed to die in the jungle. All of them were. Anyone who'd ever set foot in Vietnam were supposed to die in the place that owned all of their souls. None would ever love them quite like her. She'd forgive their little trespasses. See how her leaves lapped seductively against his cheeks, whispering secrets into his ears as he pushed deeper into her? It wasn't so bad. She knew the depths of his soul, those darkest recesses untouched by any human being. She recognized him without his rifle, all polished and pressed in his Dress Blues. She knew him for the animal that he was, and she spread her boughs wide to receive him, until he'd never dare to think of leaving her again.

"There he is, right up there!"

Alonzo knew all too well what was going to happen once they caught up with that hijacker. Murder left an unmistakable signature in the air. When men's worst notions purged together in collective hate, it took blood to bed it back down. Today, bloodletting was on the agenda. A killing could happen so easily sometimes. Ordinary people, left forever changed by an unplanned killing. He'd seen it. People who'd never given a thought to taking life sometimes did, and afterward, they'd be transformed into the same thin and ghostly thing that Alonzo had become. Just one sip from that goblet. One little sip. No one would see you in the jungle, secreted behind that curtain of foliage where the worst acts were always celebrated since time's beginning. No one saw what happened in the jungle, except perhaps whatever god smiled down on a killing with warm approval.

They had him now. Their fists began to pummel, reforming his face into an asymmetric shape. Dangling helplessly from his cordage, he was ensnarled in the same lines that had so recently saved his life, and now, they assured his demise. Poor little man in his parachute. They seized his kicking legs, and wrenched him like an oversized fruit from the garden bower. Silk ripped, branches snapped, and a hijacker crashed to the jungle floor. Red fists rose and fell. They were lifting him now. A loop of nylon whipped round his throat. His body rose, and straightened like a stick. The noose tightened. His Orioles cap fell to the leaf litter. Urine spattered in the leaves. The man's tongue, purple and questing, lapped the air for a last taste of the air deprived his lungs. Alonzo lingered at the edge of the lynch mob to watch the funny, horizontal hanging.

Death was interesting. Alonzo didn't mind looking at it. War simplified the whole process of death by stripping away all of those elaborate distractions and formalities meant to support a complex and meaningful illusion. Death is red. Death is wet. You go until you stop, and then you're done. Death is agony. Death brought an end to things like eating, and shitting. Once death stopped you, something else would take your seat at the table. The feast of flesh went on, and nothing mattered.

One time, Alonzo had seen a dog, and it was something extraordinary. It wasn't the first time he'd seen a dog. He'd seen plenty of those animals, of course. But the dog he'd seen on that occasion was no an ordinary animal. It was something special. It was a *teaching dog*.

Alonzo blinked as a fly landed on the corner of his eye. The insect wavered in the air, and eventually resettled on his lower lip. He licked it away. There were lots of flies on the hill where he'd seen the teaching dog. Billions of them. When enough flies got to buzzing all at once, it sounded like the engine to some nightmarish, invisible machine.

In 'Nam, success wasn't measured in terms of territory captured, because once an area was cleared, you just left it behind, knowing that the enemy was going to return in a matter of days. Instead, success was measured in terms of body count. Counting corpses was an obsession, and it helped to make sense of it all. It felt satisfying to organize the chaos by converting horror into a number, but that time there were too many bodies to count. He tried for hours, after all of the choppers pulled out, when the natural ambiance of the jungle returned, and it was finally safe to leave his hole, but he couldn't count them all. In the sanguine light of the setting sun, he'd paced the hilltop counting, recounting, stumbling through a blizzard of flies, and that's when he saw it. That's when it came to him.

It was just standing there, smacking and chewing in the red light. It weaved through the carnage on those thin, articulating legs, and nothing that it did mattered. It represented life, all life, rendered down to its putrid essence, propelled through a field of horror on a mindless mission to fill its mouth-hole with flesh, to squat and defecate, to lick its genitals. Nothing that it did mattered. Nothing matters. Fill the mouth-hole. Go until you stop, and you're over, and you rot in the grass, while a new thing takes your seat at the table, filling its mouth-holes, and on and on, forevermore. It was God's fault. Nothing mattered, because it was God who created teaching dogs, mouth-holes, and the flesh that filled them. That was the moment when Alonzo realized that God was insane.

"How do you like that? How does that feel? Is it too tight for you? Speak up. We can't hear you."

Alonzo watched the man strangle. He didn't care. His death didn't matter anymore than his life. Alonzo hadn't known anyone else on the plane, but he supposed that some of these angry people had. They'd lost friends and loved ones to this man, and they were enraged. Their lives had meant nothing to him, and now his life meant nothing to them. When the shadow of his parachute passed over them while they floundered in the sea, they all began to swim with renewed purpose, with the intent to catch and hold this man responsible for every drop of innocent blood in the ocean. Alonzo could see it in every flash of their feral eyes, their gritted teeth, as these once ordinary people pulled the cord around the hijacker's neck. He could see how eagerly they drank from the dark goblet, how eager they were to become hollowed out inside, just like him.

Alonzo's gaze landed upon an object sticking out of the hijacker's belt. The others were so preoccupied with their murder that no one had even noticed the revolver. Alonzo's reaction was automatic, and immediate. Before anyone could fathom what he was doing, he slipped through the mob, took the pistol, and jammed the barrel down into his throat. He'd seen enough death for one lifetime, and he was done. Someone else could have his seat at the table.

The taut body of the hijacker slackened, as his assassins all loosened their grips to turn and gawp at the new spectacle. It was almost funny. All of their eyes were on him. Even the hijacker, purple-faced and gasping, wore an expression of disbelief. He would be their teaching dog, and he'd show them the ultimate truth. He'd show them how nothing mattered, how things went until they stopped. Life was a big joke, and death was the punchline. Alonzo smiled, giggling around the barrel of the gun.

### 

28-D

Rising from the sand with a groan, he swiveled his head in the direction of the jungle, where he'd heard a single gunshot. He blinked his eyes. The hollow pop had resounded from the general vicinity of where he'd watched the hijacker's parachute float down. All around him, debris was washing up onto the beach. Seat cushions, soda cans, and worse were all rocking to the ocean's gentle rhythm. Voices emanated from all directions. There seemed to be lots of survivors. Cries for help keened over the tide's thunder hiss. Everyone needed something. The balance of the disaster was just beginning to sink in, and all that needed to be done was overwhelming.

A surge of foam rushed up around his ankles, enveloping his feet with an effervescent caress. The water was stained with blood. His blood. It was streaming down his forearm, dripping from his fingertips to bloom like rosebuds on the sand.

Lurching forward, he slogged from the sea like some Atlantean warrior, dazed and disoriented by the sights of the surface world. His left arm was completely numb. Blood oozed from his shoulder with every pulse of his heart. It looked really bad. His left leg was even worse. A clod of what looked like raw hamburger dangled from a ragged hole in the denim fabric. That certainly hadn't been there when he'd pulled on his jeans that morning.

He stopped to look himself over, running his good hand tenderly over every inch of his body. There were lots of places that hurt, particularly the two bullet holes. It struck him as oddly humorous that he actually caught himself feeling lucky to have survived the ordeal with only two bullet holes in his body, as if getting shot at all was anything for a person to feel lucky about. The upside was that he had himself a couple of brand new scars, and one hell of a story to go with them.

Hart glowered into the jungle, trying to recall every detail of the crazy event. Everything had happened so fast. He'd risen from behind his seat, screaming as he'd unloaded a revolver at a bunch of bad guys. It hardly seemed real. It seemed more like a snippet from some wild dream after a beer and chili binge. Hart might've even questioned his own memory, if it weren't for those two bullet holes. One, and two. Indisputable proof that he'd indeed stood up to a team of professional hijackers—resulting in a shootout that quite possibly brought down a commercial airliner, killing untold dozens of innocent people.

Hart began to breathe heavily. Impossibly, he was still alive and breathing, having cheated death yet again after being shot, and falling from the sky. However, what would that good fortune matter once the other survivors recognized him as being the one who'd fired the first shots? He hadn't meant to hurt anyone. He hadn't even wanted to touch that gun, but the federal agent had forced his hand. None of that was going to hold any water in a court of law, especially if the agent wasn't around to testify on his behalf. He'd be blamed for the whole catastrophe. They'd hang it on him. The instant that someone spotted him, they'd probably point, and begin to shout their accusations. An angry mob would form, and he'd be hounded to the ends of the earth like some loathsome monster.

Whimpering, Hart shuffled up the blanched strip of sand toward the emerald mountains that loomed beyond. The trees were funny looking. Palmed columns jutted skyward from a dense understory of ferns and vines. The trunks of the palms were all prickled with a yellowish bark, kind of like pineapple skin. He didn't know where in the hell he was.

Once he'd reached the safety of the tree line, he peered back in the direction of the sea. People were crawling from the water. Little cliques were forming, up and down the beach. The dead and wounded were being dragged ashore. Hart found himself thinking about the shackled man. He wasn't exactly sure why. Their lives had touched through stolen glimpses, and although the crossing of their paths had been fleeting, his brief connection to a man whose name he'd probably never know seemed oddly portentous. Hart wondered whether or not the guy had survived. Didn't seem likely. It was an awful thought to imagine plunging chained into the sea. Didn't really matter what crimes he might've committed. That was a particularly cruel way for a human being to die.

"Hey!"

Hart's ears pricked to the high pitch of the shout. He squinted into the brilliance of the sun-dappled sea. There was a boy out there. Clinging to a seat cushion, legs threshing the water, the kid was kicking over the waves like a grasshopper on the surface of a pond. When the boy hailed him with a waving arm, Hart felt his stomach drop. It was Lonny, the kid with the stitches on his knee. The last thing he wanted was to be recognized.

Hart peered from the relative safety of the trees like some oversized cryptid, as the kid paddled his way to shore. Once the boy reached a depth to which his feet could touch, he abandoned the cushion, and surged out of the surf with his skinny arms dangling limply at his sides. Behind his visage of exhaustion, the boy still sparkled with that naïve optimism common to kids of his age.

"Hi," the kid said, as he tramped up to Hart.

"Hi."

"Are you hurt?"

Hart nodded.

Breathing heavily, the kid turned back in the direction of the sea. Shielding his eyes with his hand, he scanned the horizon. Wreckage bobbed for miles upon the blue. Scattered castaways clung to scraps. "Have you seen my mom?"

Hart shook his head. "There's some people in the jungle."

"Want to go look?"

Hart turned back into the trees. "I heard a gunshot."

"Is it the bad guys?"

"I think." Hart frowned.

"You think somebody got killed?"

"Maybe."

The kid stared back into the jungle. He licked his lips. "Think maybe we ought to go see if everyone's okay?"

"I don't know." His left arm wouldn't move. He tried to curl his fingers, to make a fist, but only two of them obeyed. Something was wrong with it.

"I need to see if my mom is back there."

It was tempting to just tell the boy to go ahead, to run off and check it out on his own, thereby allowing Hart an opportunity to slip away into the trees and vanish from sight. He didn't exactly have a plan, other than to separate himself from the other survivors of the plane crash, and to go and find some medical attention on his own. He guessed that he could always use the old amnesia excuse. Did that ever actually work?

"Come on. Let's go."

Hart was feeling pretty conflicted. The kid knew him, knew what he'd done. He'd tell the others. However, the last thing Hart wanted was to endanger another life by sending Lonny alone into the jungle, into what might be a violent situation. "I can't."

"Does it hurt," the kid asked, wrinkling his nose as he stared at Hart's shoulder, "like, really bad?"

Hart nodded. "Yeah. You don't want none of this."

"I can help you, if you need help walking." The boy sidled close to Hart's right side. "Here. Lean on me, and I'll help you walk."

"Alright," Hart said, clearing his throat, eyes darting. He wasn't ready to face their judgment. He just wanted to hide. "They're back this-a-way." He pointed in the opposite direction from which he'd heard the gunshot. They could disappear together into the jungle for a little bit, Hart figured. It was the safest compromise. They could hide together until the circumstances changed, maybe presented some better options.

Lonny squeezed in close, wrapping a thin arm around Hart's back. After a moment, Hart placed his hand over the kid's shoulder. Together, they limped forward. He didn't really lean too much weight on the boy, afraid he'd squash him. He just allowed enough pressure beneath his palm to let the kid believe that he was helping.

Hart had no idea where they were going, except away from everyone else. Not easy to tell where people were though, or where they weren't. It was Hart's first time in a jungle. It confused the senses. It muted sounds. In any direction you turned your head, everything pretty much looked the same.

"Mom!"

The kid's sudden cry took Hart by surprise, prickling the hair on the back of his neck. "No-no-no. Shh." Hart patted the kid's mouth. "No shouting."

"Why?"

Hart didn't have a good reason why shouting was not allowed. He drew them to a stop. It occurred to him that taking a motherless child along with him as a refugee might actually have been a worse idea than sending the kid off alone. He'd inadvertently elected himself as the boy's guardian. What the hell did he know about parenting a child? If anything bad happened to the kid, then it was just going to be another strike against him in the eyes of the other castaways. "Well," Hart whispered, leering dramatically into the jungle, "we don't know what all is out there. I mean, there might be dangers around here, like lions and tigers."

"And bears?" the kid whispered, his eyes glimmering with excitement.

"Yeah," Hart whispered back, nodding his head, "and b—"

Both of them jolted when boughs of foliage parted, and a new face suddenly appeared. The man was wild-eyed, and speckled with gore. Lonny clung to Hart's waist, knotting fistfuls of his shirt between his fingers. Hart wrapped his arm protectively around the boy. The stranger smiled, looking suddenly relieved, as though he'd also been startled by their unexpected meeting. The man chuckled, smearing his palms over his mask of bloody grime, and over the glistening dome of his shaved head. Hart recognized the man's uniform from the plane. He hoped to God that the guy didn't also recognize him.

"You lost?" Lonny asked.

The man appeared equally confused and amused by the boy's question. He gave another soft chuckle, and shook his head. "No, but I don't have any idea where I am."

"Me neither," Hart said, shrugging his shoulders. "Truth is, I don't really remember much of anything. I remember boarding a plane this morning, and then the next thing I knew, I was crawling up out of the ocean onto a beach."

The man nodded, smiling broadly. "Isn't that weird? I feel the exact same way."

"We're trying to find my mom."

"Your mom?"

Lonny nodded.

"This your son?"

"No." Hart shook his head. "We just met."

The man appraised Hart's condition with narrowed eyes that swept him up and down. "You look hurt pretty bad, bro. I think you need a medic."

Hart cleared his throat, but he couldn't think of a smart reply.

"What's your mama look like?"

"Um, she's real pretty, with sort of longish, brown hair." Lonny pantomimed with flowing gestures of both hands. "She had on a white skirt, and a brown bead necklace."

The man snapped his fingers, and pointed at Lonny's chest. "You know what? I think I saw her."

"You did?"

"Yes, Sir."

"Where is she? Is she okay?"

"She seemed fine. Want me to take you to her?"

"Yes." Lonny beamed, releasing his arms from around Hart's waist.

"Brother, you need to just sit down and wait right there. Don't even move at all." The man took Lonny by the hand, and he backed into the vegetation. "I'm going to take this kid to his mom, and then I'll be right back with some help for you. You need to sit down, bro. You hear me? Don't move. You're losing a lot of blood."

Hart nodded, knowing that he wasn't going to be there when the man returned. The amnesia, and all ... a person in that condition would be disoriented, and probably prone to just wander off. Feeling empowered by this perfect opportunity to slip away into the jungle all alone, Hart thanked the man as he vanished with Lonny into the trees. Who else could you trust to escort a kid safely through the jungle, if you couldn't trust a U.S. Marine?

# CHAPTER THREE

22-D

"Come on, man, goddamn it! Hang on!"

Even as the fading sun slipped down into the sea, Nate kept up with the CPR. Blinded by tears, muscles howling, he pumped on the sternum of his unresponsive patient like a lifesaving robot gone haywire. Matted hair clung to his face. Spittle webbed his cracked lips. He would not quit. This man was going to live.

"He's gone."

Nate ignored the comments muttered by the group of teens who were sprawled in the sand. For hours, they'd taken shifts, but the kids had given up. They seemed content to loaf around watching him, and making their pessimistic assessments of the situation. What the hell did they know? They'd probably never lost anyone before. Not like him. They'd never lost anyone like Dawn.

"I'm telling you, man. The guy is gone."

Nate heard the kid. He felt the hand settle gently on his shoulder. Instead of lunging on him like a wild animal, beating him down into the sand, Nate opted to ignore the teen, and to just keep on pumping away at the federal agent's sternum. What these kids couldn't comprehend, and what he was loathe to explain to them, was that if this guy died, then Dawn had lost her life for nothing. He'd slowed her down on account of this man, whose bleeding carcass triggered the feeding instincts of the monster that took her. If he'd abandoned him to drown, as Dawn had subtly suggested, then this guy might've been the target of the attack. Odds were, Dawn would still be alive. She'd be sitting here in the sand right beside him, and this world around them would be an immeasurably better place. But, that's not what had happened. Nate had ignored her. He'd instead clung to this chunk of sea monster bait with the same stubborn tenacity as he still clung to the false hope that this federal agent might soon regain consciousness, and then explain what had happened up there, and where they were. That was the hardest bit to swallow. He'd put his wife in jeopardy in hopes of quelling his own anxieties, and she'd died as a result. In other words, his weakness had killed the strongest woman he'd ever known.

Every downward thrust to the man's sternum wrought eruptions of black bubbles from his bullet holes. Gore foamed from his flooded throat, and oozed from his reeking loops of exposed innards. He didn't want to admit it, but the teens were right. The guy was dead. Dead as a damned doornail.

Nate rose, kicked some sand at the corpse's face, and marched down to the water's edge. He wished that there was something solid around that he could slam his knuckles into. Nothing but sand and water, and so much of both. The ocean was such a vast grave for a little thing like her. Searching the twilit waters, he knew that she was out there somewhere, and that thought was maddening. The love of his life had been stolen by the same ocean she'd loved so much, and he couldn't do a damned thing about it. He cursed at the jealous sea, and then fell to his knees, weeping into his hands. She would forever be a part of it, disintegrated, and reintegrated into the rolling blue. The sand beneath him was Dawn's body. The surging tide was her blood.

### 

24-E

"Come on," Alex said. He knuckled Peanut's shoulder. "Let's give him some space for a little while."

"Guy's lost his mind." Peanut rose to his feet, brushing a curtain of sand from his rear end.

"Where are you two going?" Tara inquired, curling her lip in the cute way that she always did whenever asking a question.

Alex turned back toward Tara and Brett, and gestured up the beach with a bob of his head. "Away from him," he whispered, casting a furtive glance in the direction of the shuddering form whose tears continued to fall into the surf. "Come on. Let's leave him be." He and Peanut set off walking along the shore. After a moment, the other two leapt to their feet, and they came running up behind them.

Alex didn't know much of anything about the relationship between the two men, but he guessed that they were probably good friends, and that's why the guy was so upset. Maybe they were best friends. There was obviously some sort of a strong connection there. He didn't blame the guy for freaking out. If Peanut ever died … Alex didn't even want to consider such a horrible possibility. If anything ever happened to Peanut, he guessed he'd probably react the exact same way.

Best friends from Day One, when Peanut was still the little kid across the street. He was present in Alex's earliest memories, and in almost all of his best memories thereafter. Alex could still remember looking out the front windows of his home, back when he was still probably just a toddler. He'd press his nose against the glass, stare at that house across the street, and wonder where in the world that other kid could possibly be? He was accustomed to playing in the front yard with him on sunny days when their moms would get together, so when Alex observed that the other child wasn't always out there in the lawn where he'd left him, his whereabouts was the greatest mystery.

One rainy morning, Alex slipped out the front door, and went on a little recon mission to find his missing friend. He remembered hearing the screen door close behind him with a squeal and a bang as he made his way down the drive, and out into the street Somehow, he made it safely across without incident. He remembered searching the boy's yard, peering through the slats in their fence. At any minute, he expected to catch a glimpse of his little friend when all of a sudden, he heard his mama shout from the other side of the street. She looked really angry, and she was marching at him fast. Looked like a heap of trouble headed his way. You'd think that the memory of a spanking would lodge more deeply in a child's head than the unsolved mystery of where little friends go when they're not playing in their yards, but that was not to be the case. Even though he learned that all children eventually go back inside their houses, he never forgot what it was like to not know such a common thing. If he was ever punished for crossing the street, he did not remember.

Alex was the only kid in Southeast High who knew the true origin of Matthew's nickname. When he lied to an inquiring lunchroom full of kids that he'd earned the nickname "Peanut" because of his love of peanut butter, it inspired the adoption of more than a few other nicknames around the table. By the end of the lunch hour, Dan Minor became "Taco," Mitch McAlister became "Bacon," and Jeff Ruse became "Sardine," which was ironic, because Jeff's gym locker smelled just like a dead fish. However, the true story was that back in Cub Scouts, Alex dared his lifelong friend to stick a peanut up his nose, which resulted in a trip to the emergency room when the peanut got stuck, along with his new nickname.

"So, where do you guys think we are, anyway?" Brett asked, lagging a few paces behind them. "Wonder how long we're all going to be stuck here?"

As if Brett cared. It was probably Brett's dream come true to find himself stranded on a desert island with Tara Riley, but he was acting like it was some kind of an inconvenience for the sake of hearing himself speak. Alex and Peanut didn't need to speak. Not really. They had that psychic bond that best friends achieve after spending every minute of nearly every day together for almost seventeen years.

"Does it really matter?" Tara replied. "Like, odds are we're going to get rescued first thing in the morning, you know? We ought to be soaking up every minute of this beach while we still can, because once they rescue us, our whole trip is over."

"Why? You don't think they'd just put us on the next flight to San Fran?"

"Are you kidding?" Tara made a scoffing sound in the pit of her throat. "No way, Jose. This thing is a total bust. We're headed straight back to Baltimore."

"Man ..." Brett said, letting his feigned disappointment hang in the air for a few seconds. "I've been looking forward to San Francisco for a whole year."

What a load of crud. Brett had no interest in San Francisco or the Art Institute. He was the worst artist in the whole Junior class. His interest was Tara. That's it. She was the whole reason he'd started taking art classes in the first place. When Alex and Peanut learned that he was even going to tag along for the class trip to the Art Institute, taking his fakery to a new and mind-blowing level, it just about made them both want to puke.

Tara was the hottest girl in Southeast High's whole art program, maybe even the whole school, and although they'd never admit it, she was probably part of the reason why Alex and Peanut had developed their artistic talents. Since clear back in the fifth grade when she'd transferred from upstate, they'd spent many a late night discussing Tara's finer attributes. Peanut was particularly smitten. Sometimes it seemed as though Tara was all that the poor kid ever thought about. Peanut wasn't exactly a ladies' man, so all that he had to get him through puberty were his Tara Riley fantasies, along with half the other kids in Southeast High. If that girl had any idea … one had to wonder if any of the guys on this trip would have ever become art students if it weren't for her. Alex guessed that they were all a bunch of phonies. Funny, Tara might've been the only real artist among them.

"Full moon," Peanut said, hitching his chin at the silvery dome rising over the distant peaks of the mountains.

"Whoa, look how much bigger it looks than usual."

"That is so crazy!"

It was the biggest and brightest moon he'd ever seen. It was impossibly enormous. Every crater and shadow leapt into stunning detail, as though they weren't gazing upon it with their eyes alone, but through the lens of some powerful telescope.

"I've never seen anything so beautiful," Tara whispered.

"Me neither," Brett was quick to reply.

Alex rolled his eyes, and turned to face the group. "Alright, so where in the hell are we? The moon doesn't look anything like that in Baltimore."

"Auntie Em! Auntie Em! I don't think we're in Kansas anymore, Toto."

"Shut up," Peanut growled at Brett.

"Really and truly. Ideas, gang?"

"I don't know. All I know is that I just love this beach, and I wish that this moon could last forever."

"Me too."

Alex threw up his hands, and he began to walk again. He wasn't getting anywhere with them, and he couldn't take another second of Brett's swooning. Brett probably had just as much of a shot with Tara Riley as any of them, which wasn't much at all, but any attempt to match or surpass his level of adoration would be ridiculous. Alex knew that Peanut would follow him away from Brett and Tara, and of course he did.

"Okay, let's look at the facts, man," Peanut said.

"I'm listening."

"We were in a plane."

"We were definitely in a plane."

"We were in the air for what, like a couple minutes?"

"Maybe ten."

"Five to ten."

"Then all hell breaks loose!" Peanut produced gunshot sound effects, swinging his fingers through the air like a couple of smoking pistols. "Guys are getting shot and people are dying. Pow-pow-pow ... blahhhh. Then, all of a sudden, the lights go out."

"The lights flickered on and off, then w—"

"Then boom! There's a bright flash of green light!"

Alex snickered, as Peanut cowered in an exaggerated pantomime, shielding his face from some imaginary brilliance. Part of what he loved about Peanut was his limitless supply of energy. His theatrics made everyday life more interesting.

"Then, the plane came apart."

"Yeah, the plane came apart."

"And what do you know? Suddenly, we're in Bora Bora."

"Yes. Bora Bora. It seems so obvious to me, now that you mention it."

They walked together in silence. What more to the mystery were they overlooking? Dramatically recapped, but those were all of the important details. That was it.

"What about, like wormholes?"

"Huh?" Peanut wrinkled his nose.

"You know. What if we went through like a time warp or something?"

"Like, *Doctor Who*?"

"Not exactly, because we're not really in control of anything, you know? I'm thinking more like in *Star Trek*: *The City on the Edge of Forever*, except that we never actually get to meet the Guardian of Forever. We just passed right through his time warp all on our own."

"Well, there's a big problem with time warps, man," Peanut said.

"What's that?"

"They're impossible."

"Why?"

"It's the whole time travel paradox thing." Peanut halted in his tracks. "Just like in *The City on the Edge of Forever*, anytime you go back in time you're going to alter history in some way, to the point that you couldn't have ever existed to have been able to go back in time in the first place."

"That would make you the impossibility. Not time travel."

"No-no. If a paradox is possible, then time travel is not. Like, for example, say that they sent you back in time to kill your own grandpa."

"Why in the heck would I want to kill my own grandpa?" Alex snickered at the idea of going back in time to assassinate his favorite fishing buddy.

"I'm just saying, okay, that's the mission. If you succeed, then you never would've existed, and never therefore never could've been sent back in time. That, my friend, is a paradox, and when a paradox exists, the concept that created it cannot."

"But, you're overlooking one very important detail, my friend," Alex said, placing his hand on Peanut's shoulder.

"What's that?"

"Nobody in their right mind would ever kill their own grandpa, so time travel might still be possible."

"You don't even get what I'm saying, you lamebrain." Peanut shoved Alex, and Alex pushed him back. It was pretty great how even though they might've been dropped through a time warp, they were still managing to have the same fun together as always.

"Whoa! Guys-guys-guys!"

The boys turned in the direction of Brett's shout. He was still standing in the spot where they'd left the two of them. Awash in the moonlight, he stood rigid as a stick, his eyes bugging halfway out of his skull. In his shadow, Tara was crouched with her hands clasped over her mouth. She fawned to the heavens like some awestruck acolyte genuflecting before her creator"What are you freaking out about?" Peanut shouted.

All Brett could do was point. They'd never known that motor-mouth to be speechless. Poised like a weathercock with an accusatory finger aimed up at the eastern sky, he could only manage to say one word. "Two!"

###

28-D

Insects feasted around wet holes in his flesh, dabbing their abdomens in his wounds, depositing yellow clutches of eggs. He could see and feel this happening, but he hadn't the strength to shoo them away. It felt as though Mother Nature had made an executive decision to pronounce him dead, and his body had been condemned for decomposition. All of her little demolition specialists were marching through his infrastructure. Moving in even the smallest way had become almost impossible. Having crawled through the jungle on his hands and knees all afternoon, he'd finally collapsed, and while he rested, his shredded muscles had stiffened and swelled. Hart was finished. If he managed to live through the night, he guessed that the next morning would find him prone and bloated to an unfathomable state of agony, prepared like a living banquet for jungle vermin.

Hart closed his eyes, and just breathed the loamy bouquet of moist earth. Even in a strange forest, the soil itself remained a familiar and comforting smell. There was always some comfort in a certainty. Dirt was one of those certainties. It would always be down there to catch you when you fell, and it always smelled the same.

Sweat rolled down his brow. A murky droplet quavered from the end of his nose, but refused to fall. The better part of him felt ready to die, but some stubborn and nagging instinct insisted that if he didn't try to get back up now, then he would never rise again. Gritting his teeth, he tried to prop himself up on one elbow, but the pain was unbearable. Despite the fact that Hart was still alive, the qualities that he was exhibiting were rapidly shifting toward a set of attributes more closely associated with the dead. For years, he'd cheated death in every game they'd ever played, but at last, it looked like the dark angel had come to collect its due.

He'd screwed up. He shouldn't have slunk off into the jungle alone, hoping to hide from the other survivors. Whether or not he'd made the right decision in standing up to those hijackers, he should've at least faced the music for his actions. It would've been better to die with a clean conscience. That was the most unfortunate aspect of the situation. Neither God nor man ever had anything against him until the moment he'd squeezed that trigger, and that last act would be the one to ferry him into the hereafter in a tormented state of mind. As a result of one bad decision, he was sentenced to die alone, to be eaten alive by the lowliest forms of life. He could hear the bugs clicking. Shuffling wing covers, cleaning blood from their antennae, they stepped robotically over his skin. Things squirmed beneath him in the leaf litter. Things walked over him. He could feel their prickly legs, their chirring mouthparts in his wounds.

He thought about his mother's struggle in her final months, when she'd withered away in her hospital bed. Hart wondered if the cancer that had slowly chewed away her insides felt anything like the bugs that were chewing on him now. She'd been gone a long time, but it didn't seem so long. It was through pain, horror, the rawest forms of shared experience, that Hart had managed to remain connected to her in his own way. Despite all of the crashes, burns, and surgeries that he'd endured, his mother still seemed to have been the stronger one. She'd never once complained, not once during all of those treatments, not once during his formative years when it was just the two of them scraping out a living. The man who'd fathered him had only reached out to him once in his life. That was a few days after his ninth birthday, when Hart received an envelope in the mail with his name on it. Inside was a little bit of cash to put toward the purchase of a blood-red Cleveland Roadmaster.

Hart would never forget that bike. He smiled in the darkness, as a large insect crept its way up his cheek. From the moment that his sneakers had settled onto those pedals, Hart personified a missing bond with an absent father to a lifelong passion for vehicles, and to the controllable pain that came with them.

Hart blinked his eyes. It was difficult to discern what he was seeing up there in the sky through all of the vegetation in the upper canopy, but it almost looked like he was seeing double. Was that a symptom of dying? He squinted an eye closed, but the strange effect did not disappear. He saw two moons floating up there in the heavens, like a couple of bullet holes in the sky. It was becoming difficult to concentrate.

Hart spat as the insect crawled over his lips, trying to focus on the sounds of the jungle. There was that repetitive noise again. Right there. He'd been hearing the same sound ever since he regained consciousness. It was almost like a tapping, a soft pattering in the leaves, always emanating from the same spot.

Had to get up. An attempt to roll onto his side delivered an electrifying bolt of pain. It felt as though the blade of a sword was being reamed straight up through the marrow of his femur, all the way into his spine. Hart arched his back, trembling in agony, but he refused to impart a sound. Whenever he was hurt, there was always a small part of him that always wanted to cry out. As always, Hart denied his inner-child permission to succumb to that impulse. Never again. Not since the afternoon that a nine-year-old version of himself had writhed bawling in the dirt beside the twisted wreckage of his brand-new, Cleveland Roadmaster.

"I'm over here," he whispered. "Just come and get me."

So many signs of life that weren't noticeable while he was dragging himself through the underbrush were evident now. All around him, there was movement. Things crashed through the underbrush. Leaves scraped and slapped against the skin of passing bodies. The wings of unseen creatures hummed through the night air. Hart narrowed his eyes at the spot where he could still hear a rhythmic tapping. He was surprised to see that could see them, dried leaves, hopping all about on the jungle floor as falling droplets struck them.

Hart's gaze tracked upward, following the vertical trajectory from that patch of dancing litter through glistening threads that stretched, snapped and fell. Higher, through ropes of falling mucous, his gaze climbed into the forest canopy to settle upon a fringed tussock of a head large enough to eclipse one of the moons. It was monstrous, worshipped by swarms of flying pests in such numbers as to make the jungle drone. With a toss of its massive, feathered crown, the horror took a tentative plod forward, parting the trees like weeds before its breast.

Hart heard his breath escape with an audible pop, as the monster opened its throat, and flattened the jungle with an earsplitting blast. With every decibel of an air raid siren, the ascending howl shook the forest to the tips of its roots before terminating in a series of glottal croaks. At last, his Dark Angel had arrived.

###

## 24-D

"What in the hell—*was that*?" Margot said. She stopped picking at her nails by the light of the campfire, and shot a fierce glance down the beach, in the direction of the jungle. Behind her, Sandy's fingers stopped braiding her hair.

"Sounded like a wolf," said Donovan, after a few intense seconds.

"A wolf?" Dale lifted his head from the sand, where he'd been blowing gently on the coals. He looked across the bed of embers that he'd somehow coaxed back to life to sneer at the hawkish man in the tattered suit. "Don-boy. I know you're kind of a city dandy, but you know that wasn't no wolf."

"Oh, so now you're a wolf expert, too. That's great. That's really good. We needed a damned wolf expert out here."

"It might've been a train," Sandy said, still clinging to an unfinished braid of Margot's hair.

"Yeah, it was a train, Sandy. Trainload of fucking wolves."

"Maybe the circus is in town?" Dale grinned, winking across the fire at Donovan.

"That's right. It's probably the circus train. I got your ticket right here. Come over and grab it, you hillbilly. Send your ass back to Boonville where you belong."

Dale threw back his head and laughed like a demon. Obviously, he enjoyed every opportunity to bump a slicker like Donovan off-balance. He seemed to enjoy prodding him more than he seemed to be worrying about whatever animal had produced such an awful howl, if Dale ever worried about anything at all.

Dr. Kimura folded his hands in his lap. He inhaled deeply through his nose, and released the air in a tortured sigh. Although the incessant banter was occasionally entertaining, the constant background noise made it difficult to think. He ordinarily worked alone, so he'd become accustomed to long hours of silence, and he hadn't enjoyed a moment of that since he'd stepped into the airport earlier that morning. Ever since he, Margot and Sandy had crossed paths with these two men, Dale and Donovan had been polluting his ears with their constant ribbing, wearing him down into a state of cognitive exhaustion. Half-a-day without water, and those two men could still think of no better activity to occupy their minds than taking shots at one another. The constant dogging might've had something to do with Margot, he supposed. Although Dr. Kimura understood why they probably found the young, European model attractive, it only took but thirty-minutes to realize that she was just a pretty face, and not much more. She hadn't lifted a finger all day except to pick at her nail beds, or to fiddle with the ends of her blonde hair.

Donovan was the instigator. Once he learned that the only reaction he could provoke from Margot were rolls of her eyes, he grew bored with her, and began casting lazily concealed slurs in Dr. Kimura's direction. The doctor refused to acknowledge Donovan's bait, as he held himself to a higher standard than to react to low-brow provocation. Sandy proved to be even less fun to annoy. She was kindhearted, genuine, and sweet, everything that Donovan was not, and she'd been so distraught over her missing husband that teasing her seemed monstrous. Donovan was an underdeveloped brat who needed undivided attention, but he wasn't a monster.

In the end, it was Dale, the farm boy from the backwaters of southeastern Arkansas, who stepped up to serve as the shifty stock broker's sparring partner. Dale took the abuse in stride. He actually seemed to enjoy it, and he was always more than happy to dish it right back into Donovan's face. If Dale had one iota of pride, he'd long forgotten where he'd buried it. His lifelong dream to waste a whole week gambling in Las Vegas was already ruined before their plane fell to pieces, because he'd inexplicably managed to book the wrong flight out of Memphis, sending him off to what was nearly the furthest point from Las Vegas that the United States had to offer. He'd spent most of his life savings redirecting his connecting flights westward from Baltimore, only to end up here—wherever *here* was.

"Hey, Donovan." Dale propped himself up on an elbow, and smiled wryly across the fire. "Don-boy. Hey, I got a serious question for you, man. For real."

"I haven't heard nothing intelligent come out of your mouth all day. Why start now?"

"Check this out. If I laid my nuts across your nose, then would my pecker be on your mind?"

"Oh, God," Margot groaned, rolling her eyes.

Donovan tried to stay tough, but he couldn't maintain the charade. A smile cracked his lips. He began to chuckle, pinching at his nose. "That's good. I like that. I'm going to have to remember that one, you bucktoothed hillbilly. Nuts on my nose and everything. Where does he get this stuff?"

Sandy's eyes widened, but she said nothing. Just kept braiding the princess's hair, as if Margot was the perfect Barbie doll that she'd never owned. Dr. Kimura frowned. He felt embarrassed for her, intuiting that she probably wasn't accustomed to such idiotic banter. He felt sorry for her, too. Only Sandy seemed to have worse luck than Dale. Her tickets to the playoffs in Oakland were the only thing that she and her missing husband had ever won, and they'd landed her here, stripped of what little she'd had going for her in life, and probably widowed. All Dr. Kimura could do was to close his eyes, shake his head, and hope that he would soon wake up between his Egyptian cotton sheets and realize that all of this was just a twisted dream.

When he reopened his eyes, he noticed the figure of a man staggering down the beach at some distance to the north. Something about his gait didn't look quite right. Dr. Kimura rose, clearing his throat. "There is someone coming."

The high cliffs beetling over their campsite afforded a natural windbreak. The same feature would also probably provide some shelter from the elements if the weather decided to take a nasty turn. Dale had chosen the location of their camp. Dr. Kimura was inclined to trust him, seeing as how he was the only one amongst them with the qualifications to call himself an outdoorsman. If anyone here had a knack for wilderness survival, it was Dale. No doubt, the cliffs would serve them well against inclement weather, but on the downside, the limestone wall also blocked their view of anything but the thinnest strip of beach. They couldn't see anyone coming until the intruder was right on top of them. If there ever was a threat, they'd be pinned between it, a sheer wall, and the hungry sea. Strategically, it was a death trap. Dr. Kimura had voiced his concerns in this regard, but the majority of their group were more enamored by the comforting accommodations.

"You see someone?" Sandy dropped Margot's braid. She rose to her feet, hands clasped to her breast. "Who is it?" Her voice began to quaver. "Can you tell if it's my husband? He was wearing a bright orange Orioles shirt exactly like mine."

Dale rose from the fire. He slid his thumbs into his front pockets, and bounced once on his toes. "Nope. Not so far as I can tell."

"Ray is about this tall," Sandy said, holding a trembling hand in the air, at a height only slightly above her own head.

Dr. Kimura resituated his glasses on the bridge of his nose. He scrutinized every detail of the approaching stranger, who weaved a meandering path along the beach. The drunken navigation took the man all the way down into the surf, and then back up into the powdery sand. Dr. Kimura noticed that his clothing was drenched in blood. "He is injured. He needs help."

Dale and Sandy were close on his heels, as he hustled toward the battered stranger. The nearer they drew to him, the more serious his wounds appeared to be. His face was featureless beneath a mask of dried blood. When they were within reach of the walking corpse, he toppled, and collapsed into the sand.

"Don't move him. Not yet."

"Can you talk, buddy?" Dale knelt beside him. "We're here to help y—" Dale stopped mid-sentence.

"What is it?" Dr. Kimura whispered.

Dale pointed at the blood flowing from the side of the man's head. Dark bubbles also spewed from a ragged hole in the center of his face. The man's ears and nose were missing. They'd been cut off.

Dr. Kimura placed a hand on the man's forehead. Despite the suffocating tropical heat, his flesh felt clammy, chilled to the touch. All symptoms suggested that he was in a state of shock. The doctor turned to his companions. "We need to move him to the fire."

"What's your name, buddy?" Dale asked.

"Not alone here," the man whispered, beginning to tremble all over. "We're not alone." Eyes rolling crazily in their sockets, his teeth began to chatter. One hand rose quivering toward what remained of his face.

"Easy. You're going to be alright now. Hear?" Dale tried to assure him, glancing uncertainly at Dr. Kimura. "We got us a doctor here, and he's going to get you all patched up, alright?"

Dr. Kimura pressed the blades of his hands beneath his patient's jaws. He was relieved to find that his throat was not slashed. It was raw, and the skin was sloughed back, almost as though he'd been strangled with a cord of some sort, but most of the blood that soaked his chest had resulted from the facial mutilation. Dr. Kimura slid his hands down either side of the man's ribcage, feeling around for any broken ribs, bulges, any evidence of internal damage.

"Ho-lee cow." A grin spread across Dale's face. He poked the man in the shoulder with a stiff index finger. "I recognize you."

"No-no-no," Dr. Kimura whispered, waving his hands. "He's in shock. Do not excite him."

"Who is it?" Sandy asked, squatting down on the man's other side.

Dale gave a chuckle.

Donovan staggered onto the scene, breathing heavily after his short jog. Donovan's panting stopped when he got a look at the man in the sand. "Hey," he said, cocking his head, "is that who I think it is?"

"Danged right it is."

"Who is it?" Sandy asked, scowling back and forth at the two men.

"It's a damned hijacker," Dale said, smacking the sand off his palms. "The one who bailed out in a parachute while the rest of us fell down into the sea. This here's their leader, I think. He was the feller wearing that Baltimore Orioles cap."

Sandy covered her mouth. "He was sitting right across from us."

"Look at you now, tough guy. Don't feel so macho now, do you?"

"The vector," the hijacker murmured. "Got to find him."

"Yeah, you ain't talking your way out of this one," Dale said. "Looks like some of the other folks already caught up with you, didn't they? Doesn't look to me like they were too happy to see you."

"No!" The hijacker grabbed for Dale's shirt with a trembling hand. "The *others* … they want the vector."

"He cannot make any sense now," Dr. Kimura said, protecting his patient from Dale with an outstretched palm. "He needs treatment, and plenty of rest."

"Bull," Donovan said. "I say we roll his ass right into the sea, show him what it's like to dodge sharks while he treads water for an hour or two."

"I'm with you, buddy. See how the salt water feels on all them new boo-boos."

"Stop it. That's enough of that talk." Dr. Kimura rose from the sand, squaring off against the other two men. "If you care at all to know why our plane was hijacked, or where on earth we are, then you'd better—"

"Guys?"

All eyes swept toward Sandy. She'd stepped ten paces away from the squabble, where she stood gaping up into the moonlit sky. One hand fluttered over her mouth. The other rested upon her heart. "I'm not sure that we're on Earth anymore at all."

# CHAPTER FOUR

23-A

"Did you hear that?" Tara leapt from the sand. She dug her fingernails into the flesh of Brett's arm. The unearthly howl that just erupted from the jungle was the most terrible noise that she'd ever heard. "What was it?"

"I don't know."

Brett was shaking. She could feel his vibrations rippling from his core through his limbs, and his terror was only heightening her own. Like a hurricane warning siren, the howl rose from a guttural growl to an intolerable crescendo. It held the discordant climax for what seemed an impossible duration until the deafening note was finally punctuated with a series of dry coughs. Something out there had just awakened. Its intentions were made perfectly clear, and that howl seemed to be nothing if not a fair warning to anything standing on open ground.

*Run.*

That's what the howl seemed to say.

*Run. Everything with ears to hear me, run. Dive into your burrows. Swim far out into the sea, because nothing out there in the water could be worse than me. I am coming, and I only count to one.*

"Run," Tara whispered. "Oh, Jesus. We've got to run."

"Run where? There's nowhere to freaking run!"

Already, palms bowed and swayed. Treetops roiled in the moonlight. Trunks squealed, splintered, and snapped like firecrackers before toppling in the darkness with a hiss of leaves, and a muffled thud. One tree in the jungle was different than the others. Tara could discern that now. Taller, shaggier than the rest, it was the King of Trees, sentient and driven by some awful purpose. It could walk, this tree, and it was pushing its way through the jungle straight for the beach. It was coming for them.

"What the hell is that?" Brett pointed at it, his voice climbing to higher octaves. "What the hell is that thing?"

"Run!" Tara screamed into his ear, shaking his head by a fistful of hair. She grabbed his arm, and jerked him right off of his feet, down onto his rump in the sand.

"Get up, you guys!" Peanut pounded past, wakes of sand flying from either side of his feet. Alex was right behind him. Peanut swerved just enough to seize Tara by the wrist, and yanked her loose of Brett.

"Brett!" Tara shrieked. "Get up!"

Transfixed by the looming horror, Brett seemed unable to move, as though any decision he made would be a fatal one. He was paralyzed with fright, sallow prey in the glow of those parallel moons fixed upon him like a pair of owlish eyes. Their cold appraisal seemed to see no good use for humankind.

"Where are we going?" Tara shrieked.

"I don't know. Into the sea?"

"The sea? Are you out of your mind?" She'd seen the monsters that patrolled these shores. They'd all seen them. Black as the devil's shadow, they were lurking out there, searching for the kicking legs of swimmers through those unthinking, pearly eyes. This was their favorite game. Yes, Tara could feel their foreboding presence sliding beneath the waves just as plainly as she beheld the shaggy thing crashing through the last belt of trees.

The howler thundered out onto the moonlit beach, where it dipped and tossed its festooned head. Bobbing, puffing, peering askance through hidden eyes, the creature was clearly intrigued by the sight of them, but it seemed unsure of how it should destroy them. With a gaseous hiss, and a fluff of black feathers, the monster lowered its head to the sand.

"There's nowhere else to go. We've got to swim for it!"

"No!"

A few purposeful plods, and the howler began to charge. Leveling its flattened body with the ground, it emitted a disorienting trill as it thundered over the beach. Dust showered from its shags of filthy plumage. Sand flew in chuffs behind its stabbing feet. How the thing intended to kill them was unclear, but there would be some death tonight. That much was certain.

"Brett!"

Alex and Peanut both grabbed her by the arms, and dragged Tara writhing into the waves. The sea was colder than she remembered. It stole her breath away. She fell, disappearing for a moment beneath the brine, but the boys did not let go. Dragging, drowning, she emerged sputtering just as the thing slammed its shaggy face to the ground. She watched it thrashing, grinding, whipping its head skyward in a fountain of sand, as it engulfed something mangled with one flip of its maw. A tennis shoe sailed through the moonlight. It hit the beach fifty meters away with a puff of white powder.

"Oh my God … Brett!"

"Jesus Christ! What is it? What the hell is that thing?"

One of the boys was shouting by her ear. Tara didn't know which of them was on either side of her anymore. They'd become a single mass, clinging and shivering in the waves. The water was up to their necks by the time the howler had finished its meal, and swiveled its massive head in their direction. The elongated body pivoted afterward. It was perfectly balanced on a pair of legs that looked disproportionately thin beneath the woolly bulk hovering atop them. With a boar-like grunt, it came for them. The howler wanted more. Sheaves of filth rained from its thatch with every thrust of its limbs. The thing was no more deterred by the ocean than by the jungle's density. The teens clung to one another, screaming for their lives, as the monster crashed headlong into the waves.

### 

23-E

"I'm looking for my husband," Sandy whispered into the bloody hole where one of his ears had been sliced away. She peered over her shoulder to make sure that Dr. Kimura wasn't coming. He was a good man, and she was sure that he was a fine doctor, but he failed to appreciate the fact that if she didn't question his patient now, then she might not ever get a chance to do so. The guy was fading fast. Wrapped in a few extra articles of clothing that their group had reluctantly donated, and resting as close to the fire as he could safely be positioned, the mutilated hijacker continued to shiver uncontrollably. His eyes were alternately closed, or confused and wandering. What hadn't been apparent on the darkened beach where they'd discovered him was the exposed dome of skull atop his head. In addition to being strangled, and having his facial features pared away, the man had also been scalped.

Sandy couldn't bring herself to believe that survivors of their crash had committed these acts of barbarism. Without a doubt, he was guilty of a crime that had jeopardized a lot of innocent lives, but his endangerment of the passengers of that plane did not justify outright savagery. He didn't deserve to be tortured nearly to death, or to be left permanently disfigured. Whoever had taken a blade to this man's face was an even worse sort of monster than a hijacker. This was the clearly work of a psychopath.

The hijacker's eyelids fluttered open. His eyes dimmed, crossed, and then realigned, as though he'd bobbed back briefly to the surface of consciousness. He blinked through his mask of gore, white teeth chattering. Wild eyes rolled in their sockets toward Sandy.

"It's okay," she murmured, placing a reassuring hand on his arm. "No one is going to hurt you. I promise. You've been rescued. Do you understand? Nod, if you understand me."

The man searched her face with affrighted eyes. After all that he'd been through, he seemed unwilling to believe that she really meant him no harm. He licked his teeth, and swallowed. After a moment, he gave a single nod.

"Good." Sandy smiled, patting his arm. She looked across the fire. The only other person within earshot was Margot, and she wasn't paying attention. She never did. She was always in her own little world. Out of everyone stranded here, the young model was perhaps the most removed from her natural environment. Here, there was no trace of whatever wonderland she'd fallen from. Sandy imagined her riding around with a glamorous entourage, strutting the fashion runways amidst popping strobes. Here, divorced from all of that dazzle, she could only sulk like a scolded child, disconnected from the world around her, and picking at the beds of her nails. Some of them had begun to bleed.

Dr. Kimura still hadn't returned. Without much explanation, he'd taken a torch down to the seashore. He'd mentioned something about kelp. His parting instructions were to refrain from disturbing his patient's rest and recovery, but to try and keep him as warm and comfortable as possible.

Dale and Donovan were stewing over the hijacker's special treatment ever since he'd been carried back to camp. Becoming listless and secretive, the two had slipped surreptitiously away to a distance of around fifty meters, where they'd been talking quietly amongst themselves for the better part of an hour. If this patient didn't have so much information stored away inside his head, she might've been more concerned about what those two were over there plotting, if anything at all.

"You said that there were others on the island," Sandy whispered. "Were they the ones who did this to you?"

The hijacker gave another nod. He tried to speak, but only produced a croaking sound, and had to swallow dryly again. They hadn't found any fresh water before sundown, but Dale had managed to collect around a dozen cans of soda and beer that had washed up onto the beach. Consumption of these beverages was expressly forbidden without group consent. They were to be rationed sparingly, and shared in equal measures. Everybody seemed to be in agreement about that, at least, but it went without saying that if Dale and Donovan had anything to say about it, this hijacker wasn't going to be included in the distribution of rations. Sandy could see their cache of aluminum cans glimmering at the base of the cliff wall, and the temptation to pilfer just a small sip for this man was a powerful one.

"The other people—are they passengers from our plane?"

The hijacker narrowed his eyes, and slowly shook his head back and forth. There was something that he wanted to say, but couldn't. His throat was parched to the point of closure. Sandy guessed that he was severely dehydrated from the loss of so much blood, and from all the stress of whatever ordeal he'd been through. If anyone needed a sip, it was him.

"Listen. I'm looking for my husband." Sandy's lip began to tremble. She felt like she was hanging by the thinnest thread, and she was weighted by the worst kind of emotions. If that thread ever snapped, it was going to be a mess. Ray was everything to her. He was her rock, her knight in shining armor, and the best friend she'd ever known. He was all the family that she had left in world. He was it. They'd been through so much together, moving halfway across the country, and back again, losing everything, and then rebuilding it from scratch. Just the two of them. They'd tried everything to have children, but it just wasn't in their cards. That's what everyone said. But only she and her husband knew what it was like to sit at that table and keep on smiling, playing cards, while they kept getting dealt shit, hand after hand.

The first time in their lives they'd ever won anything was last week on that radio show, where she was tenth caller. She'd won them a couple of tickets to the playoffs, along with a pair of matching Orioles jerseys, hotel and airfare included. They weren't even baseball fans. How was that for a laugh? It wasn't even about baseball. It was about so much more than that. No one could possibly understand how much winning those free tickets had meant to them. No one but she and Ray. It was like a new dealer had just sat down at their card table, replacing the other jerk with a reassuring wink and a promise that from here on out, their streak of bad luck would remain turned around. They were just a couple of tickets, but they represented a brand new beginning.

"His name is Ray." A tear spilled down her cheek. Sandy wiped it away. "He was wearing an orange shirt, just like this one." She pinched the fabric of her jersey between her thumbs and forefingers, and lifted it from her chest. "He's always smiling. Very friendly and outgoing. He'd be the warmest one in any group of people." She leaned closer to the mutilated face. "Please. Did you see him anywhere?"

The hijacker made a gurgling sound. He blinked his eyes slowly, and shook his head from side to side. As she lowered her chin and began to weep, his hand slid across the sand toward her knee, and he touched her with his trembling fingertips. "Your husband ..." he whispered.

Sandy lowered her hands from her face, eyes shimmering. "Yes?"

"… is dead."

Sometimes the truth comes like a cement truck falling from the sky. You can feel its shadow. You can feel the pressure change, the temperature drop by a few degrees a split-second before its tonnage smashes you to a pulp. Sandy's heart seemed to stop. Her last breath was lodged in her throat. "No," she whispered, shaking her head.

"All but me … and one Marine … got away from them."

"Please, no." Sandy began to tremble all over. "Please, not Ray. Not Ray!" She felt sure that she was going to vomit. Across the fire, Margot quit picking at her nails long enough to cast a dramatic glance from beneath one hitched eyebrow, as though utterly repulsed by her display of emotion.

"The vector ..." Blood foamed from the gaping hole in the place where the hijacker's nose had been carved away. Neck arched, he rolled his skinned head back and forth in the sand. "Find him … or they'll butcher us ... coming ..." His lids fluttered down over his rolling eyes, and his head lolled off to one side. He was out again.

"The doctor guy told you not to talk to him," Margot said.

Sandy could see through the corner of her eye that Dr. Kimura was entering their campsite with an armload of dripping kelp. She was pretty sure that the timing and volume of Margot's comment was intended to reach the doctor's ears. Sandy always tried to find the best qualities in people, but if there were any exceptional qualities in Margot, she was doing a great job of hiding them.

"What happened?" Dr. Kimura dropped his sodden mass of vines to the sand, and rushed over to kneel by his patient's side. He was already checking the man's vitals before Sandy had a chance to respond.

"He woke up for a second," Sandy replied, choking back her tears, "and he told me that Ray was killed. Ray, and a bunch of other people."

"Killed in the crash?"

Sandy shook her head, smearing the salty streams from her face. "No. Killed by other people."

Dr. Kimura placed a hand on her shoulder. "Don't believe what he says in this condition. His mind is not right. Maybe tomorrow, but not now." He gave her shoulder a reassuring shake, glancing in the direction of Dale and Donovan. "Let's make some tea from the kelp. Speeds rehydration. Anti-inflammatory. Strengthens the immune system." Doctor Kimura patted her on the back, and smiled. "Don't cry, Sandy. He will make more sense tomorrow. Go get me one can of soda. You can help me make his medicine."

Sandy sniffed, nodded, and rose to her feet. She drew a deep breath, and gazed up the limestone wall to the double moons that had finally risen over the crest of their natural shelter. They were almost touching now, strolling hand in hand across the sky.

Christ, what certainties were there anymore? Even if Ray had been standing right beside her, reassuring her, holding her hand, not even his comfort would be enough to change two moons back into one. She could ignore the weird sounds of the jungle, endure the hardships of the situation, and even try to be strong without Ray, but two moons ... Sandy dropped her gaze back to the ground. Pressing her hands to the sides of her head, she just breathed for a while. The very sight of those tandem orbs in the sky was enough to remove all hope, and maybe even trigger a nervous breakdown.

"Where in God's name are we?" she murmured.

Get the soda. Make some medicine. Focus.

With the balls of her hands mashed to her temples, Sandy shuffled toward the swath of darkness beneath the overhanging rock shelf. It had the imposing grandeur of an ancient temple to bygone gods, fluted from eons of erosion, and polished to a shine by regular pummeling by the sea. Pale tendrils of roots squirmed their way through every crack and crevice to dangle from the cliff's face like a hoary beard. As she bent to retrieve a warm can of Tab, she heard a falling pebble rattle all the way down through the limestone whorls. It landed at her feet with a thump. Winning lottery ball.

She turned back toward the glow of the campfire. Despite the friction between the brooding castaways, it almost looked warm and inviting from a distance. The flickering glow reminded her of those endless summer nights with her family on Lake Geneva, when she and her brother would join the rabble of kids to play kick-the-can, and they'd all dart like rabbits through the ranks of darkened cottages. The grown-ups laughed and hollered around their nightly bonfires, while scads of bats looped and spiraled over the commons. Those were the best of times, back when her family was still in its prime.

Nobody ever tells a family that they're in their prime, and that one day it will be over and done. You can't see it at the time, because of that rush of constant activity. You just live in that window of time, and you take it all for granted until it's gone. That's when the realization comes, much later, in a bittersweet retrospective. Mom was young and beautiful. Dad was tanned and strong. Her brother Martin was still the ornery kid with the lopsided grin who she'd always looked up to, followed around like a little puppy, and loved with all of her heart—years before he flushed his life down the toilet. God, if she could go back to one window of time in her life, and just live there forever … like miniature people in a snow globe.

She turned the warm cylinder of soda in the palm of her hand and sighed. When Dale and Donovan discovered that she and Dr. Kimura were wasting a whole can of their precious soda on making medicine for that hijacker, they were going to go through the roof. There would be hell to pay for this. She could already hear their accusations, their screams of outrage. Something so simple as a can of Tab could be just the catalyst to pit them all against each other, and have them tearing each other apart. How sad. First thing in the morning, they would all need to start searching for water, or else their group's precariously balanced personalities were apt to topple their little house of cards.

Sandy looked down at the can of soda, and she decided that the best course of action would be to commit to being open and honest about whatever it was that they were doing, and why. Discuss it. Be democratic. Put everything to a vote. Trust was key. In this volatile situation, it was critical that they strive to be tolerant of one another, to be patient, to take the time to discover and utilize each other's unique strengths and skills. They really couldn't be more different, the five of them—well, now six—but at least they had each other, and that was something. It was important to realize that now, and not to lament that fact in retrospect.

Their group was blessed to have a skilled outdoorsman amongst them who could conjure a roaring fire from raw elements like some sort of a wizard. Who knew what other neat tricks Dale might have up his sleeve? They had a doctor in their circle. A *doctor*. Seriously, how could you possibly put a price on Dr. Kimura, with his working knowledge of natural medicine? As far as hands of cards went, theirs was not a bad one to be dealt. Her people definitely had promise, and the tight bonds that were currently missing could surely follow. It all began with trust.

A falling pebble pinged off the lip of the aluminum can. Sandy jumped, and clutched her heart. A second piece of rock landed somewhere nearby, clattering down a drift of sloughed shards. Sandy squinted up the face of the crumbling limestone wall. She could imagine it all coming down in one terrible avalanche. Their sanctuary didn't seem so very safe anymore.

Clasping the can in her hands, she backed away from the wall. The last thing that she needed was for her group to discover Ray alive and well, only to have to inform him that his bride had been brained by a falling rock. She hesitated, glancing back at their stock of canned beverages. If they woke up tomorrow to find a limestone slab atop a bunch of crushed cans, that would be a pretty disheartening way to start the day. It would be safer and smarter to store them by the fire, away from the base of the crumbling wall. She went back, and began filling the front of her Orioles jersey with cans until it sagged beneath their weight like a bulging apron.

A small shower of pebbles rattled down through the channels to hail around her. Instinctively, she covered her head, peering warily up at the overhang through the corner of a widening eye. As she rose from her crouched position, she let out a shriek when a limestone wrecking ball slammed into the sand right beside her. She winced through the spray of particles that cascaded from the impact. Running blind, spitting sand, she clutched the cache of cans to her midsection as she fled the danger zone just as hastily as her cumbersome load would permit.

Her legs slowed when she noticed the others poised around the campfire, alerted by her cry. They looked braced for anything, ready to fight to the death against anything that threatened one of their own. The sight of them all standing united, mustered into an unrehearsed defensive stance was somehow very moving. She was relieved and proud. Dr. Kimura, Margot, Dale and Donovan— maybe even the hijacker—they could all be members of a new family in this strange home away from home, and it looked as though there just might be some hope for their little family yet. In that moment, Sandy believed with all of her heart that she could trust each one of these people with her life.

The warm cocktail of emotions suddenly chilled. Sandy's brow gathered into a knot. What in the hell was that?

Her pace slowed to a jog, to a walk, until she lurched to a sudden stop. Struggling to make sense of the sight before her eyes, she stood frozen, staring past the flickering silhouettes of her new family to the nameless thing that loomed beyond them. A couple of cans tumbled from the side of her makeshift apron.

At first glance, it was just a tree swaying in the wind. It was every bit as tall as a tree, and it had that top-heavy imbalance of a canopy of wispy fronds. It might've been a tree, it should've been, if it weren't for the fact that there were no trees in that narrow path between the cliffs and the sea. There was nothing in that area but sand. That stark realization clubbed her soundly, at about the same time that the stench invaded her nostrils.

It was a feral musk, distantly familiar, but confused by the soured putrescence of roadkill. The odor reeked from the strange, new tree that had somehow sprouted and grown to maturity right in the middle of their only route of escape. It made no sense that a tree would be towering in a spot where just an hour before, there was nothing. However, if it wasn't a tree, then her mind's cogs were condemned to spin in the vast emptiness of a search that would never find a match with anything else on earth for what she was seeing.

Bobbing, dipping in the moonlight, its motions wimpled its lancet fronds. After each session of pumping, the tree gave a lurch forward. Dust billowed from its canopy with every hop. Sandy couldn't bring herself to scream, because she didn't even know if she needed to. She couldn't move, because there was nowhere to run. Her hapless new family, they had to hear something as the stinking tree shambled nearer to their campfire. They had to smell it, or sense it in some way. She wanted to warn them, but she didn't know how. She didn't trust her own perception, and if there was a threat to their lives, it wasn't obvious. Whatever it was that Sandy was seeing, if she was even seeing anything at all, was a master at concealing its intentions.

Its smell, at the most intimate level, jarred loose an old memory. In their Grandpa's barn, where her brother once used a broomstick to knock down the mud nests of the barn swallows that liked to roost in the rafters. Blizzards of angry swallows blazed through the musty corridor while he demolished their little world, warning him away from their nestlings with piping cries that he ignored, as he destroyed one nest after another with thrusts of the broomstick. Showers of dirt, eggs and hatchlings rained to the ground. Pink and translucent, some possessed only blue bulges for unopened eyes, skinned so thinly that the activity of their tiny hearts and innards could be seen by the naked eye. Others were older, feathered, with beady eyes black and bright. Sandy took them all, gathered them into the paunch of her blouse, fostering each as quickly as Martin could send them to the ground. That was the smell. The pastoral musk of baby barn swallows. As she'd lowered her head down into her blouse to assure her orphanage that everything was going to be alright—and it never was, because Martin found ways to kill them all—she'd inhaled the pure essence of *bird*. For whatever reason, the memory of that odor had quietly kept a permanent residence in some recess of her mind.

Bobbing, hopping, every aspect of the thing's behavior seemed something casually observed, but never consciously recorded, in passing instants of ordinary life. She'd seen these movements before, but what towered before her was a perversion of normality. That was perhaps most chilling. It was a nightmarish rendition of something dragged down to Hell from the front yard, demonically reconfigured, and belched back up in an unacceptable new form. The longer she stared at it, the more certain she became. It was a bird. What she was seeing was a gargantuan sort of bird, and her observations of everyday birds in the yard warned Sandy that its movements were no performance. Those types of creatures behaved in such a manner when they were inching their way toward something with predatory interest, gauging the distance to that object, verifying the target, in the moments that preceded a deadly strike.

It charged.

"Run!" Sandy screamed, dropping the folds of her makeshift apron. Cans of beer and soda tumbled to the ground. "Run!" As the thing thundered down the narrow funnel between the cliffs and the sea, it became obvious that there was nowhere to escape but into the dark and churning sea. There was nowhere to hide.

Dale and Donovan were quickest to respond. The younger men had hardly glanced over their shoulders before their legs were sprinting for the sea. Dr. Kimura staggered backward. Margot clung to his arm. It looked as though they might tumble entwined right into the roaring campfire.

The thing lowered its frilled head. Craning its neck until its body was streamlined, it emitted the guttural prattle of a fighting rooster. Clawed feet slashed through the spraying sand. It fanned its lateral plumage until its width was doubled, maximizing its breadth as if to crush all hope from hapless prey that might attempt to dodge it.

As the horror bore down on the doomed pair, the unthinkable happened. It was a sight far worse than if the monster had gnashed its serrated maw down over them, masticating their enmeshed flesh into a red paste. That would've been better. At the very least, that sort of an end might've harried Margot and Dr. Kimura together into the gilded halls of martyrdom, but to Sandy's utter aghast, Margot instead wrenched the doctor over her hip, and shoved him right into the beast's face.

"No."

Margot spun, and fled for the safety of the sea.

"No!" Sandy dumped her load of canned beverages. She charged up the embankment toward the campfire, where Dr. Kimura's screams lent discordant treble to the monster's basal growls. It wrenched its shaggy face into the sand, snorting and grunting with a sickening relish for human flesh. The muffled cries of its meal barely penetrated the damper of reeking plumage.

"Let him go!" Sandy exploded into the ring of firelight. The monster's head thrashed in the sand. Its sickening purrs were interrupted by the popping of bones. The stench at this proximity was intoxicating. Through the matted heap of pelage, Sandy discerned a yellow eye, round and owlish in shape, and burning with predatory malice. It disappeared back beneath the shifting mass, where the muted cries of Dr. Kimura could still be heard.

Lunging into the campfire, Sandy seized a burning log in her bare hands. She felt no pain. "Let him go!" She swung the fiery club over her shoulder, rushed the beast, and brought it down with a hollow clunk atop its stinking head. A flume of sparks ascended. The wave of heat knocked Sandy back, as the heap of greasy feathers ignited like a pile of tinder. Before it could rear for a counterattack, its devilish head was consumed in a ball of fire. Caterwauling, screeching like an injured chick, it bounced blindly against the limestone wall as it lumbered flaming into the night.

### 

22-D

The bloodcurdling howl, punctuated by a series of dull chuffs, was replaced by the tide's rhythmic roar. Nate stood alone on the beach. His arms dangled limply at his sides. Not in a million years could he have imagined a distraction that could've snapped him out of his grief, but that was pretty effective. Flipping through a mental rolodex of every animal on God's green earth, he failed to find a suitable match. What in the hell had made that noise? He attempted to rub the double-image of two moons from his eyes, and when they refused to merge into one celestial body, Nate had to consider the possibility that he might've lost his mind. Somewhere in the far distance, a second howl rose from the jungle in a mournful crescendo. Whatever the things were, they seemed to be communicating. Goosebumps prickled up and down his forearms. Unlike like the howl of a wolf, the eerie cries in the night did not strike him as being the least bit beautiful. This was a terrible sound.

Shaking uncontrollably, Nate turned away from the sight of the tandem moons to the sea. When he saw the doubled reflections of a thousand moons glimmering on the crest of a thousand waves, he doubled-over, and vomited on the sand. This was it. He was sure that he'd gone insane, and now he was going to die. Retching and trembling, he dropped to all fours to lessen the impact of the fall, because he felt his consciousness waning. Dawn was gone, and he'd lost his mind.

It was the sound of their screams that saved him, brought him back from the brink of madness. Nate swiveled his sagging head in the direction of the shrieks. He was pretty sure that it was that group of teens, but it didn't sound like they were fooling around. Sounded serious. Something bad was happening. He rose to his feet, squinting down the pale strip between the ocean and jungle. At the farthest reaches of his visual limits, he saw something that he couldn't explain.

The kids were all out in the water. Silhouetted by the hammered brilliance of moonlight glittering on the sea, their dark forms could be seen rushing out into the waves, but there was something else. Something else was chasing them, and whatever it was, it didn't make any sense to his eyes. The thing was enormous. It was impossibly huge, yet formless. It looked like a dark thunderhead floating over the beach, but this was no cloud. It had one of them.

"Oh my God."

Nate ran. As though life had given him a second chance at saving Dawn, at saving the man on the beach, he squeezed every ounce of speed from his pounding legs. Not another. Not one more life would be lost on his watch, or on his account. Evidently finished with the kid in the sand, the shaggy abomination turned its attention to the other teens, who'd already swam to a considerable distance offshore. In an instant, the thing was back in pursuit. It charged right into the sea like a gigantic grizzly bear. Dazzling sprays sparkled in the moonlight as the monster smashed through waves, closing the distance between itself and the screaming cluster of teens. Just as the creature drew close enough to ensure their demise, Nate beheld something inexplicable. One of the three kids abandoned the group. One dark silhouette swam back to face the monster, all alone.

###

21-F

"Alex! What the hell are you doing?" Peanut knew exactly what his best friend was doing. He was just being Alex, the most selfless human being he'd ever had the honor and pleasure of knowing. There went Alex, his other half, swimming right out of his life.

What was the point of it? Their whole life, and it had always been one shared, seemed suddenly so random, and so meaningless. If Alex's whole purpose for being born into this world was this moment, where he would spare the lives of two people by sacrificing his own, then Peanut would have no other choice but to scream.

Peanut might've started screaming because he knew he couldn't afford a massive debt that couldn't ever be repaid, but this wasn't completely true. Peanut screamed because the truth was that there was no debt at all. This was Alex, and his death, much like his life, was just a gift to those around them. The trouble was that both were gifts so amazing that Peanut felt unworthy to have ever received them. He was just the damned clown, the fool of their lifelong act, where Alex always took the role of the hero, while Peanut handled the comedy relief. It was a flawless presentation to the world around them, one they'd mastered, but in the end, the hero shouldn't lay down his life for the fool. That made no sense. It should be the other way around, but then, heroes will be heroes, and fools will be fools, and in the end, the fool will always live to tell his fallen hero's tale.

He wouldn't watch. Peanut turned his head, and closed his eyes when the howler lunged. He heard the sound, and he knew that he'd just heard his best friend's life ending. That was the worst sound he'd ever heard. It was the worst sound that ever was.

"Fucking swim, Tara!"

At the very least, his death would not be in vain. He'd not allow it. That monster was not going to eat either one of them. Peanut threshed his legs against the water, dragging Tara Riley further out into the sea. He'd swim across the whole goddamned ocean if that's what it took, but the howler was not going to eat them. Peanut pulled at the water, pulling her, kicking against the heavy fluid. He growled with every stroke, but the monster was still coming. He could hear the blasts of air from its nostrils, the sluice of water through its dagger teeth. It was gaining on them. It wouldn't give up. Peanut understood that now. He could maybe swim across an ocean, but so would the howler. It wouldn't quit until they were all dead.

### 

## 22-D

It was like watching a terrible accident in slow motion. The kids weren't going to make it. Whatever it was, it could definitely swim. The distance between the shaggy hulk and the remaining teens was shrinking by a meter almost every second. Whatever the kids had done to run afoul with this monster, Nate couldn't even imagine, but it was after them like they owed it money. The problem was that once it was finished with them, it would probably be looking for its next target, if it hadn't slated him into its queue already. Nate knew that he ought to be contemplating a route of escape, but he couldn't bring himself to look away from the horror. Some morbid part of the human mind always demanded that the eyes bear witness to that which could befall less fortunate people, even when a gruesome sight had no practical application.

In a roar of brine pulverized to foam, a new form appeared, streaked in moonlight, breaching the sea with all the power of Poseidon's Kraken. Twisting its body in a magnificent pirouette, the fantastic animal seemed to hover in midair as it unhinged its crocodilian jaws, tilted its massive head, and toppled toward its prey. There was no denying that this was the same sort of creature that had taken Dawn, nor was there any room left to deny what sort of monster it was. Nate was looking at a mosasaur.

It dropped toward the howler with the lethal precision of a deadfall trap. There was no escaping the acute angle of those jaws, and the shaggy beast seemed to sense it. It ceased paddling after the teens to gawp up at its destroyer in quiet wonderment, as though dumbstruck by the sight of a monster so much larger than itself. The yawning maw slammed shut over the howler's head, and in an instant both creatures were gone, returned to the lightless depths with a thunderclap, and sparkling jettisons.

# CHAPTER FIVE

28-D

They were inside of him. Thousands of them, squirming all around in his body. He could feel them in his mouth, in his skull, peering out at the world from behind his eyes. The insect eggs had hatched so quickly. All through the night, he felt the larvae churning purposefully in his bullet wounds, but they weren't devouring his flesh. They were doing something else entirely. Something good. By the time dawn's light gilded the overhanging foliage, Hart realized that his injuries had ceased to pain him. He was still swollen, but the throbbing agony had mysteriously abated. Some degree of natural feeling had even begun to return to his left arm. He was full of worms, but they were good worms. They were like his little helpers. That's how it seemed. Hart wiggled his fingers.

It was the strangest night he'd ever experienced. Prone on the jungle floor, unable to move, he'd been visited by things. Nameless admirers had come to lower their nightmarish heads, and sniff him, before eventually lumbering on. It was as though some angelic force was protecting him with crossed swords, keeping every beast of the night at bay. He was Daniel in the lions' den, filled with a Holy Spirit that he could actually feel squirming in his innards, and wriggling occasionally up his throat to deposit clusters of eggs on his lips. He and his worms were one. They were his protectors, and he was something of their mighty vehicle. Hart could sense that they were in the mood to travel, but where would a bunch of worms want to go, and could he even move?

Starting by wiggling his fingertips, Hart lifted his wrists from the leaf litter. He rotated his hands, and raised them up before his eyes, where masses of worms were probably gathered, peering out at their new body in amazement. But they hadn't seen anything yet. Hart groaned as he sat up slowly, blinking his eyes, gazing around at the surrounding jungle with a sort of bemused complacence. Where before the forest was a vast and terrifying place filled with enormous horrors that roared and howled all through the night, the morning light made things seem so much smaller, and more manageable. The nightmare was over. A fresh, sunny day awaited.

There was a sour taste in his mouth, kind of like spoiled milk. He could even smell it on his breath. He smacked his lips, which were coated with worm eggs. They felt pretty disgusting, but he knew better than to wipe them away. The worms had put them there for a reason, and he was supposed to leave them alone. Kind of annoying, but he guessed things could sure be worse.

Hart looked down at his leg. Yesterday's ragged bullet hole had been totally transformed. It wasn't exactly healed. Just patched. It was all glazed over with a glob of amber gelatin. He could see the worms hard at work beneath it, roiling around in the damaged tissue. They were weird, but they sure seemed to know what they were doing. He was blessed to have stumbled right into a nest of helpful worms. Yesterday's terrible anfractuosities would have snuffed the life from an ordinary human being, but he was no longer ordinary, and technically, he wasn't even sure that he was still a human being.

All his days, he'd walked the world alone. Sometimes he'd felt like an insect trapped inside a window pane, doomed to forever watch other lives passing by, but forever denied access. It didn't seem fair. What had he ever done so wrong that the whole world rejected him? He hadn't done anything. The truth was that he was just too sensitive for the world. Lots of people endured worse lots in life than he'd been given, and they still turned out to be very successful people who were admired for their perseverance. Hart had always been strong. He'd persevered through so many terrible accidents, surgeries, and trips to the burn unit, but no one admired him. No one cared. Life was just more complicated for him than it seemed to be for most people. He never could figure it out—people, that is—and why someone as big and strong as him should be made so easily broken.

Hart smiled down at the glob of amber stuff on his thigh. It was like a little window. They were trapped behind the pane, but they were on the same side of the window as him. They cared about him. He could sense that. His worms loved him for who he was, and they wanted the best for him. At last, he had friends, lots and lots of them, and he could carry them with him wherever he went.

Now, the only question was where to go? Hart looked around the dense reefs of undergrowth. He noticed the two sets of human tracks in the mud left behind by Lonny and that Marine. Hart licked his caked lips and teeth, careful not to swallow any of the precious eggs. He decided that he would follow those footprints, because he guessed that what he felt most like doing today was biting people.

###

22-D

Like a rabble of zombies, they shuffled along the endless strip of sand. The kids collected bags of peanuts and cans of soda, as they happened upon them. The beach was littered with debris. Every few steps there were seat cushions, parts of the plane, and parts of people. Nate caught himself wondering if they were the only ones who'd managed to survive the terrible night. The jungle was quieter by day. He guessed that the howlers were nocturnal hunters, but where was all of the other life on this island? Where were all of the keening seagulls that should've been picking through the grisly remains? What sort of animals did howlers eat when they weren't feeding on human beings?

They hadn't spoken much in the last hour. They were exhausted from lack of sleep, crushed by loss. They all had grief in common. The boy called Peanut had cried all through the night, his head buried between his knees. One of the two kids killed had been his best friend. They'd grown up together, across the street from one another. Sounded like they were practically brothers. Nate once had friends like that, long ago, back when he was their age. As kids approached young adulthood, they traded their childhood dependence on their families for stronger bonds with their peers. Once they got a little older, the intensity of those bonds with friends would dissipate, as they reconnected with their families in new ways, and used the skills they'd developed through adolescence to foster the greatest and most challenging bond of all—the bond with a spouse.

It had taken them both a couple of failed efforts in marriages before they found one another. He and Dawn were both re-treads. Their nomadic spirits had proved unconducive to previous relationships, where their exes were made anxious by their wandering, their dissatisfaction with an ordinary life of pink houses and picket fences. Their true love had always been, and always would be the sea. Together, they shared that understanding.

She was something of a scientific icon, particularly in the eyes of females. Dawn had played a significant role in breaking down the old patriarchal barriers that had long kept women out of marine biology. Nate was awed by her drive and determination, and enamored by her almost childlike fascination with all living things. Her passion for life and the living sea was perhaps what made her tragic end so bittersweet. Dawn's true love had turned on her.

Being eaten ... there was something so repulsive about being regarded by a larger animal as nothing more than flesh to fill its gullet. It was the most primal fear of all, passed down through our genes from those ancient ancestors who learned to fear snakes, spiders, and shaggy beasts. It was why kids were afraid of the dark. It was why people screamed. So much basic human behavior was nothing more than the genetic memory of a monkey.

Before the sun set, they had to find some shelter. Their lives depended on it. They could not survive another night like the last one. They needed a cave, a crevice, a damned hole in the ground. If they hadn't found a place to hide by the time those awful howls resounded from the darkened jungle, then it would already be too late.

"Do you think we went back in time?" Peanut asked.

It was the first time the kid had spoken since midnight, but Nate didn't have an answer. He'd have loved be able to explain what had happened, to offer an educated guess as to where they were, and why they were here, but he didn't have either. It would've been nice to have been able to cling to the hope that they'd discovered some lost island that time had forgotten, where creatures existed that could be found nowhere else on earth. The problem was the two moons floating up in the night sky.

"Alex and I were talking about it. He thought that maybe we'd gone back in time, like through a portal or something. I told him that I didn't think that was possible because of paradoxes, but now I don't even know about that anymore."

"Paradoxes? That's a pretty big word for a kid your age."

Peanut shrugged. "I like science fiction, and stuff like that. He and I both do. I mean, we did. We used to talk about that kind of stuff all the time."

"Tell me more about these paradoxes."

"Well, it's like, if a theory results an impossibility, then that makes the theory itself impossible. That's basically what a paradox is."

"Example?"

"The one I used on Alex was the grandpa-assassination paradox."

"That sounds interesting."

"If you went back in time and killed your grandpa, then you'd cease to exist."

"Yeah."

"So, if you never existed to begin with, then you couldn't have gone back in time to kill him, so that makes the whole scenario an impossibility. It could never happen."

"You guys are weird," Tara said.

"So, you're saying that time travel is impossible because it creates impossible scenarios?"

"Pretty much."

"Hmm." Nate walked in silence for a while. They all did.

"What if time's not linear?" Tara asked.

"What do you mean?"

"I'm not even sure what I mean."

Nate cleared his throat. "Well, if you think of every moment in time as being a sequential number, with the first moment being one, then two, and so on, stretching out to infinity, then that would be an expression of time in a linear sense. If number ninety-nine jumps out of place, and goes back to erase number twenty-five, then it wipes out the whole row of numbers ahead of twenty-four."

"Exactly, making it impossible for number ninety-nine to ever have existed."

"Wait," Tara said, "what if instead of time being one single thread of numbers, it's just a whole mess of random numbers, floating all around in time like alphabet soup?"

"That sounds nuts."

"Or, even better, what if there's more than one universe?" Tara smiled.

"Huh?"

"What if when you travel through time, you're not going back linearly, you're dropping through crack between moments, and falling into a new layer? Then, you could kill grandpa, and return safely back to your own place in time."

"But grandpa would still be alive in your universe."

"Yes, he would. But, if your mission was to kill grandpa, then you successfully completed your mission, even if there's a billion other copies of grandpa in a billion other universes."

"I think I like the linear idea better," Peanut said. "It's less messy."

"Fine, but even with the linear idea, there's no paradox. If ninety-nine goes back and erases twenty-five, then he just wiped out his whole lineage. It's not impossible. It's just existential suicide. Ninety-nine existed. Even if no one ever knows that he existed, he did, right up until the moment that he took out all the preceding numbers with him."

"No witnesses." Peanut grinned. "The perfect crime."

"Twenty-four saw everything," Nate said.

"But no one will ever believe him," Tara said. "Everyone will think he's nuts."

"I'm telling you, man," Peanut said, waving his arms emphatically, "this evil number from the future came back in time, and he killed my son, right before my eyes!"

Tara giggled.

Nate found himself smiling for the first time in what felt like forever, even as they passed a mass of what was probably human entrails. For the first hour of their walk, he obsessed over every bit and piece, wondering if it was hers. Not anymore. Some part of him was starting to come to terms with what had happened. Kids were so resilient. Nate admired that about them. Maybe he could borrow a little of that resilience from them. "How many other kids were on your class trip?"

Tara and Peanut glanced uncertainly at one another. "Fourteen, I think," she replied.

"I saw other people swimming to shore," Peanut said. "Before the current started spreading us all out, I saw like twenty people, maybe more."

"I hope Maureen made it," Tara whispered.

Despite what they all knew was swimming offshore, and what stalked the island after dark, Nate was pretty certain that there were bound to be other survivors. The front half of the plane had simply disappeared. It had all happened so quickly. One second, it was there, and in the next, the tail end of the plane was disconnected, and shredding apart. There were at least nine rows of passengers in that section who could be accounted for at the moment they all plunged into the waves. Six people per row. Nine rows. Probably around fifty people. Despite all that had happened in the twenty-four hours following the crash, some of those people surely had to be alive.

"Smoke!"

Snapping out of his thoughts, Nate frowned in the direction that Peanut was pointing. Up ahead, the beach narrowed at the foot of a sheer limestone wall that gently curved into what appeared to be a secluded bay. Sure enough, rising skyward from around the blind corner was a wispy tendril of gray smoke.

"Come on!" The teens began to run.

"Hey, wait a minute." Nate wasn't sure why he felt inclined to rein them back. Just being protective. "Let's keep our cool, and all walk in together."

"What's wrong?" Tara asked.

"Nothing's wrong, really. We just don't know what's around that corner, you know?"

"Might be cavemen," Peanut whispered, grinning mischievously at Tara.

"You're a caveman."

"Ooga-booga. Me Tarzan. You Jane."

As they walked into the shadow of the overhang, Nate noticed all of the tracks in the sand. There were lots of human tracks, which would've been uplifting if it weren't for the other tracks stamped over them. They were immense, with three splayed toes on each foot. He'd seen these tracks before, back on there on the beach where a shaggy beast had taken two lives. Everyone halted.

"Howler," Peanut whispered.

The tracks were chaotic, running in both directions. It looked as though a howler had come through here in the night, paid these people an unwanted visit, and then returned to the jungle from which it came. The implications were grave. They'd seen what a howler could do to people in a matter of seconds, and this one hadn't been stopped. It had come, done its thing, and had departed.

"You guys," Nate whispered, placing his hands on the kids shoulders, "I'm afraid that what we're going to find around this corner might be—"

"We know," Peanut replied, "but obviously we have to go look."

The kid was right, of course, but Nate had a pretty good idea of the kinds of things that they were probably going to see. They'd seen quite enough already. Another crushing blow to their hopes was not what they needed today.

From around the corner of the wall came a single cough.

Their eyes widened. Tara gasped, and covered her mouth. Someone back there was still alive. Nate and the teens looked to one another in astonishment, hints of smiles spreading across their faces. All at once, they began to run.

### 

28-D

The two sets of tracks terminated in a spot of strange activity, and then a single set of tracks continued on into the jungle. Hart stopped in the clearing, cocking his head at the smoldering embers in the little fire pit, the heap of clothing, and a bunch of charred bones. It didn't make any sense. Those were Lonny's clothes.

Hart dabbed at the clustered eggs on his lips with the tip of his tongue, frowning down at the collection of weird artifacts. He didn't suppose that Lonny was running around the jungle naked.

The lone trail of departing footprints were those of the Marine. He couldn't think of a reason why he'd be carrying Lonny unless the boy had been injured, which was possible. Hart prodded a blackened ribcage with the toe of his boot. It crumbled to pieces. The rest of the bones were mostly burned to ash. There was part of a jaw, and some teeth. Hart stared at the teeth, and he felt a dark suspicion begin to flare in the depths of his core.

Why would the Marine have done that?

He'd trusted that man. He'd entrusted that man with Lonny's life, and this was what he'd gone and done? It just didn't make any sense. It didn't make any sense at all.

As Hart lumbered along the trail of single footprints, he could feel his friends becoming restless. They were writhing in his mind, recalculating, as though they were alarmed by his darkening emotions, his willful shift toward an insubordinate propensity. His bullet wounds suddenly began to hurt again. The worms were threatening him by showing him that their symbiotic relationship could be dissolved, thereby returning him to a helpless state of agony. While Hart appreciated their position on this matter, there were just some things that a man had to do on his own. He could take the pain. He could take all the agony that his new masters could inflict, and then some.

Hart bellowed into the jungle, gaining speed as he lurched along the trail. Eggs spilled from his lips on swinging tendrils of drool, but Hart didn't care. His wounded leg was screaming with pain, but he didn't care about that either. It was no longer the worms in control. Yeah, Hart was still going to bite him. He'd keep his end of the deal. But he might have to do much more than bite that man. He might just have to go far above and beyond delivering the small injury that the worms were ordering him to inflict.

### 

25-B

Dale rose to his feet as a new man, and a couple of teenagers, came running without warning around the bend, and right into their camp. They were breathless, smiling, overflowing with obvious joy to have found some other survivors. However, once they noticed the mutilated hijacker, and what was left of Dr. Kimura, their smiles faded.

Things had changed. Not that their camp was ever really a happy place, but after last night's events, a pall had settled over them. The constant attention that their two patients required had not only reduced their able workers to alternating shifts of two, but unless something changed with the status of the injured men, they couldn't relocate. They were stuck in this spot. Truth be told, he and Sandy were the only reliable hands in camp. He enjoyed Don-boy's company, but the guy was not exactly cut out for hauling firewood. Neither was the backstabbing princess. She wasn't cut out for much of anything but shaking her booty up on a stage, and after the stunt she'd pulled last night, the whole group had disowned her. Margot sat alone, shunned to the edge of the sea. There was no coming back from that one. She was dead to them.

Donovan didn't even sit up when the newcomers marched into camp. He didn't move. Looked like he might be on the verge of having a stroke, if he hadn't had one already. He'd just finished dragging in his third log of the day, and the effort had just nearly killed him. It was the heat, the hard labor, probably just being outdoors. He was passed out in the sand, sprawled in a patch of shadow with his arm flung over his eyes. The island had drained all the piss and vinegar right out of him.

Dale was feeling a little whipped from hauling logs out of the jungle since dawn's break. His arms were rubbed raw from the scaly bark of the local trees, and the fancy city shoes he'd hoped to wear through streets of Las Vegas were rubbing blisters all over his feet. He couldn't cuss them enough.

Sandy was the one to get up and greet the newcomers, of course. Dale was really starting to like her. She was a good girl, probably the best of the whole bunch. While everyone else was hightailing it, Sandy had stepped right up to face that woolybooger all on her own, and she'd whopped it right over the melon with a burning campfire log. Blistered her hands up something awful. Dale grinned, chortling to himself over the memory. When that thing ran off squalling into the night with its head all lit up like a torch … well, he guessed that was probably the damnedest thing he'd ever seen.

Looked like Sandy was explaining the situation, gesturing to Dr. Kimura and the hijacker with her bandaged hands. She'd been nursing them all day, treating them according to Dr. Kimura's specifications. Odds were, that man was never going to walk again. Dale had seen enough injuries in the logging woods to know when a man wasn't apt to return, and the doctor's mangled legs were the worse injuries he'd ever seen. That woolybooger had really worked him over. The doc really seemed to believe in that seaweed tea concoction of his, but Dale guessed it was going to take a lot more than a sip of that juice to keep him alive. If they didn't get rescued pretty quickly, he didn't expect that the doctor would have much chance of lasting for any longer than a week, before some terrible infection did him in. At some point, those rotten legs were going to have to come off.

One of the teens handed something to Sandy, and then he turned, and started walking in Dale's direction. Eyeballing him, Dale chewed on his stick, observing the boy's awkward gait as he plodded through the sand. Kids his age always looked like they'd just learned to walk the day before yesterday.

"Want a sack of peanuts?" the kid asked.

"What's your name?"

"Peanut."

"I asked you your name."

"That is my name."

"Your name's Peanut, and you're handing out peanuts, too?"

"My real name's Matthew, but everybody calls me Peanut—because I like them."

"Well, damn, Peanut. I guess today's your lucky day." He accepted the sack of airline fare from the boy, smeared his palm on his hip, and extended his hand. "Thank ye kindly. I'm Dale."

"Welcome." The kid shook his hand, and then looked down at the heap of airline packages in the paunch of his shirt. "I found them all along the beach this morning. Looks like I've probably got enough for everybody." The kid smiled, nodded, and then ambled in Margot's direction.

"Uh-uh." Dale reached out and caught him by the upper arm. He frowned and shook his head. "None for her." He could see Margot staring hopefully in their direction, but he refused to look her way. "She don't get no peanuts."

"Why?"

"You see that little chewed-up Chinese feller over there?"

"Yeah."

"She's the one did that to him. On purpose." Dale studied the kid's face as he took it all in. "She don't get no peanuts or soda. You hear me?"

The kid nodded. "Yes, sir."

"Tell you what. You sneak on over there to that sleeping I-talian, and real careful, you just lay a sack of nuts right across his nose." Dale grinned, and winked. "You tell him I sent you."

The kid gave an uneasy chuckle. "Okay …"

Dale watched the kid the slogging off through the sand in the Donovan's direction. If you couldn't have just a little fun now and then, then what was even the point of living? He guessed he probably ought to go over and meet the neighbors. "No nuts for that one either!" he shouted after the boy, jabbing a finger in the direction of the hijacker.

The hijacker was finally awake. He was sitting up for the first time since they'd dragged his sorry carcass into camp. When he turned his head, Dale met his eyes with an unwavering scowl. Dr. Kimura looked pretty pleased with himself. Despite his own grievous condition, he was eager to appraise the health of the criminal he'd managed to nurse back to health. None of that was going to matter if they didn't get enough wood collected before sundown. Dale had a sneaking suspicion that there was more than one of those woolyboogers on the island, and if they didn't stoke up a raging bonfire in the middle of that path, then more folks were bound to get chewed on. Thanks to Sandy's selfless act, they'd managed to learn something pretty important: woolyboogers were flammable.

All hands were gathering around the hijacker, who seemed to be suddenly alert and responsive. Dale greeted the new man, named Nate, who seemed cut of pretty good cloth, as well as the girl he had with him. Tara was a cute one, but probably just a little young.

Hard to gauge ages when everyone's face was covered with the same layer of grime. Sandy, as Dale could've anticipated, was already trying to baby her hijacker, offering ol' Skinhead a sip of her seaweed tea. "Come on, now," Dale said, shifting his feet in the sand. "He's a big boy. You don't got to wait on him like that."

"He's dehydrated," she replied.

"Y'all know who this is, don't you?" Dale looked at each of the new faces in their camp. "You recognize him without ears and a nose? This here is one of them hijackers who blew up the plane."

"I didn't blow up the plane."

"So, you can talk now. That's good. Wonder what we ought to talk about?"

"Leave him alone."

"You know what? I've done left him alone. I left him alone all damned night, but now I think it's time this feller answered a few questions."

"You got that right." Donovan strolled up beside Dale to stare the hijacker down.

Nate squatted beside the man, studying his injuries with what appeared to be a morbid curiosity. "Who did these things to you?"

The hijacker began to breathe heavily, clenching his fists. He seemed unready, or unwilling to recall that disturbing memory. "Listen to me. We're in terrible danger here."

"No shit, Sherlock." Donovan grinned, bobbing his head.

"There are others here," he said, his eyes peering through the caked blood, still glazed with the residual horror of whatever he'd been through, "and they're not other survivors from the crash."

"Who are they?" Sandy asked.

"They're savages." The hijacker stared into her eyes.

"Tell us about what happened," Nate said.

"Some of the other passengers caught up to me in the jungle. Started beating me up. Tried to strangle me with a parachute cord."

"Good," Dale muttered.

"But, there was this U.S. Marine amongst them. A little shell-shocked maybe. He saw what they were doing to me, and he just kind of lost it. Took my gun, and turned it on himself. Stuck it right into his mouth." His hands knotted into bloody fists, squeezed and relaxed, squeezed and relaxed. "But before he could pull the trigger, those others appeared. They came pouring out of the jungle, all around us."

"The attacked without provocation?" Nate asked.

"Not exactly." The hijacker swiveled his scalped head in Nate's direction. "The Marine turned the gun on them, and he shot and killed one of them before running off. That's when everything went south. I was the only one they spared, probably because they saw me as being an enemy to the rest of you guys."

"They got that right," Dale said.

"But, it wasn't before they did all of this to me," the hijacker whispered, "and they're not finished. They'll be coming for the rest of you. They know things, impossible things, things that they shouldn't know. They know about the vector. He's the one who they really want."

"The vector, the vector. Here we go again with that mumbo-jumbo," Donovan said.

"Yeah, maybe we ought to start with the simple things first," Dale said, stepping forward, and bending down. "Who the hell are you, and what the happened up there on that plane?"

"My name's John."

"John Doe, or John Smith?" Donovan said.

"John Woodard. I was working for the United Nations, in health and disease control. What happened up there on that plane was a terrible accident. It was supposed to be a quick and clean job. We were trying to save lives."

"I believe you screwed the pooch on that one."

"What happened up there was not my fault. No one was supposed to get hurt. None of that was part of—"

"Like hell it wasn't your fault."

"If it wasn't your fault, then whose fault was it? Huh, tough guy?"

"Wait a minute," Nate said. "Let's hear what he has to say. What do you mean when you say that you were trying to save lives?"

The hijacker breathed deeply, shooing a cloud of haranguing gnats that haloed his skinned head. He closed his eyes slowly, and then reopened them. "Those weren't U.S. Marshals transporting a prisoner. They were CIA."

"Who was the monkey on their leash?" Dale asked.

"That would be the vector. We don't know his identity. All that we do know is that he's carrying a deadly virus, the likes of which we've never seen. Causes—horrible symptoms, bleeding from every orifice of the body, rapid organ shutdown. Authorities discovered him two weeks ago, wandering naked and confused through Zaire in an area known as the Ebola River Valley."

"What did the CIA want with him?" Nate asked.

"What does the CIA always want with a potential weapon of mass destruction?"

"Hang on a minute, now," Donovan said, dropping both hands in a chopping gesture. "You trying to tell us—that you're the friggin' good guy, here?"

The hijacker's eyes flicked up to lock on those of Donovan. "We have good reason to believe that the vector—as we've been referring to him—is carrying an experimental, weaponized virus."

"How can you be sure of that?" Nate asked.

"Implants. Evidence of hasty surgical procedures. Implanted technology. I saw the x-rays myself, and I'd never seen anything like what he's got sewed up inside of him. Two days after quarantine in Zaire, he was nabbed by the CIA. You do the math."

"Are you a scientist?" Sandy asked.

"Hardly. I'm just a hired specialist. My squad's orders were to return the vector to U.N. custody in Zaire, dead or alive."

"Who would've spawned a deadly virus like that, and why?" Sandy asked.

"The why part is easy. Who? That's the mystery. The Americans, Russians, Chinese … we don't know. All likely candidates, but Zaire has no international enemies, no resources or valuable territory. All they have are people. Lots of people. It was almost as if the vector was dropped into an overpopulated zone for maximal damage."

"Maybe it was some kind of an experiment," Dale said. "You know, like a trial run. Someone might've been testing out their new killer bug on some poor country, see if it's catchy or not."

John the hijacker nodded. "We believe that to be a distinct possibility."

"Guess this brings us to the million dollar question," Dale said, licking his lips, and gazing around their camp through anxious eyes. "Where in the hell are we?"

"You just said it," John said, narrowing his eyes up at Dale. Gnats fizzed around the bloody hole in the center of his face. "Hell. We've fallen straight down into Hell."

# CHAPTER SIX

28-D

Hart crashed through dense thickets, ripped down curtains of ensnarled vines. Growling, shambling through reefs of stinging nettles, he flung his numbed arm from side to side like a battle flail. He didn't care. The pain was making him crazy. They were hurting him on purpose, refusing to produce any more anesthetic. It was their way of punishing him. They wanted him to suffer for disobeying. They meant to break his spirit, to enslave his mind. Turned out, the worms weren't really his friends after all. Yeah, they'd cared for his wounds, but Hart was beginning to find out that there were some pretty stiff conditions attached to the treatment. They were just using him like a demolition derby car, just like everyone in the film industry had always used him. Whenever something came up that was too risky for their actors, they'd send in the expendable fool, the crash dummy. Taking hits for weaker masters seemed to be his whole lot in life.

He was about to show his new controllers who was really the boss. Dragging his forearm across his lips, he smeared away the slathering of yellow eggs. He was done with this. His mouth was not going to be their stupid nest. He sucked the gobbets from his teeth, and spat the next generation of worms all over the jungle. Balling his hand into a sledgehammer, he smashed his fist down against the bullet hole in his thigh, splattering the gelatinous mass, and the worms beneath it, across his blue jeans. The pain that followed was excruciating. Maybe not the best idea. He collapsed into the nettles, shivering, tears spilling from his eyes, but he refused to scream. Somewhere nearby, he heard someone else scream, but he couldn't imagine that they were any worse off than him.

It took a few seconds before the agony subsided to a tolerable level, and he was able to rise once again from the briars. The worms were furious with him. They were biting, boring, corkscrewing hot tunnels through his flesh. It was maddening. He wanted to peel back his skin from the underlying muscle, and start picking those little devils out one at a time, crushing them into between his fingernails. However, he knew that there were way too many inside him, probably thousands, and he was stuck with them. He could fight them, but not forever, because it hurt too much. Eventually, they'd break him. The freedom he'd always taken for granted was suddenly boiled down to a single choice that the worms allowed him to make: choose the hard road, or the easy one, to the exact same destination.

There was another scream, followed by a gunshot.

Hart swung his heavy head in the direction of all the commotion. Yes, there were definitely some people needing bit over there. It was starting to become imperative that he sink his teeth into someone, and he didn't think that it was the influence of the worms. It was his own decision, not theirs, and it seemed like the proper thing to do. He couldn't imagine why he'd never thought to bite anyone before.

Already, he felt the pain lessening. The little ones were pleased with his new direction in thinking. They were rewarding him for making good choices. Who was in control now? Seemed like he was the boss of them. Worms writhed in his injuries, oozing anesthetic, prepping him just like a miniature film crew for his next stunt. Hart lurched forward. Gel oozed from his wounds. Placing one foot in front of the other, he staggered toward the ruckus.

Shouts echoed through the trees. One voice was shouting, anyway. The other was unintelligible. It might've been human, but it sounded more like a bestial groan. Another gunshot cracked the humid air, succeeded by a contemptuous bellow. Hart pushed through a mossy veil, and he saw them.

The man with the revolver was the U.S. Marine who'd done the bad things to Lonny. Someone else had gotten to him first. The Marine squeezed off another shot, and then turned, and ran from the other fellow. His assailant did not appear to be armed, but for some reason he had no fear of the Marine's weapon. He chased him down, tackled him, and wrestled him to the jungle floor. More shouting, groaning, as the pair thrashed all about in the leaf litter, until the Marine was pinned face-down in the dirt. His assailant bent over him, opened his jaws wide, and sunk his teeth deeply into the Marine's neck. A garbled scream permeated the jungle, as the Marine's legs flailed against the ground.

Hart licked his lips, eyes widening. This was fascinating. Someone else had stolen his idea. It was someone just like him. All his life he'd always felt so alone, like the last of some extirpated race wandering an alien world, but right there in the forest clearing was another one. It was another lonely monster just like him.

Lowering himself to his hands and knees, Hart crept through the underbrush, circling around to the combatants' blind side. Another shriek wrought a fountain of crimson from the Marine's opened neck. The sound of his fluids spattering in the dry leaves was exhilarating, but Hart was reluctant to interrupt while the other was engaged with his prey. That seemed kind of—rude.

The attacker reared up, as though he'd caught a whiff of danger. He spun around in Hart's direction, searching the jungle. When their eyes finally met, Hart sucked a sharp breath, and his hands began to tremble. It was *him*. Hart awed over the glimmering chain still looped between the monster's wrists. Somehow, he'd managed to make it to shore. The shackled man cocked his head, studying Hart through his blood-drop eyes.

What a rare and beautiful creature.

The Marine scrambled to his feet, blood spouting from his neck. The shackled man whirled back around, ready to pounce, but he decided against furthering the chase, and he just let the man go. Finished, for the time being. He gazed back at Hart, blinking slowly, as the sounds of his prey crashing off into the jungle grew distant. This meeting between two monsters was a far more important matter.

Hart rose from his crouched position. He and the shackled man peered at each other through the screen of foliage, but neither seemed quite ready to approach the other. Hart lowered the frond in front of his face. He pinched a single leaf between his thumb and forefinger, and he plucked it gently from its stem. The shackled man quietly observed. After a moment, he also reached for a nearby bush, and he plucked a leaf of his own. They twirled their leaves between their fingers, just looking at each other.

The shackled man opened his fingers, and he allowed his leaf to flutter to the ground. Hart did the same. One of them must have flinched, because just like that, they were both moving toward one another across the clearing. They began to circle one another, as the distance between them shrank down to almost nothing. It was the final approach in some deadly dance that could end in any number of ways. Would they run together, or would one's throat soon be dangling from the teeth of the other? His heart throbbed against his ribs, chugging blood through his ears, as a couple of monsters prepared to engage.

Hart could see them. They were all squirming behind the shackled man's sanguine eyes. The clustered eggs that coating his lips were stained with his victim's blood. It helped Hart to better understand and appreciate his own condition to look upon his mirror image, and what he saw standing in front of him was perfect.

"What's your name?" Hart whispered.

Their worms were all gathered behind the portals of their eyes, all pressed against the glass with excitement. The shackled man shuffled his feet, and lowered his chin, as though embarrassed. After a moment, he opened his mouth, and he revealed that he had no tongue left in there. Only a purple nub bristling with black stitches remained. Some sick bastard had cut it out. How awful. Hart would never be able to hear him speak. They would never be able to share their stories or ideas, and that was most unfair. Hart wished that he'd have been somewhere nearby when they'd tried to do that to him. He'd have ripped open their stomachs, and pulled everything out of them. No one was ever going to hurt this guy again.

Hart lifted a trembling hand, and he touched one of the two bullet holes in the shackled man's torso. The shackled man's face stretched into a smile. He responded by raising his chained hand, inadvertently lifting the other connected to it like some entangled marionette, and he touched the festering hole in Hart's shoulder.

Worms roiled wetly against Hart's fingertips. He loved this. They were repairing him. He was already looking better. The worms would fix every ailment that ever threatened the life of Hart's best *friend*.

### 

27-D

Margot licked her cracked lips, gazing longingly at the cache of beer and sodas heaped near the campfire. She was so thirsty that it hurt. Her head was pounding, burning internally as though acid had slowly begun to displace all of the blood in her veins. She needed a drink so badly. She needed something to eat. However, she knew better than to ask, because they weren't going to share anything with her.

It wasn't fair. She hadn't meant to hurt anyone. It's not like what happened was premeditated. If they'd asked her five seconds before that thing came running at her if she had any desire whatsoever to kill Dr. Kimura, the answer would've obviously been no. It was just a knee-jerk reaction. Nobody knows how they'd react in a situation like that. You might think that you'd be all heroic, but you might as easily be mistaken about who you thought you were in a moment of crisis. Margot wasn't consciously thinking when she pushed Dr. Kimura over her leg. That action was pure instinct. Survival mode. Any one of the others who were looking down their noses at her might've done the same thing if they'd been standing in her shoes.

Out here, it was clearly survival of the fittest, and Margot knew that she wasn't the strongest, the toughest, or the fastest. She didn't have any super-amazing skills to bring to the table. She was just a girl, so already, she was at a disadvantage. From the get-go, she was probably considered to be the least valuable camp member, the most likely to die, and odds were, the first that the others would've thrown under a bus if the going ever got tough. Given those hard truths, who the hell could blame her for trying to outsmart them, and for just trying to stay alive, when she was all alone on Team Margot?

Obviously, they were going to hold her accountable for the doctor's demise, but they were also the ones who'd voted to starve her to death. Basically, she had nothing to lose by continuing to do whatever it took to stay alive. They already hated her. She was already dead to their little community. They hadn't physically thrown her out of their camp yet, but when the sun went down tonight, and it started to get cold, were they even going to let her come up to their fire to warm up? Probably not. They'd probably just start yelling at her all over again, and she'd end up having to sleep all alone down on the freezing beach, just like the night before.

Why was she still hanging around here? She didn't know. They didn't want her, and it was starting to feel awkward, but she didn't have anywhere else to go. The smartest thing would be to go look for some new people to take her in, but at this point she was already dying of thirst, and those other jerks had already combed the beach, and had hoarded all of the available food and drink for themselves. She doubted if there was anything left out there.

Whenever she eyed that pile of canned beverages, she could feel her throat tightening up. Over lunch, the others had split three sodas, and they'd shared a bunch of peanuts right in front of her. That was not cool at all. It was mean. She needed a drink just as bad as them, and they didn't even care if she lived or died. They weren't leaving her with a whole lot of options. Unless she made a move pretty quickly, it wouldn't be long before those sodas and beers were all gone, and by then, she'd be half-dead. Yeah, it was now or never.

Dale, and the two new guys were preparing to head out on some sort of a mission to find fresh water in the jungle. She'd never even been introduced to the newcomers. She only watched from afar as they gathered the empty beer and soda cans, and even made a sort of duffle out of seat cushions and a garbage bag to carry back all the water they that thought they were going to find out there. She doubted they'd find anything. Maybe they would, but once again, they weren't going to share any with her if they did. That left Donovan, Sandy, and the new girl in camp, all taking turns playing nurse to their two patients. Margot watched as the three guys said their goodbyes, exchanged hugs, and shook hands.

Finally, they set off down the beaten trail in the direction of the beach. Margot was beginning to think that they'd never leave. After pampering their spoiled patients for a short while, Sandy and Donovan headed out of camp, probably to gather some more freaking firewood. They just kept gathering more and more and more, when there was already a ridiculous pile of wood sitting there that would've lasted them like ten-billion years. Bunch of idiots.

Margot watched as Sandy and Donovan rounded the bend in the trail, and disappeared from sight. Once they were gone, she swiveled around on her butt to stare at the new girl. She was pretty. Not model-pretty, but sexy-pretty, and there was a big difference. She was definitely younger than Margot, maybe seventeen or eighteen, still naïve and impressionable. Margot kept staring at the girl until she noticed. Margot smiled at her, brushing a few loose strands of hair out of her face, and tucking them behind her ear. She knew how to appear friendly. She could be anything that a camera wanted her to be, and she pretended that the girl was a camera that begged her to be approachable, hopeful, and innocent.

"Hi," Margot said, smiling sweetly.

"Hi," the girl replied.

"Need any help with anything?"

"Mmm, I think I've got it. Thanks."

Margot rose from the sand, dusting off the backs of her legs, and approached the girl. She could tell that the girl was already feeling uncomfortable. Evidently, they'd been telling her things. "I'm sorry that we didn't get introduced earlier, but I was afraid they'd all just attack me if I tried to come over to meet you guys. I'm Margot."

"Hi, I'm Tara." The girl smiled, cocked her head, and folded her arms across her chest. "The man with us is Nate, and the other boy my age is Peanut."

"Peanut? That's cute."

"Yeah, he's something."

"Do you guys know each other from school or something?"

"Yeah, we go the same high school. We're art students. There were a bunch of us on that plane," Tara said, her smile fading.

"I'm sorry. This has been so awful for everyone."

"I know."

"Well, I'm really glad that you found us. I was hoping for some new faces around here. As you can probably tell, the people in this camp are kind of—mean."

"Really?" Tara scrunched up her face.

"Yeah. You saw how they treat me. I haven't had anything to eat or drink since the accident. They won't share anything with me."

"Why?"

"Basically, they hate me." Margot nodded in self-affirmation, tightening her lips, looking off to one side, and … there were those tears, right on cue. She sniffed, and wiped them away. "Sorry," she said, giving a halfhearted chuckle, "it's just been hard." More tears streamed her cheeks, as she let her face crumple.

"Why do they hate you?"

"They didn't tell you all about it? I'm surprised."

"No. I mean, well, you know, they said something about it or whatever, like, at the fire last night … I guess that guy fell, and got attacked, or something?" Tara said, gesturing toward Dr. Kimura.

Margot started to roll her eyes, but caught herself, and pretended to wipe tears from them again. She nodded, and cleared her throat. "We got attacked last night, by this gigantic thing."

"So did we."

"You did?"

"Yes."

Margot gasped, feigning horror, and covered her mouth. "Oh my God."

"Yeah," Tara said, nodding as tears filled her eyes, "it was pretty much the worst night ever. Kind of hard to talk about."

"I'm sorry." Margot gave the girl a half-hug. "Yeah, pretty much the exact same thing happened here. But, that thing came charging into camp, you know, and everyone just scattered. Everyone was screaming, pushing, scrambling everywhere just trying to get out of the way, and he crashed right into me! He tripped over me, and fell. Well, today they're all mad at me because I didn't stop, and like, help him up, and for that I am truly sorry, but hello? When something like that is charging at you, it's not like you have tons of time to think clearly."

"Well, no."

"So, I didn't even think to stop, or stop to think, or whatever. I just ran, just like everyone else. Yeah, I should've stopped, and I should've helped him up, but I didn't, and now I guess I'm paying with my life for that reaction, because they've cut me off completely."

Tara eyes widened with empathy.

"They ran too, let's not forget. All of them did. But I guess I'm the bad guy because I just happened to be closest to him when it happened."

"Didn't the other lady like, grab a burning log though, and like, hit the howler over the head with it?"

"Yes," Margot said, unable to refrain from rolling her eyes that time, "and for that, I admit, she is a hero. I am not. I'm just a regular person, and I was scared out of my freaking mind."

"We swam clear out into the sea to get away from ours, and when we did, this huge—"

"Can I ask you for a favor?"

Tara cocked her head, and frowned. "Sure. What—"

"I am *so thirsty*, honey. They won't share with me. I haven't had a drink in two days. I saw you guys brought in some drinks of your own."

"Sure," Tara replied. "I don't care if you have one of ours. Yeah, we found a whole bunch of cans this morning, and bags of peanuts."

"Dale said that I wasn't allowed to have any peanuts."

"Pshh. I found some of them. I guess I'll share my peanuts with whoever I darned well please."

"Oh, my God. Thank you so much." Margot's hands were trembling as she cracked open the can of soda, and peeled off the metal tab. She choked as the first swallows of warm cola rushed down her parched throat. It was so sweet and delicious. It was the most wonderful drink of anything that she'd ever taken.

"Hey!"

Still guzzling, Margot glanced through the corner of her eye at the form of Donovan, marching around the bend. She knew that he'd probably try to grab the can from her, so she intended to drink it down to the last swallow before he snatched it. Already, Tara was squaring up to him, probably ready to defend her own actions more so than the can of soda, but any line of defense was helpful.

"I knew it. I friggin' knew it. Soon as we left, I told Sandy, she's going to raid our stash. She's going to steal all our stuff. Boom. Here you are."

"Excuse me," Tara said, "but those are not your supplies. I collected that can, and that bag of peanuts. They're both mine, and I gave them to her."

"See, that's where you're all wrong, kid. There ain't no 'I' in 'team,' and there ain't no 'Margot' in this one. All supplies belong to all of us, and they ain't to be shared with her!" Donovan brushed past Tara, and he slapped the can hard right out of Margot's hand. What remained of it vanished into the sand.

"Are you crazy?" Tara shrieked. "You just wasted soda!"

"No, you did. You wasted it on her."

"She's a human being!"

"Not in my book. That was a human being right there." Donovan pointed at Dr. Kimura, who tried to sit up, but slumped back down. "He was the only doctor on this whole friggin' island, and she threw him to the beast! No. We don't reward bad behavior with soda and treats. Give it here." Donovan raised his upturned hand to Margot, and beckoned for her bag of peanuts with a fluttering gesture. "Hand 'em over."

"She gave them to me," Margot said, looking to Tara with pleading eyes. "They're all I have. I haven't eaten anything since—"

"I said hand over the nuts, or things are going to get ugly."

"Please!"

"Leave her alone!"

"Hand them over!" Donovan drew back his hand, and seized Margot by the collar with his other. "I swear to God, I'll slap the taste of that soda right off your lips."

"I said, leave her alone!" Tara grabbed hold of his wrist, and attempted to yank it loose of Margot's shirt, but Donovan reached across her, and slapped Margot across the mouth. Tara screamed, raking at his face with her fingernails.

The truth was, the slap hadn't really hurt Margot all that much, and she was so glad that it had happened. Donovan was playing a more corroborating role to her side of the story than Margot could've imagined if she'd written a goddamned script, and handed it to him. She clutched her face, wailing, and collapsed dramatically into the sand, balling her body protectively around her bag of peanuts. She noticed the can of spilt soda. While Tara and Donovan grappled, she reached between their legs for the tipped can, and returned it to her lips. Little sandy around the rim, but she managed to salvage another couple of swallows. A fleshy smack from above brought a screech of pain and surprise from Tara, who fell to the sand beside her. Blood dripped from her lower lip. Margot fought back the crazy urge to snicker, because he'd actually struck her pretty hard. This was all playing out so perfectly.

"Donovan ... stop it." The feeble voice of Dr. Kimura could barely be heard over the fray. He'd managed to prop himself up on an elbow, but it didn't look like he'd be upright for long. Flies swarmed around him. His head wagged like a rotten mushroom on its stem.

"You broke the rules! You both broke the rules!" Donovan shouted, stabbing an accusatory finger at the two girls lying in the sand. "This camp has rules that you obviously don't respect, so you can both get the hell out of here. Want to steal our food like a couple of rats, huh? Let's see how you like living out there in the jungle with all the other frigging rats. Get out! Now!" Donovan kicked sand into their faces.

"I was just trying to help her!" Tara cried.

"Yeah, you were. You fucking rat!"

"Donovan ... please."

No one turned to acknowledge Dr. Kimura. They heard his voice, thin and wavering in the humid air, but they behaved as though they'd heard nothing at all. His health was fading so rapidly that some part of them already dismissed him as being dead.

"But, they all left to go get water," Tara said, "and they're going to wonder what happened to me when they get back."

"Don't worry. I'll tell them all about it. You're done in here, and there ain't no coming back. Got that? Both of youse. Done!"

The girls glanced at one another. Margot was amused to see that Tara wore an absolutely mortified visage, as if the whole snowball of events that led to their sudden exile was the first time in her charmed life that she'd ever been publicly humiliated. Probably a good lesson for the little bitch to learn. Welcome to the real world, Margot thought, barely able to conceal her smug vindication. "Come on," she said, picking herself up out of the sand. She jammed the sack of peanuts down the front of her shirt, glaring straight at Donovan while she did it. "Let's go, and find ourselves a higher quality of people."

### 

## 22-D

"So, what do you do for a living, Dale, if you don't mind me asking?" Nate said, trying to catch his breath in the jungle humidity. Sometimes it felt more like water in the lungs than air. The new group members had all endorsed Dale as being the most suitable guide for their mission, touting his abilities as an expert woodsman, but "expert" was a relative term. The people endorsing him had only known him twenty-four hours for crying out loud, and now, Nate worried whether or not he'd made the best decision in allowing Peanut to come along. If anything happened to the kid, he didn't think that he'd be able to live with himself.

"Hogs and logs, man. Hogs and logs."

Dale had a terse way of communicating. It seemed to be a trait that was pretty typical amongst the men of small town America, almost as though they didn't want to say too much, and risk appearing foolish in some way. That, or Dale just preferred to bait his listener into doing all of the talking while he heckled them. If that was his strategy, it was effective. If most guys from small towns employed the same bait-and-heckle technique, it was no wonder why nobody ever said much. However, it didn't seem like there was very much was at risk. Nate wasn't a proud person, and he preferred some friendly conversation over silence. "So, you have a hog farm, do you, and some sort of a logging operation as well?"

"You're a good listener."

"I guess you'd probably know a thing or two about trees then, wouldn't you?"

"Not these 'uns, if that's what you're getting at."

That was, in fact, what Nate was getting at. Seemed like every conversational direction he took, he ran straight into another wall. "So, you don't see any species of trees or plants around here that you recognize?"

"Not a one."

"Interesting. I'm an engineer. I design submersibles for marine research. My wife is … she *was* a marine biologist. She could identify every fish, every animal living in or around the sea. She was a remarkable woman. I lost her in the crash."

"That's a damned shame."

Nate nodded. "Yes, I certainly thought so." He didn't know why he was talking, or what he was even trying to say. He hadn't had a chance to open up to anyone about his loss, to vent some of that emotional toxic waste that had been building up in his core since the moment Dawn disappeared beneath the waves. In truth, he hadn't even really begun to process his wife's death, and what it meant to his world. He was still in a sort of numbed phase that had been following his initial shock and horror, and he wasn't sure what phase ought to come next. "She was eaten by a mosasaur."

"A whose-a-what's-a?"

"It's a—a kind of prehistoric reptile that used to hunt the ancient seas."

"I'll be dogged."

Nate nodded, ducking beneath a thorny branch. "It's extinct. Well, at least it should be. It hasn't existed on earth for millions and millions of years, and there appears to be a whole breeding population of them in the waters all around this island."

Dale snapped a twig off a bush, and sniffed the broken end. He wrinkled his nose, and made a face. "We tell y'all about that woolybooger we seen last night?"

"The uh, the … yeah. We'd been calling them howlers. The kids were. We had quite a run-in with one ourselves, down on the beach last night." Nate cleared his throat. He almost hated to bring up the next point. Even by the light of day, it still rattled him to his core. "I'm sure that you noticed the two moons in the sky last night?"

"Yep."

Nate slipped a little on the muddy trail that they were following. Dale referred to it as a game trail. It slithered all through the jungle in what seemed a pretty purposeful manner, rounding boulders and thickets only slightly to maintain a steady bearing. Dale seemed pretty certain that it would lead them to water, eventually.

"So, the kids and I were discussing a few possible scenarios this morning," Nate said, "with respect to where we are, how exactly we got here, and we all basically came to the same conclusion—given the two moons—that something pretty extraordinary has happened. Given all of the evidence that's all around us, it doesn't leave a person with much choice but to at least consider the possibility that we're not simply stranded on a remote island that supports a variety of unique species. I mean, I hate to be the first to come out and say it, but unless a second moon just popped into existence overnight—and I'm not saying that's not what happened—then there's at least a possibility that we've somehow—"

Dale made him jump when he suddenly pressed an index finger to the side of one nostril, bent slightly at the waist, and jettisoned a great rope of snot from the other. The glob cartwheeled through the air to stick to the trunk of a tree. He smeared his bare arm beneath his nose, sniffed, and kept right on hiking.

It was hard to believe that another human being in the same unfathomable circumstances could appear as unaffected as though he were tramping through his own logging woods back in Arkansas. Nate was awed by this incongruity. Dale's reticence was bound to be contagious, because you could only talk to a snot-covered tree for so long before falling into silence yourself. Nate had been quietly hoping that their search would turn up more than just water. He was hoping for new people, other survivors, maybe a big group of them who'd fared better. Not that he disliked Dale, or his group. They just seemed to be struggling. There was a whole lot of tension back in that camp, and he wasn't exactly looking forward to spending the night in their cloud of funk.

He wasn't sure what to make of John's tale. The mutilated hijacker had seemed just a little out of his head, expressing far more worry over those other people with whom he'd run afoul than the more obvious threats of the howlers, dehydration, starvation, or lack of medical treatment for his injuries. By Nate's estimation, any chance of there being other people on this island was nothing but a good thing. A local tribe of indigenous people would have all of the knowledge and survival skills that the castaways were lacking. If there really were natives, then they could be their salvation. The nutcase who'd fired a shot at them had screwed-up royally, that much could not be denied. However, there was no doubt in Nate's mind that if the opportunity presented itself, he could lead a peaceful negotiation into some sort of a truce with them, but he'd probably have to gag Dale and Donovan before doing so.

"When do you think we'll find water?" Peanut asked.

Dale stopped. He turned to the boy, as if this new subject matter actually had some value. "The jungle critters who made this trail are taking us on the most direct route to it, little buddy." He pointed through the trees at the jagged mountain ridge that loomed ahead. "See the way them peaks are kind of corrugated? Like an old sheet of tin roofing?"

Peanut frowned. "Yeah."

"Well, them furrows were all carved out by water. Fresh water, from the sky. We're headed for that deepest one, right-smack in the middle where all them other little ones converge. You follow a game trail that's aimed for the deepest hollow, then I guarantee you'll find yourself some water."

"Cool."

"Trouble is, we ain't going to be making this hike back and forth every day."

"What do you mean?" Nate asked.

Dale shook his head. "Well, it makes a whole lot more sense to me to move our camp right to the water, than to keep hauling water back to camp. You want this to be your job, starting tomorrow?"

"No, I guess not."

"See what I'm saying? There ain't enough manpower to keep firewood stocked, to haul water, and hell, we ain't even started to talk about building a shelter, a big fence, and learn to start hunting and trapping …"

"I'm ready to start hunting," Peanut said. "I want to kill a howler, for Alex."

"Wait a minute. So, you're in this for the long haul?" Nate said. "I mean, you're talking about building a permanent fort way back there in the jungle. There's not going to be any hope of being spotted by a ship or a plane back in there, and that pretty much drops our chances of getting rescued down to zero."

Dale looked Nate up and down. "There ain't going to be anybody left to rescue if we don't move our camp closer to water. That's the long and short of it." Dale set his jaw, and resumed hiking, as though the conversation was finished.

Nate skipped to catch up with him. "If we decide to do what you're suggesting, then how do you propose we transport our injured clear back into those mountain valleys?"

"I ain't suggesting or proposing anything. We either do it, or we die."

"We should probably start making some spears," Peanut said, "just in case."

"I don't think that a pointed stick is going to be very effective against a howler."

"I'm not just talking about howlers," Peanut replied. "We don't know what's in these woods, but we need to be ready to defend ourselves against whatever."

"I agree," Dale said. "We'll work on making us some weapons tonight, around the fire."

"But what if something attacks us this afternoon?"

Dale reached into his pocket. He fished around for a few seconds, and then produced a pocket knife. "Here," he said, tossing it to Peanut.

Peanut's eyes lit up. A hint of a smile curled his mouth as he flipped open the gleaming blade. He tilted it in the sunlight, and snapped it closed again. "Do I get to keep it?"

Dale placed a hand on the kid's shoulder, and gave him a shake. "I pronounce you our designated hunter and warrior. Yes, you can keep it, but I might need to borrow it from you now and then. Deal?"

"Deal."

"Sharpen a good stick later on, if you like, but right now, finding water is what's most important. We ain't got time to waste. I don't know about y'all, but I don't want to be stuck out here in these woods much after sundown."

The trail ascended a steep ridge. Nate tried to step wherever Dale stepped, following closely, but not so close that he'd catch another whipped branch across the face. That was a lesson that only needed learned once. He still couldn't get over how quiet the island became during the daylight hours. It was probably the absence of songbirds that made the jungle seem so deafeningly still. You didn't realize how much they contributed to the background noise of an ordinary day until their voices were removed from the ambiance. There was no wind. The only disturbance to challenge the profound stillness was the rustle of their own footsteps through the litter. When they stopped walking, the silence was profound.

Where were the howlers? Something that huge would have to have trouble finding itself a place to hide during the day, unless there were only a few of them on the island. What about the other animals? Obviously, there were other forms of life, or they wouldn't be walking along a beaten trail. Nate scanned the trampled mud beneath their feet. There were plenty of footprints, alright. They were three-toed, like the howler, but much smaller, about the size of a human handprint. There was something vaguely familiar about them. He supposed that they reminded him of shorebird tracks, only larger. Based on their comparative size, Nate imagined a bird roughly the size and shape of an emu.

Cresting the ridge, they paused to peer down into the depths of the succeeding hollow. The jungle plummeted into a dark rift where trees grew sideways, reaching horizontally to snatch at rays of sunlight. More impressive than the canyon below, however, was the sight of endless ridges and hollows rippling the land before them to the reaches of their visual limits. Nate felt suddenly very small. As he gaped over the boundless expanse of rainforest, he found himself wondering if this was not an island at all, but just the very edge of an entire lost world.

"Hey," Nate whispered, slapping at Dale's arm. "Look right there." He could see something, an animal of some sort, clear down in the paunch of the hollow. It was pale, mottled, and covered with downy plumage that draped over its humped back. Through the thick vegetation, he only managed to steal a glimpse of whatever it was before the mysterious creature shuffled off.

"Look!" Peanut pointed at the horizon's edge, where scythe wings carved slices through the sky. Their villous forms spiraled over the jungle in a dark promenade.

"What are they?" Nate whispered.

"Dragons," Peanut replied.

They sure did look like dragons. With their ornamented heads, and their long, whip-like tails, they looked every bit like sky dragons. It felt as though they were living in the cover art of a fantasy novel, and for that moment, at least, their lost world felt amazing. God, he wished that Dawn could've been there to share the moment with him. Her adoration for nature's wonders would've enabled her to appreciate a sight like this one on a level that the others couldn't even begin to comprehend. She would've seen so much more than the shapes of dragons in the sky. She'd have seen living history, animal heritage, and biological links, expanding her whole comprehension of the living world in an almost mathematical orgasm that would've stolen her breath away.

"Well," Dale said, snorting and lobbing a wad of sputum far out over the hollow, "let's go find that watering hole."

# CHAPTER SEVEN

21-A

A cool drink from cupped hands would be just the remedy. A splash over his flushed face would bring him back around, and chase the darkness away. That's what Alonzo had hoped would happen, but when he finally collapsed on the bank of a crystalline stream, he realized that water alone could not save him. He was too far gone.

He gazed down at his own reflection, distorted by the water's flow, and by the ruby droplets raining from his open throat. Alonzo watched what little remained of his natural essence be spirited away by the current, until there was nothing left. His injury had ceased to throb. That was strange. The dangling flag of skin was numb to the touch, yet it churned like a net full of eels. He felt the flap of skin jiggle wetly against his shoulder as he spun around to scan the jungle for his pursuer, and saw nothing of the shackled man.

Once again, the jungle had pinned him down for a death stroke, and at the penultimate moment, she'd changed her mind. It was her deadly games, her flippant nuances that assured Alonzo that the jungle was female. Alonzo tried to keep her at arm's length and out of his head, but like any woman, she would have no less than the whole of him. She wanted him in her, alive and bestial in his entirety, while some dark part of her yearned for him to die in her arms, just to see what it would feel like to lose him forever. Today, she would have it both ways.

He could feel himself evolving. The transformation was happening right now. Evolution only confused a teaching dog's fundamental lesson in the pointlessness of existence. A new visage would mean new lessons, and the underlying message would become complex. Lessons within lessons evaded Alonzo's understanding, leaving his mind to flounder in the vagaries of strange, new layers of life's ultimate truth. Perhaps it was not as simple as it once had seemed, back on that smoldering hilltop in Vietnam. Do we all just go until we stop, or were there those amongst us who stopped, then got back up, and kept on going?

The humanoid form that attacked him was not just a man. There was more to him. Alonzo sensed a vastness about him, as though he too was a thing that had managed to keep going when it was supposed to have stopped. The mysterious possibilities of the universe were expanding in Alonzo's mind. His jungle goddess was behind it all. He was sure of that. Something of her essence had been imparted into him, delivered through one savage bite. What secret had his lover, creator and destroyer whispered into him through the mouth-hole of a new breed of teaching dog?

Alonzo tapped the water's surface with a trembling index finger. His face appeared so deathly wan, his eyes so vacant yet shimmering with a new sort of madness that he didn't recognize. Enough battlefield casualties had taught him well to know the face of a dead man, and the face leering up from the stream was that of a corpse. When he collapsed at its edge, his body had bled out. He'd gone until he stopped. His life was done.

Chirring insects in the trees kept him aroused, hovering by a thread over death's brink. He'd twitched, shivered on the end of that thread cast down into the precipice like a baited fishing line. That's when something ascended from the dark abyss. It rushed up from below, yawned its vast maw, and it swallowed him whole. Enveloped in the darkness of its gut, Alonzo wriggled with larval futility as the entity digested him, assimilated him, until two bodies and souls had merged into one.

They were speaking to him, those insects. He could hear their collective voices as she reeled him back up from the netherworld's depths, but he was unable to comprehend their cacophony of alien tongues. At the moment he erupted to the surface, sucking air as his stiffened form writhed in coagulated blood, the words of insects made strange and sudden sense to him. Theirs was a singsong dialect of ancient anthems that proclaimed their allegiance to one of a million sects.

They were his friends, the ones inside of him. There were lots of them hard at work to preserve a body fit for only for death, all brewing some necromancer's formula that refilled his shriveled veins. It was a gift, but he sensed that it wouldn't free. No gift ever was. They'd restored him in exchange for some favors that only he could provide for them. This would be a symbiotic relationship of give and take, not unlike that between spouses.

"It's you," he whispered, awing down into her eyes gazing back at him from behind his own reflection in the wishing pool. It was God herself manifested in a new and clever way, one in which she would at last have the whole of him. Thoughts, flesh, and thoughts of flesh would be shared, forever merged with his jungle lover as one creature divine.

### 

## 28-D

They ran, paired, and single-minded for the chase. They ran as one with a forest world that contorted around their hurtling forms. Outgrowths seemed to lift, bow, and recede from their path with every juke through that labyrinth of light and shadow. Theirs was a predatory privilege known only to the wild things that bounded over feral plateaus towering over the fearful lowlands of their prey. They alone knew the steps to the instinctual dance, gyrating over the huddled masses they'd soon invite to a timeless climax where the stage would invariably be soaked with one performer's blood.

Panting, heaving, they leapt thorny barricades with effortless grace. They jagged around one another, forever jostling for that coveted spot in the lead where they knew first blood would be spilled. Bursting into a clearing, some groaning thing stirred from its diurnal slumber to swivel its massive head, but it did not give chase. Just as the great bear pardons the pack of wolves, the shaggy beast recognized them as fellows in blood sport, and it had no urge to quarrel. Through its black shag of down, one saucer eye parted wrinkled lids. A translucent membrane slid away from a burning portal straight to hell. The round pupil constricted to a pinhole in the sunlight.

Hart threw back his head and howled as they thundered past the stinking hulk, and he heard the shackled man echo with his own mournful bale. They'd no need for words in this game, because theirs was a bond forged over thousands of generations of deadly pursuit. These were ancient lessons coursing through their veins, and somehow they knew all the ways of taking lives just as completely as the author of the killing book.

Crashing back into the trees, they resumed their quarry's trail. Crimson spatters bejeweled the leaves, and smeared branches wherever he'd passed. Great pools splashed the ground wherever he'd paused to catch his breath. Here was a red handprint stamped onto the trunk of a tree. There was a lake of gore where he'd stumbled and fell. They were nearing the end of the trail, and the shackled man gibbered with excitement. No greater thrill in this world exceeded that of the final reckoning, when they at last bore down on their terrified prey.

The shrieks of surprise were met with growls, primal roars, as Hart and the shackled man slammed into their flank. He felt some ribs shatter beneath the force of his impact. It felt so natural, so right, his teeth rending flesh, and squeaking against bone. The warrior's painted faces were twisted into masks of horror. Hart threw his arms around two skinny necks, and he squeezed their heads together until he heard two pops. The worms didn't approve of fatalities, but both Hart and the shackled man somehow understood the art of pushing violence to the brink, of satisfying those primal urges imbued by the ancestral savages of their strange lineage, while staying within the graces of their handlers. They would obey their hidden masters, and pass on their precious eggs, while still relishing the destructive power of their enhanced attributes. Skulls cracked, teeth rained into the leaves, limbs dangled, and eyeballs bulged strangely from crushed orbits.

The shackled man gave a yelp through his mouthful of flesh as one lunged, blindsiding him with a thrusting spear that reamed him through. His flesh tented and popped. A glistening spearhead emerged briefly, and then retracted. It plunged again into his ribs. The shackled man fell skewered and snarling into the mud.

Trembling the jungle all around him with a primeval roar, Hart smashed through the knot of puny defenders. A jawbone split. A nose crushed beneath his fist like a bloody bug. A stone hatchet impacted with the base of Hart's skull, blinding him with agony. Whirling on his attacker with a woof, and a great slap of his hand, he ruined the symmetry of the painted man's face. With that, the skirmish was over. Painted people writhed in the leaves all around them. Only one escaped. His left arm swinging at an unnatural angle, he crashed away into the forest, leaving the pair of battered predators to lick their wounds.

### 

23-E

She emerged from the trees, oozing sweat, with clouds of gnats fizzing around her head. Her legs buckled drunkenly beneath the weight of all the logs slung over her back, lashed together with strips of airliner upholstery. With every step through the powdery sand, her ankles threatened to roll, as she heaved her way down the beach in the direction of the cliffs. Beneath her feet were the retreating tracks of the enormous monster that she'd driven away. Unable to go a step further, she released her burden with a small cry of exhaustion, ringing her burning and bandaged hands. Sandy thought she might vomit. Having worked in the suffocating humidity since dawn with only her sip of rationed soda around noon, her blood had thickened to the consistency of hot gravy.

She doubled over, placing her hands on her knees, and just breathed, watching droplets of sweat pock the sand. In her condition, she couldn't afford to throw up. She needed every ounce of liquid that remained in her body. However, the acrid stench of campfire smoke hanging in the humid air only worsened her nausea, recalling the reek of burning feathers, the sickening purrs of the monster as it crunched Dr. Kimura's bones. Rising, she staggered away from the spot, as if all of those bad memories were somehow affixed to it, and she lumbered in the direction of the roaring sea. A little swim would draw some of the heat from her body. As she neared the shore, she hesitated, pausing to stare at a black column of smoke that was billowing up from behind the limestone wall.

It didn't look right. Something was wrong back at camp. When she and Donovan left an hour ago, their campfire had almost burned down to a pile of white ash. They'd agreed to conserve wood during the daylight hours, to save it all for a bonfire that they'd need to build nightly to block the narrow path against any threats that might come lurking in the darkness. By the size of the plume gushing into the sky, it looked as though their entire stockpile had somehow gone ablaze.

"Oh, no."

Foregoing her afternoon bath, Sandy turned from the sea, and began to jog. Her next thoughts were for her patients, Dr. Kimura and John, who might've lacked the strength to move to safety if a spark from the untended fire had somehow ignited the nearby woodpile. How bad would she feel if anything had happened to them? She was especially worried about Dr. Kimura, who couldn't possibly escape the blaze on his own. Her pace increased to a run. As she tore down the narrow path between the cliffs and the sea, awful scenarios flashed through her mind. However, when she rounded the final bend, nothing she'd imagined even came close to matching the sight before her eyes.

Donovan sat alone on the beach, gazing out to sea. He held a full beer in his hand. Crushed cans, catching the light of the afternoon sun, glimmered in the sand all around him. In the center of camp, an inferno raged. Every log that they'd gathered since sunrise, every stick and twig, were consumed by flames.

"Donovan?" Sandy plodded up to the young man. His countenance was slackened by the effects of alcohol on his dehydrated body. He pulled a swig of beer without looking her way. "What the hell is going on?"

Her heart pounding in her chest, she whirled in all directions, appraising the madness of the situation through unbelieving eyes. Both patients lay prone in a new location at the base of the cliff wall. The clear ruts through the sand suggested that they'd been dragged to the furthest point from camp. To Sandy, it appeared as though they'd just been thrown out like yesterday's garbage. The girls were nowhere to be seen. "Why are you drinking? Where are Margot and Tara?"

Donovan shook his head.

"What do you mean you don't know? Who moved the patients? Why is all the wood burning?" She stormed around in front of him, and squatted down so she could look into his bleary eyes. "Donovan," she said, lowering her voice to a steady tone, "tell me what happened here."

"We need to get rescued," he said, averting his eyes, gazing past her to the farthest reaches of the sea. "Got to signal a ship."

Sandy noted the number of scattered beer cans. She was fairly certain that he'd consumed them all. What was he thinking? The other guys were going to kill him when they returned. "Donovan, where are the girls?"

"Gone."

Sandy leaned to the side to make eye contact. "What do you mean, *gone*?"

Donovan shook his head.

It was then that she noticed all of his injuries. His face and arms were covered with scratches. Claw marks. A chill whistled up through her core. Something terrible had happened.

Donovan took another drink from his can, and pointed seaward. "Thought I saw a ship out there earlier. Tried to signal them with some smoke, but I don't see it no more."

He didn't look right. It was more than just the alcohol. Something inside him seemed to have devolved to a state of weird complacency. She rose, and marched across the campsite, past the intense heat of the roaring bonfire. She noticed a few peanut wrappers dancing in the swirling thermals. How had Donovan managed to completely lose his mind in the space of the hour or so that she was gone? None of this seemed possible, even for a man with a fiery temperament like him.

"Dr. Kimura? John?" Sandy felt the urge to run to them, as if she really believed that if she ran quickly enough to them, then somehow she might be able to change what some part of her already knew. A grimace twisted her face. Fists balled to her temples, she gawped down at their glazed and unblinking eyes.

Insects wandered over their faces, rising and settling upon their lips, crawling in and out of their open mouths.

"Oh, my God. Oh, my God." Her voice thinned to a tremulous whine, as a dark shadow of realization passed over. Her life was in danger. She had to leave, right now, and never come back here again.

### 

## 21-F

"Come here, you guys! Get a load of this!" Peanut shouted, ripping away at the undergrowth that concealed his hidden treasure. He emitted a titter of delight when at last he exposed a large portion of the thing. He ran the palm of his hand over the rusted metal panel. It looked like it had been there for half a century, just rotting quietly in the middle of the jungle.

"Guess this island might be inhabited after all," Peanut said, beaming at the two men as they came sauntering up, and relishing the way their expressions heightened from annoyance to disbelief. A smile spread slowly across Dale's face. Nate bent to examine the ancient ruin of what had once been an automobile.

"I'll be god-danged," Dale muttered.

"What kind of car is it?" Nate asked.

"Says here it's a 'Hybrid,' whatever that is," Peanut replied, pointing to a rusty emblem with a peeling leaf on it.

"Well, it's a Ford," Dale said.

"It says 'Escape' down there."

"A Ford Escape Hybrid?"

"What's Hybrid mean?"

"Two models combined into one, maybe?" Dale said, pulling at his nose. "Maybe it's something Ford only markets overseas?"

"How long do you think it's been sitting here?" Peanut asked. "Looks like it's been down here forever."

"Twenty years, at least," Dale replied.

"I'd guess longer than that," Nate said. "Maybe closer to fifty."

"Fifty years? Hell, that'd be 1921. This look like a damned Model T to you?"

Nate shrugged. "You said twenty years. It doesn't look any more like a Model T than it does anything from the forties."

"You got me." Dale shook his head. "To be honest, I ain't never seen a car like it."

"Maybe something experimental."

"Got to be."

"How did it get here?" Peanut asked, polishing the leafy emblem with the pad of his thumb. "Looks like it fell right out of the sky."

The three guys stood and stared at the old wreck, hands on their hips. No one could come up with a better theory. There were no roads anywhere.

"Maybe it fell off a ship, and a tidal wave came along and washed her clear up inland," Dale said.

"Or, it fell from a helicopter."

"If there's choppers flying over this island, then that'd mean there's civilization within a hundred miles or less," Dale replied.

"I like the sound of that."

"What if," Peanut said, lifting his hands slowly before his chest, as if he were about to catch something between them, "this is some sort of experimental island where the government does all kinds of weird experiments on cars, animals, maybe even people. So, when the hijackers veered our airplane too close to it, they had to shoot it right out of the sky."

Nate hoisted his eyebrows.

Dale glanced at Nate, chewing thoughtfully on his lower lip.

"Oh," Peanut muttered, looking down at his feet.

"Hmm?"

"The two moons."

"Fuck." Dale turned his head and spat. "Tell you what. I'm about getting sick of this."

"Sick of what?" Nate asked.

Dale snorted, as though his question was highly amusing. "Sick of what?" He turned on a heel, laughing up at the sky. "Sweet Jesus." He smeared his face with both hands. "Got me grinning like a mule eating green briars." Dale laughed through his hands until they fell, revealing tear-filled eyes. "Holy shit, boys. I'd say break time is over. Come on. Let's go find us some water before we all lose our ever-loving minds. Goodbye, Ford Escape Hybrid, whatever the hell you are."

"Still, it's a good sign," Peanut said, skipping to catch up with Dale.

"And how's that?"

"It's manmade. Doesn't it feel kind of good to see something manmade after looking at nothing but leaves and dirt all day?"

Dale stuck out his lip, raised his eyebrows, and nodded. "Yeah, I guess it kind of does, now that you mention it."

"Guys. Wait a second."

Peanut turned to the sound of Nate's voice, just behind him.

"Everybody stop for a second, and just listen."

Frowning into the jungle, all three stopped. Nobody moved, or even breathed. Peanut cocked an ear toward the bowels of the hollow, from which the beautiful music of flowing water was emanating. "Oh my gosh," Peanut whispered, eyes brightening.

Wordlessly departing, Dale half-ran, and half-slid down the slope of the ravine, grabbing for branches and tree trunks along the way to keep from tumbling into the abyss. Peanut and Nate dogged his heels, employing the same tactic. Peanut added a baseball slide into his repertoire for controlling speedy descents, while Nate implemented an occasional butt skid. The further they descended to the bottom, the more intimate the enchanting burble of liquid became.

"Woohooo!"

The shrillness of Dale's whoop resounding through the forest prickled Peanut's skin with a sort of electrified joy. He heard a weird squeak escape his throat as he tumbled down the slope's footing, and through a soft bed of weeds. Dale was already up to his waist in the middle of the stream, throwing cascades of clear water into the air with great sweeps of his arms.

"We found it, buddies!" he cried. "Come on in! The water's fine!"

A flattened spade head thrust up through the foam, splitting wide and pale in a bristled grin. Forelegs paddling the air, a slimy form lunged from the stream. Before the joyful smile had even melted from Dale's face, he'd disappeared in a churning whirlpool of speckled coils and clouds of mud.

"Jesus Christ ... Jesus Christ almighty ..." Nate's mournful exclamations were muted by the vastness of the hollow, and the murmuring stream. Nate paced the riverbank with a mindless guise of some purpose, but already the cloud of dark debris was being harried downstream by the current, revealing none but the last set of tracks imprinted by Dale on the river's muddy bottom. In a flash, their outdoorsman was gone.

Peanut heard the rhythmic gasps of his own breaths, the buzzing insects in the forest canopy. He stared down into the water where seconds ago, a friend and mentor was clowning. As his mind gradually processed what had just transpired, he felt the shock of what he'd beheld start to simmer, and then to boil.

"Hey, you need to step back away the edge of that water! Didn't you see what just happened?"

Peanut felt Nate's grip on his arm, pulling him backwards, controlling him. In a sudden fit, he yanked his arm away, and turned to shove Nate harder than he'd ever shoved anyone in his life. Both hands slammed into the man's chest, dumping him back onto his rump in the weeds. "Shut up! I told you we needed to make weapons!" Peanut screamed, feeling his eyes fill with hot tears. "I told you so! You stupid asshole, if we'd had spears then that wouldn't have happened! He'd still be alive!"

"Peanut ..."

"Don't even!"

"There's nothing ... if we'd even had a rifle, there's nothing ..."

"Bullshit!" Peanut whirled away from Nate, wiping tears that he knew were more for his best friend Alex than for Dale, as he felt his throat start to constrict. He didn't want to cry again. He'd cried enough for Alex already, and something was changing. He could feel it. Something inside him was growing, while something smaller was dying in its shadow. Storming off into the jungle, he seized a thin tree with both hands, and he began to throttle it back and forth, grunting with every wrench of his hands. The feel of something strangled in his fists, the sound of splintering wood, it was darkly satisfying. The base of the tree gave an anguished snap, and he smashed it to the ground. Standing on it, he pulled Dale's knife out of his pocket. The blade came open with a little click. Now, the tears were for Dale.

"We couldn't have known that thing was in there," Nate said, in a low and steady voice.

"We should have known. We should've expected it." Peanut sliced away at the last strips of connecting bark. Once the base was free, he bent the opposite end beneath his shoe, and snapped it off it just beneath the canopy. "There's always something. Always. You can't go in these woods unarmed. You can't ever let your guard down. There's something that wants to kill you behind every tree, in every river, under every ocean wave." He took the knife to the basal end, and began stripping away wood shavings with rapid thrusts of the blade, while rotating the handle of what would soon enough be his spear. "But you better believe I'm going to be ready when it happens the next time. I'm not going down without a fight. Alex and Dale didn't even have a chance, but I will."

Through the corner of his eye, he saw Nate standing there with his arms dangling at his sides. He knew that it wasn't Nate's fault, and he also knew that Nate had lost somebody precious to him as well. It wasn't fair to take it out on him, but Peanut felt like he needed to make it known to somebody where he stood in this world. He wasn't going to be treated like a child any longer. He was through with that stage of his life. His childhood had come to a violent end at the exact moment when he'd watched the best friend in the whole universe die right in front of him.

"We need to talk, whenever you're ready," Nate said, "about what to do next, and where we probably ought to go."

Peanut glowered down at the sharpening point of his spear, feeling a little bit better with every stroke of the knife. "Yeah?"

"Yeah." Nate shuffled his feet in the leaf litter. "We'll still need to fill our water cans. Those people back at camp are counting on us, and it's getting late in the day. Trouble is, without Dale, I'm not one-hundred percent sure how to get back."

Peanut stopped scraping.

"I mean, I know we have to climb back up that slope, but from there … well, Dale was pretty much leading the way all afternoon."

Peanut looked back up to the distant ridge line. It was a very long way back up. Nate was right. Dale had served as their unofficial leader, and on some level they were counting on him to lead them back. The game trail was forked in a hundred different places where other trails converged. It had seemed pretty straightforward on the way in, but using the same method to get back out, without Dale, was bound to be a much more difficult endeavor.

"Here's what I propose, and you can tell me what you think. I know that we travelled roughly northward, bearing northeast as we went up into the mountains. Rather than trying to follow the same winding game trail all the way back to camp, it might be smarter to follow this river downstream, where it will more than likely dump into the ocean. Then, we just follow the beach south back to camp."

Peanut nodded. "But down there on the beach, that's where the howlers come out at sundown."

"That's true. That seems to be a favored hunting ground of theirs, and that's exactly why we need to move quickly, and get back to camp before nightfall."

Peanut looked off to the canting position of the sun in the western sky, shining through the leaves of the forest canopy. It was already starting to drop toward the horizon. "How much time do you think we have? About three hours of real daylight left?"

"I'd say that's probably a good guess."

"Alright." Peanut nodded his head, and released a long sigh. He dabbed the pad of his thumb against the pale point of his new spear. Before they set off, part of him wanted to apologize to Nate for shoving him, for getting so angry. It felt like the right thing to do, but he wasn't sure how to do it.

"I'm sorry I gave you a hard time about wanting to make a weapon," Nate said. "You're a young man, and an equal. I should've realized that, and let you make your own decision in that regard. I will from now on. You feel kind of like a son to me out here, and I guess I was just being overprotective. I don't want to lose you, or anyone else."

Peanut cocked his head at Nate, and cleared his throat. "It's okay. I'm sorry I acted like a jerk. It was nobody's fault. It just happened."

They turned back to the river, and stared at what was once a vision of hope and joy, and was now just another source of despair. They were running out of chances to find hope in this land, and that was a crushing feeling. "I'm sorry you lost your wife," Peanut said, glancing up at Nate.

Nate put his hand on Peanut's shoulder. "I'm sorry that you lost your best friend."

# CHAPTER EIGHT

23-E

"Margot! Tara!" Sandy stood on the rim of a great precipice that seemed to drop straight down into the bowels of the jungle. It was getting late. She'd followed the trail of footprints and upturned leaves for more than an hour, and she'd still not heard a response to her cries, or any sign of humanity whatsoever except for one oddity that had looked like a rusty, old car.

She wasn't even sure whose tracks she was following anymore. Sometimes they looked human, and at other times, more like those of clawed animals. The jungle soil was spongy, and it didn't leave the clear imprints, just dull depressions. The human prints could have been left by the girls, or just as easily, by the guys. Her only hope was that the tracks didn't belong to that band of savages that John described, which could mean that she was following them straight into a hostile camp. Regardless, she couldn't go back to the beach. She had to warn the girls, if she ever found them, that Donovan had revealed a very dangerous side of himself.

Upon discovering the lifeless bodies of Dr. Kimura and John, she decided against pressing Donovan with any further questions. Her hunch was that Donovan had smothered them as soon as he had the chance, because he believed that they were taxing his own chances of survival by depleting the limited resources. To some extent she had to agree, but she would never agree to euthanize a person who had a desire to live. That was murder, plain and simple, and she believed that dehydration, hunger, and the stress of their situation had driven Donovan to murder. All it took was a little alcohol, and probably the voiced disapproval of Dr. Kimura. Some weak part inside of him had just snapped, and before he knew it, he was on top of the helpless doctor, choking the life out of him.

Of course, it was also possible that the two men had simply passed away. It was unbearably hot, and those guys were dying from blood loss. She'd been gone over an hour, maybe closer to two. Hard telling exactly how long she'd been away. Dry wood was not easy to find in a humid jungle. Everything was either alive and green, or rotten and filled with termites. Nothing seemed to lie dead for very long here.

Either way, Donovan had most definitely flipped his lid. He'd burned all the wood, drank all of the beer, and that kind of irrational behavior was enough to convince Sandy that she ought to not pester him anymore. With his back positioned to her, as he sat staring out to sea, she'd collected the last reserves of soda, and slipped quietly out of camp along the narrow trail. Sandy hadn't felt very good about taking the last of her group's rations, but her only other option would've been to leave them with Donovan, and in his confused mental state he'd surely have consumed every drop. If she ever found those who remained of her shrinking family of castaways, then she would redistribute what little she'd salvaged. She figured that if the guys made it back to camp, then they could deal with Donovan in their own way, but Sandy felt that it was her moral obligation to try and warn the girls.

"Margot!" she cried, hearing her own desperation reverberating through the jungle. It was a heartless, aversive sort of place that had no love for human life. "Tara!"

The sun hung low in the western sky. Probably not a good idea to keep yelling at this hour, or risk drawing unwanted attention to her location. No telling if those howlers had just happened to be on the move at that hour the night before, or if nightly hunts by those horrible creatures were something that she could always come to dread whenever the sun settled down into the sea.

The trail slithered down into the hollow. She could see the turned stones, skid marks where people had slid and stumbled. It looked steep. Drawing a shaky breath, Sandy took the first step in what became an even more rapid descent than she'd anticipated. She could hardly move slowly enough to keep her eyes fixed on the footprints. A root caught her toe, and she shrieked as her ankle twisted, and folded beneath her leg. She grabbed for a tree trunk as she toppled, but her nails only raked the bark. Tumbling, rolling, her body quickly picked up speed, cartwheeling through brambles, and slamming over rocks, until she landed in a battered heap at the bottom.

She clutched her sprained ankle, rolling back and forth in agony in a shock of weeds at the bottom. The pain was so intense that it took her breath away, made her start to perspire. She felt lightheaded, and nauseous. It was perhaps the dizzying effects of pain that made her question what she thought she was hearing as some sort of an auditory mirage. Closing her eyes, she controlled her breathing as best she could, and just listened to what sounded like the gentle burbling of a nearby brook.

It couldn't be.

Sandy's eyes flicked open. Her dry tongue lapped at her cracked lips. Wincing from sharp bolts of pain that stabbed at her ankle, which was already beginning to swell, she forced herself into an upright position. Right before her was beautiful, clear stream of flowing water. Whimpering, she dragged herself toward it. Her gaze hesitate on a pile of wood shavings next to a broken off sapling. She gave a weak laugh of relief. It was the guys she'd been tracking, no doubt about it. They'd been right here, sitting and whittling in this same spot, probably not much more than an hour ago. Sandy imagined the relief and joy that they too must have felt when they'd happened upon this friendly branch of fresh water.

"Dale!" she tried to shout, but her parched throat produced only a rasp. She needed a drink. She needed a long, cold drink. She dragged herself up to the river's edge, and she plunged her face down into the wonderful water. God, it felt so good. She was going to drink like a deer until her stomach couldn't hold another drop, and afterward, she might just roll on in, and enjoy that little bath that she'd been denied back there on the beach.

Lifting her drenched head from the water, she gasped for breath. A broad smile spread across her face, and she began to laugh for no reason at all. She didn't care. If a howler came charging after her tonight, at least she was going to die with a bellyful of cold, fresh water, and somehow, that made the thought of dying seem a little bit better. She washed the mud from her hands like a raccoon, and then pushed back her hair, wiped the water from her eyes. She pinched the fluid from her nostrils, gave a sniff, and then gazed down at her own reflection.

A face with bulging eyes stared back, bloated and pale. It was not her own. Half-engulfed in the mouth of an enormous salamander, Dale gaped back at her from the bottom of the River Styx. The unblinking pearl eyes of the monstrous amphibian stared too, while saffron gills fanned on either side of its discus head.

Thrusting herself away from the river's edge, Sandy crab-walked back into the weeds. When the pile of sharp wood shavings bit into the palm of her hand, a new and terrible version of the men's afternoon on the riverbank became evident. They weren't sitting around whittling for pleasure. They were desperately making a spear. They needed a weapon to stab that dead-eyed monster flattened on the muddy bottom with poor Dale, their only hope for survival, clenched in its toothless maw. Sandy balled her fist into her mouth, threw back her head, and began to scream.

### 

22-D

They froze in their tracks. Neither had to ask if the other had heard her scream. They just reacted, spinning back in the direction from which they'd just come, and charging back into the darkened hollow. No telling which of the girls was in trouble, but it was almost certainly one of their own. Not one more. Not one more was going to die on his account.

Peanut was already way ahead of him, with an eager spear in hand. Younger, faster, stronger, the teen was better equipped to handle whatever dangers awaited, but that didn't mean that Nate wasn't feeling conflicted about not calling the kid back. He'd made a promise, after all. He'd assured Peanut that he would be considered an equal from here on out, a fellow man who could make his own decisions. The problem was that Nate was once a kid of his age, and he remembered that most of the decisions he'd made at that time were usually pretty stupid ones. The kid would have to learn the same way he'd learned, back in the school of hard knocks, that reacting impulsively and physically to a perceived threat was rarely ever the smartest choice. Nate had to wonder, as he watched Peanut's form growing smaller as the distance between them spread, if he'd have reigned back another grown man outrunning him, or if he was just being unfairly biased on the basis of age?

Who was he kidding? The kid was right. They should've all made spears. This place was no state park with marked walking trails, tame wildlife, or public restrooms every hundred yards. There was no other way to react to a threat in this jungle than with some sort of an impulsive physical response, which went against a civilized lifetime of training the male mind to always calm down, and think things through. That didn't always work here. The only choice that a man in a place like this really had was to either stand up and be a man, or sit down, so the man behind you can have a better view of what's attacking your people. This was exactly the sort of world in which humankind was forged. Its inherent dangers at every turn were what made us so violently reactive, so prone to praise our castes of warriors and conquerors, because it was by the spilt blood of our heroes that the rest of us survived.

Peanut, like all young men, wanted so badly to be one of those heroes. Who didn't? What guy at his age desired anything more than to earn the respect of other guys, and the adoration of the girls, by charging out there to kick some ass, and take some names? Honestly, that never really changed, even decades after high school was over. It just evolved from schoolyard showboating and fights to the more complicated arena of your career, where you still did your share of showboating, and you still beat down the competition, but you did so with your mind, and your talent, rather than with your fists. Same as it ever was, always had been, and always would be. Boys will be boys.

Eventually, he could see them. It was Sandy, and thank God, she didn't appear to be in any immediate danger. Peanut was kneeling beside her, homemade spear in one hand, with his other resting on her shoulder in a consoling manner. Yeah, he was still just a kid, but one day, hopefully, if he was lucky enough to survive that long, he had all the right ingredients for becoming a good man.

"No, we can't go back." Sandy was crying, and shaking her head, as Nate jogged onto the scene. "We have to find the girls. They're lost."

"What's happened?" Nate asked, struggling to catch his breath.

"Donovan's snapped," Peanut replied.

"He burned up all the firewood—said he thought he saw a ship, or something—and he drank all the beer. He's completely drunk right now, and ..."

"And, what?"

Sandy cupped her hand over her mouth, her face pinched. "Dr. Kimura and John are both dead."

"What?" Nate knelt on the other side of her. "The hijacker?"

Sandy nodded.

"But he seemed to be coming around pretty well, just as we were leaving."

"I know," Sandy said.

"Dead?"

"Their bodies were moved, dragged clear out of camp, and the girls are both missing."

"You don't think Donovan had anything to do with ..."

"I say we go back there right now," Peanut said, "and put a foot in his ass."

"No," Sandy said. "We can't go back there. It's not a good place anymore. All the wood and rations are gone. Here. I brought you these." She opened up the fold of her shirt and handed them each a can of soda.

"I kind of have to agree with Peanut," Nate said. "I mean, what if those girls get back there before we do? If Donovan has really flipped as badly as you say has, then what do you suppose he'll do if no one else is around to protect them?"

"Tara is the only friend I've got left who's my age," Peanut said, "and if anything happens to her—I'm all alone."

"You're not alone," Sandy replied.

"You know what he means," Nate said, "and it's not like we have much choice. We certainly don't stand a chance of surviving the night in this jungle. At least back there ..."

"What?" Sandy threw up her hands. "What have we got back there? We've got nothing back there. That's what I'm trying to tell you. There's no food, no water, no fire, and now there's no one left to make another one." Tears spilled from her eyes, as she gestured toward the spot in the stream where Dale disappeared. "I saw him down there. I saw it, with him."

"You saw it? The thing that took him?" Peanut leapt to his feet, scanning the water, spear shouldered. "Where?"

"It was right there," Sandy replied. "I only saw it for a second."

Peanut growled at the water. "If I could just see that thing just one last time, I swear to God ..."

"Come on," Nate said, throwing Sandy's arm over his shoulder. "Looks like you've got yourself one hell of a bum ankle."

"I twisted it coming down the hill."

"You want to give me a hand here?"

Peanut lowered his spear. He turned begrudgingly from the stream, and positioned himself on the other side of Sandy. They counted to three, and lifted her to her feet. The sprained ankle was already beginning to resemble an eggplant. Nate didn't want to say anything, but he knew by looking at the severity of the injury that it would've been better if she'd broken it. Ankles sprained that badly took a long time to heal. "Maybe you can use that knife of yours to whittle her some crutches tonight." Nate winked over Sandy's shoulder.

The jungle all around them shook beneath a roar so deafening that it knocked the three of them back down into the weeds. They covered their ears, but it didn't stop. The blast kept coming in an ascending tone that eventually held to an earsplitting crescendo. After what seemed an eternity, the howl ended in chuffing, demonic laughter. The hijacker was right. This place was Hell, and by the sound of things, they'd managed to wander right down into Hell's deepest pit, where the devil himself had awakened.

"What do we do?" Sandy whispered. "Oh my God. It's coming to get us."

There were only three options, so far as Nate could discern. They could head downstream to the beach, where the devils all liked to dance by the light of their double-moon, they could sit here and do nothing, which was just as certain of a death sentence, or they could try and make a run for it back uphill.

Nate pointed to the slope behind them. "At the top of that ridge, there's an abandoned vehicle."

"I saw it." Sandy nodded vigorously.

"Let's go," Peanut said, grabbing Sandy beneath her arm.

Nate took the other, and they lifted.

Heaving their combined and awkward bulk up the slope, they moved as a single, crippled creature. Behind them, they heard branches snapping, or were they whole trees? The howler seemed to have picked up their scent, or perhaps it had pinpointed the exact spot where it had heard Sandy's scream, because it was pushing steadily through the lowlands in the direction of the river. Loose dirt sloughed beneath their steps. It dropped them to their knees, while stones tumbled downhill. They grabbed for every branch, every sapling for support, but every step taken by one dragged the weight of two others behind it. They had to synchronize their steps, but Peanut's legs moved so quickly. Nate could barely match his pace.

Behind and below, a great tree splintered and fell. They heard the splash of its canopy in the river. It was coming. There was no way that they were going to make it to the top before it spotted them, and ran them down. In Nate's mind, the choice was pretty simple.

"You take her," Nate said, throwing Sandy's arm off his shoulder. He gave them a parting glance, and then turned back downhill. Not one more. He would be next, but not either one of them.

"No!" Peanut shrieked. In a split-second, the kid had him in a headlock.

"Get off me, Peanut. You'll get us all killed!" Nate grappled with the teen, whose thinner arms were somehow wirier, and more difficult to wrestle into submission than those of a grown man.

"Then we'll all die together," Peanut said, "but nobody is going back alone. Not again. I won't ever watch that happen again!"

Nate realized that even the most altruistic act of sacrificing your life to save those of your friends could in fact be a selfish one. He wasn't the only one around here who without the strength to carry the burden of another death. Peanut was no different. "I'm sorry.

I'll try my best to keep up. I promise, but you'll have to get her to the top."

"Swear to God! Swear to God you won't ever stop, and you won't ever turn around!"

Nate nodded, and raised his right hand. "I swear to God. It'll have to catch me, drag me down." Another tree cracked like a rifle report, and careened down into the river. "Now, go!"

Peanut scrambled back up the slope. Nate was close behind him. Even with Sandy's crippled weight on his back, the kid was able to match Nate's pace. Her burden approximately equaled the differential between their two decades in age. Long steps, big reaches, brought them closer and closer to the top, as the mighty crow of the howler resounded through the woods. They heard a great splash, as the predator crossed the river in a single step.

"Don't turn around, Nate!"

Nate dared to steal a glimpse back over his shoulder, and the sight of what was tearing its way up the slope behind them was enough to stop a weaker heart from squeezing off another beat. A greyhound bus swaddled in buffalo hide lilted over gigantic ostrich legs. The sheer scope of the thing was astounding, but it was the disproportionate size of its pompous head that really drew the attention of the eyes. Bobbing with every plod, the topknot thatch of wispy feathers concealed all but the faintest suggestions of a face. There were eyes, red as burning embers, but any other facial features were left up to the imagination, aside from fleeting glimpses of discolored and broken teeth. There existed no creature, real or imagined, that was more horrifying than a howler.

"Faster! God, go faster!"

Sandy seemed healed by the power of terror. Pulling loose of Peanut's shoulder, she knuckled-down, and galloped uphill in great lunges with her one good leg. The technique was working. For an instant, she was keeping up with the uninjured men, until a loose rock sliding beneath her single foot brought her crashing to her belly.

It was over, and they seemed to sense it. They'd had a good run, the three of them, faring better than most in a world where humans had no business being alive. Nate collapsed beside Sandy, held her tight, and turned to face the horror. Peanut hoisted his spear, bracing it against his hip in a stance meant to inflict a parting injury to their predator, a scar on the monster's hide, by which their last stand would be remembered.

As the howler's matted jaws unhinged their racks of yellow daggers, the thought occurred to Nate that just a day ago, they were just three strangers sitting on an airplane. Unconnected, happy and complete, their lives were isolated from one another by their differing backgrounds, ages and agendas. From the moment that they'd boarded that airliner, they'd never have guessed that in a few short hours they'd be stripped of the most precious people in their respective worlds, whose absences would be replaced by a couple of perfect strangers who happened to be seated around them in nearby rows. Their lives would crash together, and would culminate on a jungled slope where they'd be forever united as fodder for a monster that had no place in their world. In another life, they might've been good neighbors, coworkers or old friends. They might've gotten together on weekends to enjoy backyard barbecues, sporting events, or an occasional summer fish fry where they'd tip back brews and laugh about their little triumphs and problems well into the twilight hours. In any timeline, they'd probably have been good friends. Nate could almost see envision some alternate timeline where he and Sandy were espoused, and Peanut was their son, or where all three of them were siblings, because there was no doubt that the three of them would forever be connected by this terrible end.

Nate took Sandy's hand. He was proud to die with these two. It wasn't a fate he'd ever have chosen, but it was one he was willing to accept. He considered himself fortunate, more fortunate than he probably deserved. He'd been blessed with a happy childhood, a loving family, a home, and he'd sailed the oceans with his soul mate, his mermaid, the love of his life. In his final seconds Nate closed his eyes, squeezed Sandy's hand tightly, and he thanked God for all that he'd been given—and to his amazement, God replied.

From the ridgeline came a blast of sound so tremendous that it halted the looming howler in its tracks. Clouds of litter billowed downhill in a rush of fetid air that swept the ground of all debris in its path. Loosed earth and stones came spilling down the slope.

Trees snapped and toppled. Scabrous columns dragging whole root balls slammed to the ground, bouncing, and rafting right past them down into the gully.

A new challenger had arrived. Bristling with garish plumage, the creature thundered right over the top of them, tail slashing, to slam headlong into the howler with all the force of a derailed train. Entwined, they toppled, shattering trees like Popsicle sticks. Flesh ripped up like old carpeting. Bones popped. The challenger was a different sort of beast, streaked in lurid patterns of black and orange that warned in nature's common tongue of coloration that this was no creature to be tested. The jagged beak sprung wide as it lunged for the howler's throat. Clawed forelimbs plowed ruts through the dark feathers. Rear legs slashed at the howler's belly, until innards bulged and spilled into the leaves.

Enraged by the stink of its own viscera, the howler rolled, ripping loose of its attacker with a thrust of its legs. Blood fountained from either side of its lacerated throat as it rose to its feet, entangled in a glistening net of its own intestines, and flung its gaping maw over its opponent's smaller, parrot-like head. Immediately, every seam in the newcomer's skull began to fold.

Had the brawl of beasts not been half so deafening, the three spectators still wouldn't have needed spoken words to seize this obvious opportunity for a retreat. Running, limping, clawing their way uphill, they fled the certain death that they'd somehow been spared. When they finally stopped, the trumpeting howls of victory were far below them, but they were still too frightened to speak. Piling through a shattered passenger window, they crawled between the seats to form a sweaty huddle in the back of the wayward vehicle. They leaned on one another, clung to each other, but said nothing. Not a word, lest they utter some displeasing word that might change the mind of whatever god had intervened.

Hours later, when the silver edges of the tandem moons peered down through the canopy, Nate closed his eyes, just breathing and wondering if there had ever been more than one moon on their planet? If so, when, and what was the fate of the missing twin? His psyche practically demanded that he lean in that direction, because there was nothing else on which to lean in any other. If they were still on planet Earth, and if their home planet had once hosted two moons, then that still evidenced a deficit of hundreds of millions of lost years, but at least they were still at home.

Nate was not a particularly religious man. He supposed that he believed in some sort of a higher power, some seat for the human soul that flew off like a locust when at last the flesh failed. His logistical dilemma was that human souls weren't even supposed to exist for eons. God hadn't created them yet. So, in the scope of Judeo-Christian philosophy, would an afterlife have awaited Dawn when she showed up on her Creator's doorstep millions of years before Christ, millions of years before that god had even dreamt of humankind? How would that play out? If you exist before your species was created, then once again, you had a time paradox. Nate's eyes flicked open. Moon shadows bobbed on the rotten floorboards of a vehicle that was not unlike them in the sense that it somehow existed many millennia prior to being invented. If things could exist apart from time, in one form or another, then that suggested that all things, all matter, all energy, had no beginning and no end, eliminating the need for a suddenly irrelevant creator. Was God the ultimate paradox?

No, he couldn't bring himself to believe that. Not here, when he needed a god on his side more than ever, when he had to believe in some sort of organization behind this screen of entropy. Where in time were they? These things, these shaggy howling beasts, they resembled nothing he'd ever learned about in school. The only enormous creatures ever known to inhabit the earth were the dinosaurs, and the creatures that inhabited this jungle did not in any way resemble those pebble-skinned, cold-blooded, reptiles lumbering around in science books—unless those books were all very wrong.

Nate's eyes brightened. What if everything they thought they'd ever known about the prehistoric world was inaccurately imagined? What if the dinosaurs were reeking shaggy things that howled up to double-moons? Nate glanced up at the two celestial bodies. They were hovering so closely tonight that he was sure they were going touch. He imagined them bouncing lightly off of one another with a cartoonish sound effect, and a little poof of stardust.

Sandy glanced at him, but she didn't ask him what he was thinking about. He was glad. He didn't feel much like talking right now. Certainly, he didn't want to describe his silly daydream of colliding moons, or his fear that their loved ones might've arrived at Heaven's pearly gates only to find a posted sign that read, "Coming Soon."

"Listen," Sandy whispered, curling her fingers around his own, squeezing his hand tightly.

"I hear it, too," Peanut said, stiffening in his seat.

"What?" Nate asked. He couldn't imagine what the two of them were hearing. He strained his ears beyond the rusted walls of their sanctuary, through the insulating layers of vegetation, the chirring barrier of sound produced by the nightly choir of insects. "Is it a howler?"

Sandy shook her head. She and Peanut gazed at each other from across either side of Nate, and they began to smile, as if they were sharing some private joke. Just as he was about to become irritated with them, he finally heard it. God, he heard it, and when he recognized the sound, he experienced a jolt of the wildest emotions surging through his mind.

Pirouetting notes piped eerily through the night, spinning, spinning, like a leaf falling from the jungle canopy, drenching the forest in an almost clerical ambiance that imagined a dervish of spectral entities, twirling spirits of the dead, until the Baroque intro was annihilated by drumsticks hammering at the sultry night air, and the gritty roar of a psychedelic guitar. The discordant, throbbing music champed along to mostly unintelligible, throaty vocals of a singer who drawled over the acid metal in a manner that suggested he was bombed clean out of his mind. *"In a gadda da vida, honey, don't you know that I'm lovin' you? In a gadda da vida, baby, don't you know that I'll always be true?"*

The relief they shared was something euphoric, something mostly crazed. Here was the equivalent of a trumpeting bugle, the thunder of a thousand hooves. It was the sound of the cavalry charging to the rescue of a few surrounded soldiers who'd been holding a desperate spot of ground against terrible odds. Where before the well of hope had run dry, there sprung suddenly a fountain of promise.

Two sounds, juxtaposed, thrown together into a bed where they were made to writhe together for two whole sides of the same record album. Here, in the literal Garden of Eden, blared the pinnacle of rock and roll decadence two-hundred-million years before that anthem would ever be written. It was weightless yet heavy, sanctimoniously obscene. The product of a forced union between angel and demon was something delicate, yet armored, bristling with spikes. It was the *Iron Butterfly*.

"Let's go find it," Peanut said, nodding his head to the beat.

"Oh my God, let's go find it right now!" Sandy shouted, her eyes glimmering with madness.

"Okay," Nate replied, resisting a fit of hysterical laughter that threatened to come cachinnating up from his core. "Let's go find it right now!"

# CHAPTER NINE

28-D

It wasn't fair. It wasn't supposed to have happened like this. Their long road together had only just begun. Hart crooned over the crippled body of the shackled man. He crawled along beside his best and only friend, who'd lived so feral and free just minutes ago, and could now barely drag his useless legs behind him through the weeds. The spear had severed his spine, and the worms couldn't fix it. The injury was hurting him something awful. Hart could tell by his weak hoots, the sheen of sweat on his skin, the tendrils of drool whipping from his lower lip. The overlapped outline of his halved spinal column surged grotesquely beneath his skin with every hitch forward.

How could that promise for a shared eternity in their jungle paradise have been such a blatant lie? The worms had never mentioned that there were some things that couldn't be fixed. They'd failed to warn them that there were risks, and that their charmed lives could come to an abrupt end. They'd been cheated. The worms had been cruel enough to show Hart just a glimpse of that happiness he'd forever been denied, opening that window just a crack to the world he'd forever watched passing him by, just enough to let him smell the sweet summer breeze, before slamming it right back down over his fingertips.

Hart threw back his head in a mournful wail. Lifting his trembling hands, he searched every scar on his face for some glyph of hope, some remembered story of a hard hit taken when he'd managed to find a way to get back up again, but something was wrong. He couldn't remember any of the stories behind his scars. He couldn't recall anything. How had he gotten here, clear out here in the middle of this jungle? Was he born here? Had he lived in this forest his entire life? Only this groveling thing in the weeds evidenced that there had ever been another creature like him, but this creature appeared to be dying. What had happened to him? Was he the one who'd injured this man?

Gritting his teeth, Hart clenched a fist, and he bashed it repeatedly against the side of his own skull. There was something wrong with his brain. He felt like he should've been able to remember all of these things, as if they'd happened just moments ago, but his mind was failing to record memories.

It was worms. The worms were eating his brain. He could feel them in there squirming against his skull, devouring memories, digesting thoughts, projecting their own dreams on the old screen of the decrepit theater that was his mind. How long before they'd completely hollowed him out into a mindless husk that just plodded around? Maybe he'd reached that point already.

Hart dropped to his knees, and gently rolled the shackled man onto his back, exposing some gruesome wounds to his chest and abdomen. The man cried out, but Hart did his best to calm him. He stroked his bald head, and gazed down into his blood-drop eyes. There were worms squirming around behind his eyes. Hart could see them, and he understood that this man was suffering in much the same way, losing a battle to the same invaders. The man's chest was heaving. Covered in mud, blood and leaves, he whimpered with every exhale, mouthing some word that he just couldn't seem to produce.

A wrecked bicycle, Hart remembered, red as the blood that trickled from his knee. Hart closed his eyes and clung hard to that memory, the very last that remained in his mind. It wasn't just a bicycle. That bike was his father, and he'd killed him. It was the worst agony he'd ever felt, before or since. Every bone was shattered in a briefly imagined connection to a man personified in a boy's bicycle.

"Don't take it," Hart whispered, his lip trembling. He could feel them burrowing in, targeting his last memory as if to them it was something sweet as candy. "Please, not that one! Leave it alone!" That memory was the root of every scar that had followed, the foundation of the monster he'd become. It was the last time he'd cried, the first time he'd experienced pain, and it had driven him on a lifelong mission to experience more. Hart required pain because he felt that he deserved it. He deserved to hurt, because he'd always needed something for which he was too proud to ask.

"Help," Hart whispered, shuddering all over, as worms chewed into his final scrap of memory, devouring his foundation, his red bicycle, and his father. "Help!" he bellowed, his mouth stretching into a grimace. "Somebody help me!"

Ironic, that he'd finally reached a point where he was no longer too proud to beg for what he needed, and he was losing the ability to speak, and to remember what it was that he'd even been crying out for.

Hart lowered his fingers to the shackled man's wound, and he dabbed them gently in the blood. Lifting his arm to the height of his chest, he brought his fingers in to rest on his sternum. In a matter of minutes, he wouldn't remember what he needed, but he could always leave a note.

H.

E.

L.

He wrote the first three letters of a word in the center of his own chest, before his fingertips ran out of paint, and his mind lost purchase on what exactly it was that he was writing. Hart dropped his chin, and he stared down at what he'd done. Although he couldn't recall why he'd painted those letters, he was convinced of some deeper meaning, some purpose that a better part of him had once intended. He'd leave it there.

Thrusting his arms beneath the unconscious man on the ground, Hart lifted him, cradling him like an oversized infant swaddled in chains, and he rose to his feet. The jungle beckoned. He lurched forward with a single step. Loops of chain swayed and jingled. There was no real plan. He was just a vehicle, and something else was driving. It turned him, this governing presence. It rotated him on his heel, peering out through his dead eyes, as it listened to the sounds of the night through his dead ears. They were one, but Hart's percentage of the whole was miniscule. The presence seemed to have an interest in the sound of distant music. Hart recognized the song. At least, that miniscule part of him did.

His feet rose and fell with a mechanical rhythm. So did the footsteps of the other things, all around him. The creatures of the night still loved to follow him. They found him interesting, in the sense that he probably looked and smelled like prey to their predatory senses, but some old instinct in the back of their reptilian brains knew better than to eat one of his kind. Something was off, and they knew it, but they would still follow him. A horde of scavengers would always follow, because that nightmarish cast of creatures intuited that wherever Hart went, he'd leave a trail of death behind him.

### 

23-E

Sandy's eyes widened as her fingers parted the veil of leaves. Before her loomed a wall of towering posts, bound together with rough cordage, and hacked into points. The wall's footing was a perilous slope of riprap, millions of heaped stones that not only served to anchor the base of the posts, but as another layer of defense on this hilltop fortress. The wall was a simple obstacle, but its design prevented great leaps or ramming charges by the behemoths of this world. She couldn't imagine how long it would've taken to collect so many stones, and to haul them to the top of what appeared to be an extinct volcano, one rock a time. Between the wall's posts jutted thinner spikes, spaced about an arm's reach apart, and positioned at forty-five degree vertices to the wall's base. Swaying bridges spanned a number of guard towers that peered over the wall at regular intervals. In the darkness, it was difficult to determine just how large of a fortress this spiked wall contained, but she couldn't see an end to the progression of pointed posts in either direction.

The music was deafening. She wasn't much of a fan of psychedelic rock, but as they'd climbed up the slopes of this hill, the song struck her as being one of the most beautiful she'd ever heard. It was like a siren seducing them ever deeper into the dangers of the night.

To remain safely huddled inside of their vehicle until dawn's break would have been the conservative choice, but the grinding beat of *Iron Butterfly* triggered a spontaneous impulse in all three of them to find the source of that music before the longest rock and roll song that was ever recorded was allowed to come to an end. There was someone else behind that wall. It wasn't passengers from their plane. It wasn't some savage tribe of cannibals, as described by John the hijacker, nor was it a nomadic band of troglodytes. Obviously, they'd been here a while, and they were brilliant. They'd managed to harness the power of electricity. They'd managed to make a stand in this violent world, and most exciting of all, they had no qualms about announcing their presence for everyone to hear.

"Wait a sec," Nate said, grabbing Peanut's shoulder as he took the first step out into the clearing. "We probably shouldn't go charging straight out into the open."

"Why?"

"I just—think maybe we should wait a while."

"But, they're from our time," Peanut said. "*Iron Butterfly* is ours. Maybe they hit the exact same time warp as us. They might even be from Baltimore!"

"Come on. No other plane out of Baltimore has ever vanished into thin air like that. We don't have any idea who's behind that wall. It could be a trap."

Peanut shook his head. "I don't think so. They're advertising. It's their way of letting us know that they're strong, friendly, and that they can defend themselves."

Sandy looked at Nate, and then back to the looming wall. She hoped that Peanut was right. In fact, she'd never hoped for anything so hard in her life. Whoever was up there blasting the night with their music seemed to be expressing a pretty clear interest in attracting visitors, and there was no telling how many others before them had already been beckoned to this same hilltop. She still wanted to believe that he was alive and well, and maybe that he was here. She couldn't help but feel hopeful when this was the best chance she'd ever had of reuniting with Ray since the crash. All people were drawn to the sound of music. If they played music every night, and if her husband was anywhere alive in this world, Sandy believed that he would be here. If not tonight, then eventually.

The song ended. Unseen speakers gave a static pop, and the eerie sounds of the forest resumed their place on the usual concert stage. Insects rasped in the leaves. Somewhere in the distance, a howler unleashed its terrible cry. It seemed to go on forever, before chuffing out into stillness.

"I'm with Peanut," Sandy said. "I want to go."

"I'm not against either of you," Nate replied. "I'm not saying we don't go in. I'm just saying that we ought to, you know, spy on them for a while."

"I can't. I cannot do it. I'm done." Sandy shook her head. "I'm through creeping around out here in the bushes. I'd rather die in there in the next five minutes than spend another hour out here in this jungle."

"I need to find Tara," Peanut said. "If she's not already in there, then maybe there's somebody who can help me find her."

Sandy nodded furiously, her eyes moistening with tears. "Yes. That's what I'm thinking. My husband could be in there right now, waiting for me."

"Alright, alright, but just—let me do the talking, alright?" Nate poked a finger at Peanut's chest.

"Whatever you say, *Dad*," Peanut said, rolling his eyes.

"Okay," Sandy replied.

Nate took a deep breath, exhaled, and then parted the last boughs that concealed them. "Okay, gang. Let's do this."

Hand in hand, their cobbled family of perfect strangers stepped forth together from the jungle, and into the fort's earthen yard. They'd only emerged for about five seconds before a shrill whistle peeled from one of the guard towers. Sandy felt her throat tighten. Her heart began to pound, as a second and third whistle keened from adjacent towers. It was not a pleasant sound. Whatever instruments were being blown were tuned to a note most disturbing to the human ear. It felt like her ear drums were being lanced with a quivering needle.

The trundling resonance of rolling cogs preceded an outpouring of defenders. Bearing spears, hatchets, and what looked disconcertingly like modern rifles, a platoon of naked and painted warriors rushed across the yard, all piping their terrible whistles. Nate had been right in his hesitation to approach this place. It was she and Peanut who were being delusional.

"Stop it. Put that damned thing down." Nate seized Peanut's spear as the kid assumed a defensive stance. He grappled with the boy for control of the weapon. At last, he overpowered him, yanked it from Peanut's hand, and threw it into the shadows.

"You told me I was making my own decisions!"

"You're not making mine for me. You want to get us all killed?"

Sandy imitated Nate, lifting her hands slowly over her head. At first stubborn, and unwilling to submit, Peanut finally obeyed when the defenders drew close enough that they were able to see their faces. Whistling warriors closed in all around them. Eyes bulging, cheeks puffing on slender reed flutes, they pointed all manner of weapons in their faces. Their various skin tones suggested a tribe of mixed races, with hairstyles that were as unique as the painted designs on their bodies. Some wore dreadlocks. Others plaited their long hair into braids, while others shaved their heads right down to the skin.

"Get on your knees," Nate whispered, as he lowered himself to the ground.

Sandy followed suit. Peanut remained standing. Defiant to the end, he refused to kneel.

The warriors glanced at one another, as though they were either confused by this behavior, or just unsure of what to do with them. One amongst them stepped forward, handing his stone hatchet off to another tribesman. He was dark-skinned, with a closely shaved head, and teeth that appeared to be gilded with some type of shiny metal. Swaggering up to Peanut, he retrieved a strange object from a pouch on his hip. He lifted the thing, glossy black, rectangular, and thin as quarter-deck of cards, and he aimed it directly at Peanut's face. The boy began to palpitate, gritting his teeth, as he cringed away from the mysterious instrument.

"Please," Nate said, "he's just a boy." Nate rose to his feet, and he stepped in front of Peanut. "Use it on me instead."

The warrior cocked his head, and frowned. He grinned, glanced around at his painted brothers in arms, then snapped his glare back around at Nate. Leveling the device with Nate's face, he tapped his finger against the opposite side, and the instrument flashed as brightly as the midday sun. Nate blinked, wide-eyed, and stumbled backward.

"What did you do to him?" Peanut shouted. "What the hell is that thing?"

The warrior was showing the device to his comrades, who all seemed to be getting some enjoyment from a private joke. At the sharpness of Peanut's tone, the warrior's scowl returned. He brought himself nose to nose with the boy. "iPhone, punk! What year you from?"

"What year?"

The warrior cleared his throat, and softened his approach to a condescending level. "What year was it that you left behind, when your punk-ass came here?"

"Nineteen—nineteen seventy-one."

"Seventy-one?" The warrior grinned, and turned his back on the boy, jabbing his thumb over his shoulder. "And this punk thought we was the cavemen."

An enormous warrior in dreadlocks stepped forward. He looked them up and down. "Got any open wounds? Slept overnight in the jungle?"

"No," Peanut said, shaking his head. "Just scrapes and stuff."

"How about your fine ass?" the first warrior asked, pointing his device at Sandy. "Got any boo-boos? Need me to look you over?"

"Yeah, strip down. I want a look."

"Drop them drawers, baby."

Sandy began to breathe heavily. A dozen sets of hungry eyes were crawling all over her. The men were all starting to push closer. She knew that whatever move she chose or chose not make at this moment would determine how these men would regard her, and therefore, what they would or would not do to her. If she obeyed them, and removed all of her clothing, then they would take her submission as a sign of weakness that would easily be dominated. If she refused their order, then she risked appearing insubordinate, and probably earning a beating. Both roads would end in the same violation. Her hands were clenched on the bottom of her shirt. She didn't know what to do. "We slept on the beach," Sandy said, "and we've got no open wounds."

"On the beach, you said?"

Sandy nodded. The warriors all looked at one another, as if she'd said something that was inadvertently of importance, or incriminating. They spoke English. They all seemed to be American, but there was no telling how long they'd been here, how devolved they'd become. If these were the same savages who'd mutilated John, it wasn't obvious to her that they were utterly lacking in humanity. A little rough around the edges, maybe, but they didn't seem like psychopathic barbarians. "We understand that there was some sort of an altercation between our people and yours—"

"Sandy," Nate said.

"Well, they weren't our people. That's what I'm trying to tell them. I mean, we were all on the same plane, but the one who shot—"

"Gag 'em and bag 'em."

Seized by a clutch of grabbing arms, she was dragged into their midst. Groping her, squeezing her, they pinioned her arms behind the small of her back. A knotted rag was jerked into her mouth, and tied behind her head. She watched the same bonds being fastened to Nate and Peanut, until a sack of reeking cloth was dropped over her head. It smelled sour inside, like aged and ample saliva. She could see nothing but the dark stains on the fabric as she was marched blindly ahead.

If there was some negative association with their camp on the beach, then that could only mean that they'd discovered it already. Donovan. They'd seen the great plume of smoke rising up from the bonfire, and they'd followed it right into their camp. When they arrived to find Donovan drunk and combative, sharing space with a couple of mutilated corpses, what were they to think of anyone who might be associated with that man? Who knew what else Donovan had done since she'd left him, or what his reaction might've been when a band of painted warriors charged into camp? Knowing Donovan, it wouldn't have gone well at all.

Unseen arms dragged her along through some sort of a gate that grumbled mightily behind them until it closed with a metallic clank. The ground was hardened here, almost paved. She could feel the gaps between pavestones beneath her feet. Her ankle was howling with pain, but she did her best not to limp, or to show in any way that she had a highly sensitive part of her body, or she feared it might be used against her in some torturous way. The thought of being restrained while someone twisted and wrenched on that swollen ankle was too horrendous to consider. She couldn't let them find out.

"Take her up to Dr. Bendu. Put the rest of them on the poles. Keep them bagged and gagged. We don't need them talking to the others."

The others?

They almost certainly had Donovan, but whom else? The missing girls? The desire to see if Ray was amongst the other captives was almost enough to make her cry out in desperation.

The footpath on which the warriors led her inclined. She could feel the burning in her calves and hamstrings as they ushered her up an ascending trail into some cavernous tunnel where their footsteps resounded sharply against the walls. Here, the glow of lights on either side of her permeated the stinking bag over her head. Only now could she discern that the stains on the fabric were blood. A huge, irregular splotch darkened the sacking in front of her face, as though the last person to wear the fetid article had died suddenly and violently, face-down in a lake of blood.

The arms wrenched her leftward into another corridor, where the light faded to absolute blackness, and gradually returned with greater brilliance than ever before. She could hear the crackling of a fire. Each snap and pop reverberated keenly off of close stone walls.

"Sit."

Hands pressed down on her shoulders. A foot snapped at the back of her knee. Sandy allowed her legs to fold beneath her, but her swollen ankle made it awkward to sit in any other position but flat on her butt, with her legs outstretched in front of her. She hoped to God that no one would stumble over that bad foot, or she would scream with pain.

"What have you brought me?"

The new voice echoed off the cavern walls. There seemed an intelligence to the man's inflection, discernible in his careful annunciation of each word, and his measured tone. There was an accent that she couldn't quite place. The root was British, but its edges were softened with a sort of patois. Possibly African? What unsettled her was that the intelligent aspect of his voice also bore a seductive quality, possibly even depraved. Even men who were perhaps once filled with promise could be hardened to perversion and cruelty.

"She's from the camp down on the beach. We picked up three more of them."

"The vector?"

The silence that followed suggested that a negative shake of the warrior's head had been the reply. She wished that she had some information to give them on the whereabouts of the vector. She could always lie, if that would buy her time, but she felt that sticking to the truth would be her best course of action. The awkward silence was horrifying, leaving her to imagine what suggestions were being made by body language and gesture, if anything was happening at all. They were possibly just staring at her, appraising her body for its most basic worth.

"Let me see her."

In a flash, the reeking bag was snatched from her head. The room exploded into view. She stifled a shriek in the pit of her throat when she saw the face of the man seated by the fire. Raised scars decorated his cheeks in patterns of oceanic swirls, and his teeth, they were all filed into points.

"Pretty, in a way," the man said, stoking the coals with prods of his wizardly staff. He continued to smile at the fire for a spell before licking his lips, and turning back to her. "Tonight, you're going to testify," he said. "You're going to testify on behalf of yourself, and you'll testify on behalf of every member of your group. What you say is final. Do you understand?"

Sandy made a whimpering sound through her nostrils. She nodded tentatively to his question, although she remained unsure of what exactly he meant by his strange request. The room all around her was an unholy marriage between the darkly eclectic nostrums of a witch doctor, paired with the technical fitments and brilliant disarray of an inventor. Shelves and workbenches all around were cluttered with clay pots, anatomical remnants, and disassembled bits of machinery.

"I am Dr. Bendu, head of the Science Guild here in Briggstown," he said, with a dramatic sweep of his outgrown nails, "the City on the Edge of Forever."

He gave a couple more pokes to the firewood, releasing a flume of crackling sparks, and then rose from his seat. He took a few steps toward the rough sill of what appeared to be a window that was chipped right through the wall of his Stone Age laboratory. "Yesterday, we saw you fall from the sky into the Garden of Eden. You were lucky to land in the sea, and not into the highland crags like my fellow Africans and I." He twisted his staff between his hands, and then tapped it against what sounded like a wooden leg beneath his tunic.

Dr. Bendu turned from the window to stand over Sandy. He sucked at his sharpened teeth. "We have but one reason for maintaining a civilization here in Briggstown, rather than running loose through the jungles of Eden like a pack of feral dogs, as many others have chosen to do. Our singular purpose here is to find a living vector. We are here because of them, and we were all meant to die here alongside them. However, those who implanted the technology inside the vectors underestimated the will of humankind to survive in a world where survival was not deemed possible. For more than a century, the citizens of Briggstown have invented ways to overcome this living hell where they've condemned us, but very soon, we will make our phantom enemies pay dearly for their crimes against humanity. You see, you've arrived in here in Briggstown at a very historic moment, when humankind stands poised to launch its first counterstrike in a war between the ages."

Lowering himself to a squat, Dr. Bendu reached out with a hooked finger, and pulled the knotted rag from her mouth. He smiled as she licked her lips and swallowed in an effort to wash the sour taste out of her mouth. Chuckling softly, as though he'd been through this ordeal many times before, he rose to his feet with a grunt, and moved back to the open window. "Bring her over here."

Sandy felt strong hands curl beneath her arms, and lift her to her feet. With her hands still tied behind her back, she feared that if she toppled from stress and exhaustion, she'd be unable to catch herself as she crashed to the cave floor. Her handlers seemed to sense that possibility, and they kept hold of her as they eased her up to the window.

"I think that she presents little danger to us here. Cut her loose, please."

Sandy felt the strokes of a sharp blade between her wrists. It made her a little nervous, but soon enough, the cutting was done. Her hands were free again. She raised them before her chest, and rubbed her wrists.

Below, the seated forms of several people were bound to posts jutting up through the pavestones of a torch-lit plaza. The silhouettes of other structures could be discerned beyond the ring of firelight, but they were indistinct in the shroud of darkness. Armed guards stood behind each of the prisoners, whose heads remained concealed beneath those bloodstained bags, but Sandy immediately recognized Nate, Peanut and Donovan, by their attire. The other two looked to be female. Although they were bruised, battered, and barely clothed, they resembled Margot and Tara. It looked to be a foreboding stage that was all set for some dreadful ultimatum.

"We waste nothing in Briggstown. We can't afford it. Resources are scarce, and often dangerous to obtain, so we salvage everything that we are fortunate enough to find. People are no exception. We need people to grow, to expand our small gene pool, and to survive. We need skills and talents, able bodies and minds, but the foundation of every relationship is trust, and that is why before your citizenship can be considered, you must testify. Understand?"

Sandy hesitated for a few seconds before nodding.

"Good. Easy questions first." Dr. Bendu smiled sweetly. "What is your name?"

"Sandy," she replied, her voice cracking. She cleared her throat, swallowed, and then repeated herself.

"Sandy," he said, placing his clawed fingertips together before his lips, "if you had to classify your role, thus far, down there on that beach where your little group was camping, what would you say has been your role, in a single word?"

Sandy's eyes flicked back and forth over the paved commons, across the row of prisoners bound to poles. "Nurse," she replied.

"Nurse?" Dr. Bendu nodded his head. "We can always find good use for those who possess medical acumen, or even those whose altruism drives them to care for the sick and wounded. We can perhaps use you, here in Briggstown, but there are many other positions yet to be filled. When you look down at those people, what else do you see?"

Her eyes drifted from one end of the tethered lambs to the other, and back again. Her gaze halted on Peanut. "I see a young warrior," she said, with a conviction that surprised even herself.

"Which one?"

"The teenage boy, second from the end, on the left."

Dr. Bendu smiled. "He looks like he might be a little young to me, but we'll see how well he fits into our Guild of Bad Faces." He extended his right hand through the window, made a fist, and popped his thumb skyward. Below, a guardsman paced from one end of the row of captives to the other, staring all the while up at Dr. Bendu. When he walked behind Peanut's pole, Dr. Bendu dropped his arm. The warrior produced a long, curved blade. He knelt behind the boy, and severed his bonds. The sacking was pulled from his head. Peanut looked around with a dazed expression before rising to his feet. After a moment, he followed the guardsman out of the plaza, and into the darkness beyond.

"Artist," Sandy said, smiling down at Tara, whose open devotion to the fine arts was the girl's most memorable contribution to the conversation they'd enjoyed during their short visit over lunch with their group, back in camp. She'd showed off a tattoo on her ribcage that she'd designed herself. She said that all her life, she'd dreamt of nothing else but attending an art school in San Francisco. It was her hard lobbying that eventually brought her high school's trip to San Francisco to fruition.

"Art is a powerful influence on a civilization. It forges a society's culture. It inspires direction, and it raises morale." Dr. Bendu thrust out an arm, and a thumb snapped up into the night. Another guardsman patrolled the shadowy backdrop until he passed behind Tara's pole. Dr. Bendu's hand dropped, and the girl was cut free.

Sandy frowned. For a moment, she thought that she might've misidentified Tara for someone else. This wasn't the same girl she remembered. Below, a ragged and disheveled figure moved so slowly, limping, shuffling her feet across the pavestones with the gait of an elderly woman. What had once been a beautiful teenager's face was bruised and misshapen to a frightful perversion of its original form.

"You are fortunate that those two girls were captured ahead of you." Dr. Bendu turned to Sandy, and chilled her blood with a salacious smile. "It's been more than a year since new females arrived in the Garden of Eden. Sometimes we can be—how shall I put it—overzealous, in our manner of welcoming new females."

Sandy recalled her own moment of terror out there in the Briggstown yard when they'd surrounded her, bullied her, and made veiled threats to physically assault her. She'd never felt so vulnerable. "Don't you have laws against that kind of abuse? What kind of civilization allows that to happen?"

"There will be plenty of time to explain the structure of our society if you are selected to be a part of it. Now would be the time to testify on behalf of any quality people who might remain down there. Do you see any?"

The shock of seeing the results of whatever horrible ordeal Tara and Margot had endured at the hands of Briggstown's police force was not a sight so easily shaken from her mind. The ramifications for herself, and for what might yet lay in store for her, and for the other women, had her mind addled with trepidation. What kind of society was she pledging to join, and worse, recruiting others in its servitude? She felt terribly conflicted, but there seemed no choice in the matter. They either learned to survive amongst these people, and to live by their rules, or they would die like animals in the jungle.

"Sandy, are there no useful people remaining down there?"

"Y-yes, there's ..."

She couldn't think straight. Sandy folded her hands against her lips, and stared down at Nate, knowing that his life might be hanging in the balance between her silence, and whatever role she blindly assigned to him. He was a good man, but one of unparticular quality. She couldn't remember what he said he'd done for a living in the world they'd left behind. She knew him to be loyal, trustworthy, kindhearted, and a fatherly figure toward everyone around him, but what specific position would he fill in a Stone Age society? He didn't seem to have the stomach for any sort of brutality, or the youthful fitness demanded by hard labor. Nate was philosophical, intelligent …

"Scientist," she said, blurting the word with a heavy breath, as though she'd just survived some narrow escape.

"Scientist?" Dr. Bendu tilted his head, hitching a thoughtful eyebrow. "What sort of scientist?"

"He's—an engineer, I believe. Very scientifically minded. Brilliant."

"I'll assess his level of intelligence myself. He'll be working right here in the lab, under my authority. I've been without a competent assistant for many months now. Which man is he? Right or left?"

"Left. Over there on the left. All the way on the end."

"Excellent," Dr. Bendu replied. He gave a thumbs-up, and within a few moments Nate was cut free. He rubbed his wrists by the flickering light of the torches until he was ushered away into the night.

Sandy knew what was coming next, and she dreaded it. Only Donovan and Margot remained. What practical use this society would have for a hawkish broker and a fashion model was difficult enough to imagine, but to further complicate Sandy's dilemma was their selfish and untrustworthy character traits. She suspected that they were exactly the sorts of people that Dr. Bendu was screening against, and she had to come up with something quickly. The witch doctor was staring at the side of her face, and he was no longer smiling. His mood seemed to be dropping the temperature by degrees, the longer she faltered. He could sense her hesitation to endorse them. He could see that she was struggling.

"Sandy, what I'd like for you to do instead of testifying for these people, is to testify against one of them. Survival of the deserving majority is at stake. If either of those two cannot be trusted, if they've displayed selfish or violent tendencies that might one day jeopardize the survival of a person of higher quality, then please, point out that individual now."

Her gaze swept from Margot to Donovan, and back again. It was hard to discriminate between the two, really. Dr. Bendu had aptly described both of them. They were both guilty of disloyalty. Both had behaved selfishly, in ways that did in fact jeopardize the lives of more valuable group members. However, she supposed that if she had to choose one as being more disloyal, more dangerous to a group than the other, then her choice would have to be Donovan. Margot, at least, had behaved impulsively. Her only real crime was that of failing to suppress the powerful instinct of self-preservation when her own life was endangered. Donovan's behavior, on the other hand, seemed very much premeditated. He and Dale had been plotting the night before. They'd made their intolerance of pampering the injured quite clear. Donovan had actually taken the time to sit back in the wings, and decide to commit the ultimate form of treachery against the same group to which he'd pledged his loyalty.

"You are protecting the lives of your friends, and the lives of everyone else in Briggstown, Sandy, by helping me cut the chaff from the wheat. Which of those two must go?"

"Him," Sandy whispered, lilting her chin in the direction of the man in the tattered suit with the stained sack over his head. He looked so pitiful. This was probably the lowest point in his entire life, and she'd just made it worse for him, somehow. Despite what he'd done, or might've done, she felt so sorry for him. She couldn't bring herself to say his name aloud.

"Why him?"

"He stole from our group, drank all our rations. He burned up all of our firewood."

"And?"

Dr. Bendu moved closer, until she could feel his breath on her neck. God, he was like a living polygraph machine. He seemed to be able to sense whenever she was hiding information, and he had a keen ability to extract it.

"And—he may have killed two people."

"Killed people?"

Sandy nodded. "Today. Two people who were badly injured, people whose lives we entrusted into his care."

"You entrusted people's lives to this man, and you suspect that he broke your trust by murdering them in cold blood?"

Sandy closed her eyes, and nodded. "Yes," she whispered.

"Sandy …" he said, crooning into her ear. He raked his clawed nails gently through her hair. "Sometimes the right thing can be so hard to do, but you've done the right thing for everyone tonight. Don't you see?"

Sandy sniffed, and nodded. What he was saying did make sense. She didn't enjoy the job of thinning her own flock, but who else would possess the insight to point out dangerous individuals but one of their own group members? It made sense.

Dr. Bendu turned to the window. His fist shot out like the arm of Lady Justice. The thumb flicked sideways, and it dropped into a downward position.

Sandy couldn't bring herself to look away, as one of the remaining two guardsman stepped forth from the shadows. She watched him slide quietly behind the pilings. Donovan tilted his bagged head as the guard drew near.

"Are you going to send him back out to the jungle, all alone?"

"Sandy. Weren't you listening to a word that I said? I told you that we waste no resources in Eden. Not a single, solitary scrap."

The curved blade floated behind Donovan, and then swept around the pole to settle beneath his chin. Donovan's scream was accompanied by the trill of whistles. Unseen warriors all around had been waiting for this moment. They rejoiced it. Their piping chorus charged the air with demonic energy.

His legs played in red gouts that spewed down his stomach. The eager blade tilled back and forth through the yawning slot. When it struck his vocal cords, the timbre of his shrieks changed to sheep-like bleats, then squeaks, until the communicative organs were severed. Still, his feet kicked, while the only sound was that of steel slopping back and forth through wet folds of meat. The knife grated against vertebrae. His head lolled with grotesque flexibility, as a new stain spread over the crotch of his slacks. With a terminating crunch, his legs leapt and fell in a single spasm, as his bagged head tumbled down into his lap, and trundled a short distance across the pavers.

Quick as a cat, Dr. Bendu had seized her from behind, pulling a blade of his own up against Sandy's throat. Something had changed. It was as though his patient and charming ruse had been nothing but a sheepskin, and the wolf was now upon her. She could feel the burn of the razor edge nipping through the outermost layers of her skin.

"Please, don't!" In that moment, Sandy knew that she would say or do anything to be spared Donovan's fate, anything but what she'd just witnessed. The irony did not escape her that the very sin for which she'd judged Margot was one she was now willing to commit.

"Rolling heads and pooling blood," Dr. Bendu said, purring into her ear with warm chuffs of his ineffable breath. She could feel his whiskers scratching her cheek, his stiffening pelvis pressing into her behind. The blade of the knife was pulled so sharply beneath her jaw that it was lifting her up onto her toes. "Welcome to Briggstown, Sandy. I think you'll like it here a lot. Only one last question, Sandy. You or her? That's it, and then we're finished. One of you lives to see the morning sunrise, while the other will be butchered and brined in our kitchen larder. You or her?"

"Her!" Sandy shrieked. The blade kept pulling, pulling, tilting her chin to the ceiling. She felt warm trails of blood rolling down her throat, while Dr. Bendu's smearing fingers rubbed it all over her chest.

"What do you mean, Sandy?" he replied, pinning her body against the windowsill with a vicious thrust of his hips. He was dangerously aroused. "Her? Her? I'm a little confused. Do you mean that you want her to live, or that you want her to die?"

"Die!"

"If you mean it, shout the order." Dr. Bendu's tongue lapped her earlobe. His free hand chased rivulets of blood beneath her shirt. "Tell the guard to cut her fucking throat!"

"Kill her!" Sandy cried, sobbing. Tears poured down her cheeks. "Kill her!" Her own voice was a haggardly squawk, as though some witchman's spell was changing her into a horrid form more befitting of her treachery.

"Tell him to cut her throat. Cut it. Cut it." Dr. Bendu thrust rhythmically against her. "Tell him to cut her head off."

"Cut her throat! Cut her head off!" Sandy cawed his echoed words like a bloodthirsty, devilish muse.

Dr. Bendu shivered from head to toe, obviously delighted by the power of having absolute control over another human being. After breathing deeply for a while, he began to chuckle softly. "I quite enjoyed that, Sandy. Did you? I didn't guess you'd have it in you so soon. Did you? However, it was all just a fib. That guard would never touch her without an order from me, and I'm not ready to see her die. Not yet, anyway. I've got a special use for her in mind. There's quite an important project underway that is very near completion, and I think that your naughty friend down there would do nicely as a scientific Guinea pig—if that would be alright with you, of course?"

"Y-yes."

"Lovely." Dr. Bendu said. He clicked his tongue, and sighed. "I almost forgot, the Bad Faces already staked a small claim to her, which is their right for capturing her, and delivering her to me. If you don't give the Bad Faces what they want, then they're liable to cause trouble around town. Get my drift?"

Dr. Bendu lowered the knife from her throat, and Sandy collapsed upon the windowsill. She watched blood droplets fall from the cusp of her chin to flower hotly upon the beige stone. Stepping up beside her, Dr. Bendu raised his arm, and rested the blade upon his forehead. A dramatic pause was followed by a pantomimed slice across his brow.

The guard below responded with a nod. The stained sacking was jerked from Margot's head, and cast off to one side. Wide-eyed and trembling, she peered around the flickering plaza, but when her gaze came to rest on Donovan's headless corpse folded strangely at the waist, Margot began to scream. Twisting her arms against her tether, she screamed and writhed against the pole until her neck suddenly straightened beneath a fistful of her long, blonde hair. Her voice lowed a mournful wail as a blade floated out of the shadows, hooked around her stricken face, and settled just beneath the young model's hairline.

# CHAPTER TEN

21-F

The one who'd captured her was awarded his prize, and he placed it atop his head. Clinging to the ragged flaps of hide, he twirled his new wig of flowing blonde hair. Backlit by roaring flames, the warrior gyrated around the campfire, smeared and glistening with the rendered fat of the butchered ones. Stones rose and fell upon smoldering femurs. Heads lowered, and slurped steaming marrow from the slab. All around, painted monsters howled from frescoes in a jungle of shadows cast by firelight flickering through heaps of red bones. Here, life's destruction was something celebrated, and haphazardly enshrined. Dancers hooted and piped their death whistles, hitching around the bonfires, clapping lithe hands to an ancient rhythm of scuffed feet brought with them to this world from another. They were a group unto their own, both bound and isolated by a common tongue that no one understood. The Africans captured the attention of the more prominent bands, whose watchful eyes observed their scalp dance, but dared not interrupt.

Peanut crouched along the wall of the reeking cave that served as a barracks, fetid with rotting remnants of the scavenged, and the leavings of the living. Nothing was sacred here, where the strongest postured and pushed, suckling skins of palm wine as they drifted from one fire to the next, predating on the weaker. Spats of violence erupted. Blows were thrown, and articles of perceived value changed hands. There was the sense that one's life could be deprived in an instant, and forgotten even more quickly. It was only a matter of time before the ravens fell upon him. They'd already robbed him of Dale's pocket knife, his driver's license, and even a handful of worthless coins, but amongst people like these, there would always be something more to take. After they'd stripped you of every worldly possession, they could still take your body, your innocence, and your last shred of hope for a better day. They would keep taking until every gobbet of marrow had been licked from your blackened bones.

The shaved warrior from the yard came reeling out of the mob. It took a few seconds before some spark of recognition hardened his glare, and he came staggering toward Peanut. His gang remained seated by their fire, but they watched his every move like solemn spectators to some requisite rite of passage.

"Acting all bad out there in the yard. Who bad now? Who bad now, punk? You think you want to be a Bad Face? You?"

"Come on, T-Lo. He's just a kid."

"Shut up, Gavin. How old are you, punk?"

"Eighteen." Peanut drew his knees up to his chest.

"Speak up, boy! I can't hear you!"

"Eighteen."

"What they call you?"

"Peanut."

"Peanut? That sound like a gangsta name, but you just a little punk." He bent down, placed his hands on his knees, and glowered nose to nose with Peanut, breathing wine fumes in his face. "You ain't got the juice to roll with the Bad Faces, you little punk-ass, white boy."

"Ain't no races in Bad Faces, T."

"We the Bad Faces. The *Bad Faces*. You know what that mean? Mean when somebody needs cut up into pieces, we who they call. When something comes through that wall, we who they call. Blood is our business. You can't handle it. I can see it in your eyes. Look at you. You about to cry."

"No, I'm not."

"You ain't, huh? Still think you bad?"

"No."

"No? You got to be bad, punk, but you ain't. That's the problem. What you going to do when one of your people needs dealt with? You'll be the one gets to cut they head off. You think I'm playing?"

Peanut shrugged.

"Ha-ha. Yeah, go ahead, act bad. We'll see. Tomorrow, we'll see." T-Lo rose, stumbled sideways, and then turned to traipse a meandering path back to the campfire.

"Come here." One of the other men beckoned to him with a sweeping arm.

"Me?"

"Yeah, you. Get up, and get over here."

Peanut rose, dusted off his behind, thrust his hands into his pockets, and sauntered over to their fire. He guessed that he was in for some more abuse, but it was probably better than sitting alone against the wall, where he felt like an easy target. He guessed that he liked the idea of having a designated group of antagonists, rather than serving as a whipping post for everyone who happened to walk by.

The man who'd called him over leaned back on his haunches, and he looked Peanut up and down. The other warriors addressed him as Gavin. His name was muttered on a pretty regular basis throughout the cave, as though he possessed some clout. He wasn't a big man, really. He looked just as rough as the others, tattooed, scarred and filthy, but what caught Peanut's attention was that underneath the outer layer of grime was a keenness in the manner of his observations.

"You need to understand what you're getting into with us," he said.

Peanut suppressed the urge to reply. Gavin let his statement hang in the air for what felt like an awkward eternity, as Peanut stood over the circle of seated men like a shameful spectacle presented for their amusement. He wanted to sit down, but he wasn't sure that he was being invited to do so.

"It's just blood and guts, day in and day out, without any glory. Am I right?"

Most of the men nodded, after casting Peanut a hard look. They all stared down into the pile of glowing embers, as though they were deep in thought, or entranced by the flames. No one had anything to add.

"Even if that sounds like a life you might want, wanting it ain't going to be enough. At the end of the day tomorrow, we decide." Gavin made a sweeping gesture with his index finger. "You're rolling out with the first patrol, at sunup. Better be on your best game."

"Hunting?" Peanut regretted asking the question before the word had even slipped out of his mouth. Anything he said was going to be wrong.

"What's the hardest shit you ever seen?" T-Lo asked.

Peanut cleared his throat, and rocked back on his heels. "My best friend dying right in front of me, on the first night here."

"How he died?"

"Got killed by a howler."

"By a what?"

"A howler."

"A howler? Fuck is a howler? Some kind of werewolf or something?" T-Lo looked around at his fellows, wearing a huge smirk on his face. "I ain't knew we had werewolves in Eden."

"No, it's—you know, those big, shaggy things that hunt down along the beach at night. We call them howlers, because they howl at night."

T-Lo laughed right into the fire. He pulled a swig from his wineskin, passed it to his left, and wiped his bare arm across his mouth. "Ain't nothing surprises me no more. Howlers and shit. What you first called them, Dre?"

"I ain't called them nothing," the enormous man in dreadlocks to T-Lo's left replied, while sucking petulantly on the wineskin.

"He called them, *Mamaaaaaaaaaaa*!"

Half of the men around campfire erupted into laughter. Although the Bad Faces seemed to advocate a kind of solidarity, there were divisions throughout their ranks. The five guys in T-Lo's group were obviously tight, based on their joviality and body language, while Gavin's sullen entourage was an uncomfortable contrast. The mood was precariously imbalanced. Even out in the yard, these men revealed the same quiet alliances. The other knots of warriors seated around smaller fires throughout the cave kept to themselves, rarely making eye contact with Gavin and T-Lo's men. If there was a method of segregation amongst the Bad Faces, the rules weren't obvious.

"They called rexes," Dre said, in the deepest voice Peanut had ever heard.

"T-rexes," Gavin said.

"Nah-nah, I'm the only T-whatever in Eden. They just rexes."

"You mean, like tyrannosaurus rexes?"

"Tyran-no-saur-us rex-suz?" T-Lo said, stiffening his neck, and wrinkling his nose in an exaggerated imitation.

"Just rexes."

"But, the creature I'm talking was all covered with like, feathers and stuff."

"What's your point, kid?"

"Hold up. What year you said you was from?"

"Nineteen seventy-one."

"Ah, see? They ain't had no feathered dino's in seventy-one," Dre said. "They ain't had all that yet. T-rex still be stomping around buck naked like some busted-ass Godzilla."

"It ain't like that. It ain't like that." T-Lo waved his hands, as though erasing words right out of thin air. "Right here in Eden's what it really is, son."

Beyond, the pale light of the doubled moons glimmered through the entrance to the cave. The paired celestial bodies appeared to be even more hopelessly in love than they'd been the night before. Peanut stared at them, and blinked.

It was a strange and almost sickening revelation to be robbed of the last shred of hope that they were simply marooned on an uncharted island. It was so much worse than that. It was the absolute worst. There was no way to even quantify the gravity of the fact that he would not likely see his family, his friends or his school ever again. They were completely out of his reach, and to acknowledge that fact was almost enough to make him sick. Lost in time, with no way of getting back home. Not ever.

"I don't get it" Peanut said, collapsing onto his rump in the dirt beside Gavin.

"What don't you get?" Gavin replied.

"Did all of you come from different years?"

"We came together in ninety-six," Gavin said, gesturing to the men around him with a tilt of his head. "Those guys came together in eighty-seven. There's a few here from twenty-twelve. What was Red from? Twenty-twenty?"

"Yeah."

"He was the furthest one out, then. He's dead."

"Future boys. That's where we get our iPhones," T-Lo said. "Them dudes past two-thousand. When one of them falls out the sky and lands on my beach, they iPhone be my phone."

"Can you call people?" A surge of yearning welled up inside Peanut's chest. Never in his life had he wanted to hear the sound of his mom's voice so badly, some words of encouragement from his dad, even something from his stupid sister. He missed all of them so much. Knowing he'd never be able to say goodbye to them produced the most intense feeling of loneliness he'd ever imagined, because his family and friends were not anywhere on this world, and they wouldn't be, for millions and millions of years.

"Nah. You can't call nobody. Shit just says, no service," T-Lo said, frowning down at the confounding piece of technology in his hand.

"What good is it then?"

"They got cameras," Dre said, "and little timers and stuff. Show him, T."

"Check this out," T-Lo said, tapping the glowing screen. "You can flip the camera around like this, and bam, now you got a mirror. Damn, I look good."

"Show him, man."

"Whoa!" Peanut gasped at his own awestruck reflection peering back from the little screen. It was like seeing himself live on a miniature TV.

"Dr. Bendu builds batteries out of rolled coins and vinegar. That's how he keeps these guys under control," Gavin said. "That, and the wine and brew. Just like candy for a bunch of little kids."

"You just mad 'cause you ain't got one." T-Lo polished the screen of his phone against his loincloth. "Ain't nobody controlling me."

"You're being controlled right now. You're just too dumb to realize it."

T-Lo's head snapped up. He narrowed his eyes at Gavin, who sat ready to return the icy glare. The raucous ambiance of the cave fell into a sort of lull. Campfires crackled and popped. No one but those seated around their fire could've heard the comment, but the tension seemed to be contagious.

"Briggstown ain't a bad place to live," Gavin said. "It's as good as it gets in the Garden of Eden, and the Bad Faces are the top guild in Briggstown. Trust me, there's other people out there right now living a lot worse than we are."

"What the hell you telling him all that for?" T-Lo said, gaping at Gavin in profound disbelief.

"What's it really matter?"

"You don't need to be advertising that shit."

"He'll either earn it tomorrow or he won't. What's the difference?"

"Ain't nobody ever told us that shit. We had to figure it out our damn selves. Why don't you go outside and just yell to everybody how good we got it up in here?"

"It don't matter, T."

"He'll make it or he won't."

"It's good to be a Bad Face," one of Gavin's men said, folding his tattooed arms across his chest. "First dibs on everything."

"Meat, wine and women."

"Choice cuts. Believe that."

"This is a man's world," Gavin said. "That's as straight as I can put it. Only the strongest survive."

"We got dibs on females," Dre said. "Nobody else but a Bad Face can claim a female for his own. Nobody else can touch her."

"Everybody else has to share whatever's left, whether its females, food or drink. Not us."

"Why is that?" Peanut asked.

"Can't believe y'all telling him this shit," T-Lo whispered.

"Because they know we'll kill them," Gavin replied.

Peanut looked around the fire at the other men's faces, hoping to see a smirk, some sign that Gavin wasn't being serious, but the expressions were grave. He wasn't joking. Peanut felt his mouth go dry.

"You in a good place, Cuz, if you make the cut."

"Briggstown is guild rule," Gavin said. "There's no chief, president or king. There's no governing body. What we've got instead is a bartering system between guilds, and in that pecking order, the Bad Faces come out on top. We protect them, and we intimidate them. They tolerate us because they have to. We protect them, and they provide us with the things we need. That's how Briggstown works."

"If I make the cut tomorrow, then when do I get a wife?" Peanut asked. Tara was on his mind. If he didn't claim her, then one of these men surely would. The thought of losing his only connection to the world he'd left behind to one of these barbarians made Peanut feel desperate, even a little savage.

"Listen to his ass. You see why you shouldn't have told him?" T-Lo said. "This buster ain't even earned his rexes, and you got him talking about wives, and shit. You got to earn your female, son." T-Lo yanked at a thong around his neck, where a small clutch of black feathers were bound.

Peanut looked around at the necks of the other men. He hadn't noticed the little talismans before, probably due to all of the grime and paint on their bodies. Everyone in the Bad Face's camp wore the same decoration.

"Nobody, and I mean nobody, wears rex feathers but us," Dre said. "We wear them because we the kings of this joint. You earn your rexes, and then you be a Bad Face. Everybody in Briggstown will know it. Nobody ever going to mess with your lady, because she gets one, too. Dudes see one of these around her neck, and they go clear around her, or they get they ass whupped. You know what I'm saying?"

"We own Briggstown. Every once in a while, we've got to go in there and remind a few of them of that fact, but not very often."

"How do I earn one of those?" Peanut said, his eyes shimmering with avarice. He wanted to wear the rex feathers so badly. He wanted Tara. She was all that mattered, and he saw that clearly now. Whatever it took to claim her as his own, he'd do it. Ever since middle school he'd fantasized about her, and this world provided him a unique opportunity for a guy like him to really be with her, for always, and in every way that he'd imagined. No one in Briggstown even knew her the way he did. They'd grown up together, walked to class together. He knew her artistic soul. No one else in this hellhole was going to lay a finger on her, because she was his, and if anyone touched her—he'd kill them.

"Got to spill blood," Gavin said.

Peanut nodded. He was ready for whatever test they put in front of him. "I'll spill blood. I'll spill some blood right now."

"Listen to this punk talking some shit."

"I'm not a punk," Peanut said, turning to glare into T-Lo's eyes, "and I'm not joking."

T-Lo straightened up, and he cocked his head at Peanut. The thug seemed to be staring right into his mind, searching for weakness. Peanut made sure that he wasn't going to find any. He puffed up his chest and returned the glare, just the way Gavin had done.

A wicked grin spread across T-Lo's face. "I know what's up with your ass." He nodded his head slowly, pinching his chin thoughtfully between his thumb and forefinger. "It's that little honey, ain't it now? It's that little girl them Hutus dragged in today. Am I right, or am I right?"

Peanut felt the bottom drop out of his stomach. He didn't want anyone to know that. He didn't want anyone to know how desperate he was to claim her, but T-Lo had him over a barrel, and he couldn't think of anything to say in reply. The skin of his face became warm, and then hot, but it wasn't embarrassment. It was rage.

"Yeah, she fine. I seen her, too. I might even have to get me some of that tonight."

"No, you won't," Peanut whispered.

"What you said? No? You know how many of them Hutus already got to her, today?" T-Lo whispered back, as though they were sharing some delicious secret. "All of them, Cuz. All of them. They all got a piece of that ass today."

"Shut up." Peanut didn't even recognize the sound of his own voice. His fists were balled and quivering. If he still had Dale's knife, he'd have stabbed it right into T-Lo's eye, and then he'd have kept right on stabbing some more.

"Don't be mad at me, son. Be mad at them Hutus if you want, but that's they right. That's they right to do so. They *Bad Faces*, son. That's what it mean. Get it, now? First dibs on everything, son. On *everything*."

"He's right," Gavin said. "That's the martial law we enforce, and they all tolerate it, in exchange for protection. Make no mistake about it though, they're our bitches in there. All of them. We own them."

Peanut was shaking uncontrollably. He didn't know where to direct so much hate, but he wanted to direct it at T-Lo, if only to wipe that smug grin off of his ugly face. He couldn't believe it. He couldn't believe what he was hearing, what things these people around him had done to an innocent flock. They were nothing but a gang of Stone Age thugs who dominated and terrorized hapless newcomers to this godforsaken place after they'd already lost everything they knew and loved.

"You don't understand it yet, but you will. This is the way society works in this type of a situation. It's the way it has to be."

"No, it doesn't," Peanut replied. "It doesn't have to be this way."

"This is a man's world," Gavin said. "There's no ignoring that fact. If you want to live in a fantasy world, you can, but it'll be out there with them, with the little people. Sure as hell won't be with us. We only take top quality."

Peanut just breathed, calming himself until he guessed he was able to speak. He turned to Gavin. "What do I have to do?"

"There's a big migration of 'saurs headed our way. They'll be passing through any day now. Long-neckers. Thunder lizards. A herd so huge that it'll stretch from one end of the coast to the other for weeks on end. Happens every year around the Moon Kiss, when the moon orbits swing them almost close enough to touch," Gavin said, pointing to the glowing orbs in the cave entrance. "Big meteor showers. Weather takes a nasty turn. Tides roll over the barrier reef, flooding clear up into the jungle. That's when we know the big boys are coming back to the beach, and running their migratory route just offshore. It's our best source of red meat for the whole year."

"That's why all them sea monsters be crowding up on the beach," Dre said, "and why all them rexes be moving down from the interior. They know what time it is."

"Slaughter time," Gavin said, sucking his teeth.

# CHAPTER ELEVEN

23-E

Sandy was shaken from a dream in which she and Ray kept passing. Round and round, they passed each other through a bank of revolving doors that spun them in and out of a bank's tropical atrium, on and off the noisy streets of Baltimore, and back again. With every pass, they caught a glimpse of one other, and could almost touch through the pane of plate glass. She kept shouting, but Ray couldn't hear her. If he would just stay put on one side or the other, then she'd come around to meet him, but he couldn't seem to understand what she was asking him to do. What was the matter with him? They kept passing, swiping their hands against the glass, clawing at the frame, until her fingernails splintered, blood streaked the glass, and Sandy began to scream.

"Wake up."

She moaned when a rough hand jostled her a second time. She rolled over, and found herself squinting over the glow of a clay oil lamp at the creased and swollen face of Briggstown's barber surgeon, Meyer. She recognized his bearded face, but it took her a while to remember where in the heck she was.

"We've got a patient, and I'm going to need your help with him."

"What time is it?"

Meyer frowned at her, and shook his head.

Sandy sat up, and rubbed her eyes. She didn't know why she'd asked such a stupid question. It was nighttime, and apparently, it was also time to get up. As she rose from her reed mat, the memory of horrors beheld just hours ago came rushing back into her head like the sudden recollection of a nightmare. She gasped, covering her mouth, and thought that she might get sick.

She'd killed two people. She was no better than Margot. When the chips were down, and fate forced her hand, she'd chosen to save her own skin over the life of another. Donovan's execution had come as an awful surprise, but by the time they got to Margot, Sandy knew exactly what was stake.

The guilt was almost incapacitating. She'd judged Margot, sentenced her to death for the same sin that Sandy was ironically committing by doing so. Along with everyone else, Sandy had judged that girl harshly, outcast her. The sad part was that she knew they wouldn't have reacted so hotly if it had been Donovan, rather than Dr. Kimura, that Margot had thrown to the beast. It came down to the value of human resources that had been wasted, and the fact that she hadn't repented over what she'd done, by way of some emotional display. That was definitely a factor, but whatever they'd been expecting of her, Margot was unable to give. What was it, anyway? If their demand was remorse over a spontaneous incident that resulted in fatality, then what would that kind of remorse even look like?

Donovan was gone, just like that. They'd butchered him on the spot like a hog. Donovan was funny. He was an entertaining character around the campfire who kept things lively, and light. Sandy was still trying to find practical uses for him, reasons to spare him from that fate. Perhaps, she always would, spinning that terrible situation round and round inside her mind like some damned revolving door that never led her anywhere. Their lives would forever be her burden, and their ghostly faces would forever be leering at her from the opposite side of the glass. Sandy caught herself scratching at her forearms, staring down into the dirt at nothing. Yeah, that's what Margot's remorse would've looked like.

"Are you about ready?"

"I'm sorry." Sandy brushed her hair back out of her face with her fingers, wishing she had a hair tie, a clip, a bobby pin, anything. "What's the situation?"

"Well, it's a bad one," Meyer replied, turning toward the curtained portal that led down into the old network of lava tunnels. "He came in the east gate around an hour ago, pretty beat up. Broken bones and lacerations, possibly some internal injuries."

"One of our warriors?"

"Well, of course it is."

"Oh, no." Sandy grabbed Meyer by the upper arm. "It's not the boy who I came with, is it—around eighteen?"

"No, but it'll be him eventually, if not tonight."

"Why would you say that?"

The doddering bulk of Meyer eclipsed the light of the oil lamp, casting his oscillating amplitude all over the walls for a dizzying effect. If he'd ever been a medic at all, back on the other side, Sandy guessed that he'd have been something of a curmudgeonly relic, an old throwback with enough tenure to skate through his last years to retirement.

"Oh, you been working this hospital long as I have, you start to notice certain things," Meyer said. "Not so much who shows up most frequently, but who doesn't show up. Get my drift?"

"No," Sandy replied, "I guess I don't."

"Hmm, well, I don't like to talk about other guilds, but my observation has been that there seems to be a group of Bad Faces who run a sort of racket over there, sending the fresh ones out to try and prove themselves, and that almost always gets them killed. The youngsters do whatever they're told out of fear or respect, I'd imagine, but that same bunch has been running things that way for almost twenty years."

"How long have you been here?"

"Well, I came over in ninety-one, but I've been here in Briggstown almost fifty years, longer than most. Wrap your head around that one, and you'll need some aspirin." Meyer cleared his throat with a rumbling hack, and spat something substantial against the ground. "I was just a boy when I came over. My mama and I. Been here ever since."

She was dying to ask him if the citizens of Briggstown were free to come and go, but she didn't want to raise any suspicion of malcontent too early when that question was bound to answer itself eventually. She also knew better than to ask Meyer about his mama, when she'd detected that telltale softening of his voice. It was so sad. A lonely, wobbling troll who'd haunted these lightless whorls for half a century was once an orphan stripped of all that he'd ever known, and abandoned here, in this City on the Edge of Forever. These tunnels were his entire life.

She could smell the astringent stink of their home brewed antiseptic, and heard the moans of the infirmed. They were getting close to the so-called hospital, which was just a cavern beneath their dormitory that featured an underground spring, and a flat slab of sandstone on which to operate. It was stocked with oil lamps, fashioned surgical instruments, strange nostrums and remedies. Every medicine was blended strictly to the specifications of a detailed logbook penned by one Captain Benjamin Briggs, the nineteenth century founder of this colony, after whom Briggstown was eventually named.

To the best of her understanding, Captain Briggs and his entourage were the original human castaways in the Garden of Eden. They were the true survivors who'd not only erected the fort's massive walls around the rim of an extinct volcano, but they'd also developed the fundamental skills that were still employed by all of the guilds. Captain Briggs was a warrior, doctor, scientist, artist and inventor, all rolled up into one. It seemed to Sandy that he was a pretty remarkable man, one to whom far more credit for Briggstown was owed than men like Dr. Bendu would have newcomers believe. Sandy liked to imagine Captain Briggs rolling in his grave over the devolution of his once astonishing sanctuary in a savage land to what was now, under guild rule, little more than a human trap.

A recovered automobile's stereo system was rigged to a bank of vinegar batteries in clay casks. The sounds were piped nightly over the wall, amplified through a system of rawhide bullhorns. Newcomers to Eden invariably followed the sound of music through the twilit jungle until those rolling doors slammed shut behind them. Once those gates closed, especially if you happened to be female, then you were regarded as little more than Briggstown's property, and were absorbed into a caste. Only warriors seemed willing or able to venture freely beyond those walls to hunt and forage. Meyer hadn't specifically stated that others were forbidden to leave, but Sandy suspected that if she ever had any doubts about Briggstown being a trap—and she didn't—then, all that was required to test her theory was to attempt to leave.

Meyer wobbled past the slab, where four patients groaned and shivered. Without casting a glance in their direction, he made his way over to the great hearth, and struck up a gasping rhythm with an enormous bellows. The flames leapt higher with every downward thrust, until the hospital was brightened by the roaring portal. Meyer tossed a few logs lackadaisically into the fire, smacked off his palms, and wobbled back over to the cutting slab. He put his hands on his hips, and he glowered down at the twisted mess of a human form. "I don't guess he's going to make it through the night."

"Oh, um …" Sandy smiled through her teeth at the patient, and rose tiptoed to whisper into Meyer's hairy ear. "Maybe we shouldn't say things like that right in front of the patients."

"Why?" Meyer's bulging eyes, the downturned corners of his wide mouth, gave the distinct impression that he might at any moment unleash a sticky tongue to snatch a fly right out of the air.

"Well, I think it might be a good idea to try and keep their spirits up, you know?"

Meyer didn't appear to know. Perhaps he'd spent too many years down in the caves. He stared down at the patient, blinked his bullfrog eyes, and licked his lips. "Secure his wrists and ankles, if you would. I'll need to fetch a particular device."

Muttering to herself, she squatted beside the patient, and assured him that everything was going to be alright. That wasn't exactly the truth. She had no clue what Meyer was up to, and until she landed on Eden, she'd never had any medical experience. Back home, she worked down the block from a hospital, so medical professionals were always a part of the neighborhood scenery. She found their world intriguing. At the local café, she enjoyed eavesdropping on their oftentimes gruesome conversations over lunch break. Their lives seemed more interesting than her lot in life as a secretary. Yeah, their jobs were probably intense, and they surely went home covered in every sort of bodily fluid, but at least those nurses could jump into their cars at the end of each day feeling good about the fact that they'd actually helped people, all day long. How amazing would that feel? Nurses put positive energy out into the world every time that they pulled on their scrubs, and Sandy envied them for that.

The patient on the slab in front of her emitted a thin moan. Sandy sighed, and clasped her hands before her chest. This wasn't a typical hospital, to be sure, but Sandy intended to do a damned good job, to help lots of people, and to be the best nurse that she could be, under the crude circumstances.

The wrist and ankle restraints were loops of heavy gauge copper wire reeved through metal stakes driven into chinks in the stone slab. She got to work, securing his ankles first, followed by the wrist of his right hand, but she wasn't sure how exactly she should go about securing what remained of his left arm, if it even needed securing at all. She supposed not. She left it lying crookedly at his side, at the small risk of receiving one of Meyer's quizzical frowns.

Nearly every part of the warrior's body appeared to be injured in some way. She had to look past the hundreds of abrasions that spangled his filthy carcass, and focus only on those injuries that demanded immediate treatment. His left arm was a mangled mess. Dislocated from the shoulder, the bones were pulverized beneath the skin. His throat was ripped out, and bubbling forth a blend of mucus and blood. His left orbit was crushed inward to the bridge of his nose. The eyeball once housed there had burst from the explosive force, and its contents had dried where they'd dribbled down his chin. The left side of his jaw bulged outward like a bruised potato, and his swollen tongue protruded between fragments of shattered teeth. It looked as though he'd either fallen from a great height, or something of stupendous mass had slammed into the left side of his body with the force of a runaway train.

Sandy cocked her head, narrowing her eyes at the injury to his throat. The flesh was torn, peeled down to his collar bone, but the wound originated at a crescent-shaped divot in the side of his neck, about the size and shape of a set of human teeth. That was peculiar. Who would bite into the throat of a fellow human being, rending and thrashing like a rabid dog? Honestly, she preferred not to know. It was easier to believe that whatever had sunk its teeth into this man's windpipe was something other than a human being.

"You just relax now," she said, stroking the patient's forehead, as Meyer reentered the hospital cavern with what looked like a stainless steel rod in one hand, and a bladder of dark, sloshing liquid in the other. "The doctor is back, and he'll get you all fixed up."

The man's undamaged right eye fluttered open for the first time since she'd been at his side. Drool rolled from between his parted lips. He arched his neck, emitted a mournful groan, and turned to gawp at Sandy.

She leaned in close, peering deeply into his single eye. Something was weird in there. Sandy scooted on her knees around the man's head until she'd relocated to his right side. From this angle, she could maybe get a better look at it. Using her thumb and forefinger, she spread his eyelids, and stared down into the squirming organ. Sandy wrinkled her nose, poking a fingernail gently against the eyeball. Segmented masses churned and recoiled from her touch. "Hmm."

Meyer waddled up, breathing laboriously, and sank down onto one knee beside her. The steel rod in his hand was actually hollow, and sharpened on one end to a needle point. He began to affix the sloshing bladder of liquid to the dull end of the hypodermic that was aimed at the inside of the patient's thigh. "Antibiotic cocktail with a powerful hallucinogenic stimulant. This should either liven him up for a while, or send him into the hereafter like a friendly slap on the ass."

"Wait a minute," Sandy said, pawing at Meyer's arm. "Come up here, and have a look at this."

"What exactly are we looking at?"

"I don't know. It's like—there's something inside of his eye. Something alive." Sandy screwed up her lips. "It almost looks like it might be worms. Have you ever heard of such a thing?"

"Worms, you say? Inside of his eye?"

"Yeah, whole bunches of little critters, see? Right there."

"Get back! Get back! Good God, get away from him!" Meyer shouted, as he staggered to his feet, and stumbled away, clutching his chest. He dropped the hypodermic to the stone floor. The needle rolled musically from its tether to the bladder.

"What on earth is the matter?" Sandy edged over to the medic's side, shifting her gaze from Meyer to the moaning patient.

"I thought they were just a myth," Meyer muttered, wiping his brow. "Fifty years, and I've never seen them. I can't believe they're really real."

"What?"

"Nurseworms!" Meyer stabbed an index finger at the ceiling, turned on a heel, and waddled back off in the direction of the hospital stores. "It's a lethal contagion described in the final entries of Captain Briggs' journal. Nurseworms were the very malady that wiped out the original colony in just a matter of days, but in the century since their passing, not a single other case has never been documented—until tonight."

"What should we do?"

"Move the other patients away from him, if you would. Drag them clear over to the far wall, but don't get too close to that one. Ho-ho, if he bites you, it's over!"

"If he bites me?" Sandy grabbed the wrists of the patient furthest from the infected warrior, and began dragging him across the cave floor.

"Indeed," Meyer replied, while banging around in stone cabinets chiseled into the pumice walls. "It was Captain Briggs' own daughter who got lost in the jungle overnight. By the time they found and rescued the child, she'd contracted nurseworms through an open wound on the bottom of her foot. She was the first documented case, but once they brought her back into Briggstown, the malady spread like the Black Death." Meyer popped the stopper from a clay jug. He leaned down to sniff the bung, and recoiled. "These are nasty parasites, voracious little buggers that bore tunnels all through the brain matter, affecting judgment, and altering behavior." Meyer hefted the jug off the floor, and tottered back across the cave to the restrained patient on the slab. "Biting is the mechanism by which they're most commonly transferred, because the saliva contains great quantities of their eggs."

"Ew." Sandy watched Meyer swing the jug over the patient, slopping the pinkish medicine all over his body. The man coughed, lolling his head back and forth, as if to avoid the fumes. "He got bit. Look at his neck."

Meyer halted his application process. He stooped to gawk at the gruesome injury to the man's throat. "Yes, I believe you're right. He didn't come about them naturally, by any means. I'd say we may have an epidemic of nurseworms on our hands."

"Why do they call them nurseworms?"

"Ah, because they heal!" Meyer exclaimed, as he heaved a great splash of fluid over the patient's face. "They tend to the injuries of the infected, and restore them quickly to health. From an evolutionary standpoint, it's presumably meant to increase the longevity of their host, and therefore, the likelihood that the worm colony will be spread. I suppose there might even be some medicinal use for the little buggers if they didn't always burrow straight for the brain, but the fact is, they're just too dangerous to keep around."

Before Sandy could react, Meyer snapped a wooden matchstick against the back of his front tooth. Flame spat from his bullfrog mouth. The tiny flare arched through space to engulf the infested patient in a ball of fire. The warrior's back arched, his legs straightened, and his wrists curled over his shackles. Sandy watched his fingers creeping through the flames. She covered her mouth and screamed for him, as roiling masses of worms came spewing from his eye sockets like bundles of hot wires.

"What the hell's going on down here?" A cloaked man cowered in the doorway. He shielded his face from the intense heat with a fold of tanned hide.

"Nurseworms!" Meyer screamed, pointing at the inferno. "They've already made it inside. Go and tell Dr. Bendu that we've got nurseworms! Run!"

Sandy shrieked with a mix of surprise and pain, as one of the other patients whom she'd dragged across the room seized her by her sprained ankle, and sunk his teeth all the way to the gums. Falling to the cave floor, she clawed the ground for a stone, a stick, anything to knock him loose of her, but there was nothing but powdery dirt raking through her nails. Using the heel of her other foot like a maul, she raised her leg, and slammed it down on the snarling head, again and again, until it lifted its face to leer at her through its worm-infested eyes. She jerked her foot loose of its grip, leaving it to ponder the sudden throbbing inside its skull, as dollops of eggs rode vines of slobber from its quivering lips to the cave floor.

She crawled away, scooting backwards away from the growling thing, clutching a wound on her ankle that she knew was infected. Once she'd hitched her way to a safe distance, she bent over her ankle, and lifted her hand. Hundreds of yellow eggs, no bigger than grains of sand, were already bursting, one after another. Wriggling larvae disappeared into the crescent-shaped wound, and plunged into her flesh. "No," she whispered, shaking her head from side to side.

It wasn't fair. She'd tried so hard to be one of the good ones, a hard worker and a helper. She stood by every move that she'd made, except for the moment when she was called up to testify. Was this her penance for that single slip? Was that all it took? Just like Margot, she'd committed a single sin, and for that she was unforgiven.

Icy cold, yet hot, she choked in the astringent fumes as a cascade of pink liquid sluiced over her. She didn't have to turn her head to know what was happening, or why. His labored breaths bubbled in his lungs, as the toad physician administered a dose of his only medicine to her deadly affliction. Gouts of gasoline slopped over her head and back, until mats of sodden hair hung down over Sandy's face. She wished that she had a hair clip, a bobby pin, anything.

She heard the snap of a match against Meyer's front tooth. As the spitting stick flitted through the air, her last thought was that life had never played fairly, from Sandy's beginning to her untimely end. No family, no children, no one left in the world to mourn her loss, she was simply going to vanish in an underground inferno like so much garbage, as if she'd never even existed at all. For all their uphill struggles, she and Ray had never once been lucky in life, but that had never stopped them from pushing forward, from being genuinely good and productive people, and from making positive plans for a future that never came to pass. Flames consumed her with a woof of expanding air. Sandy was going to be a nurse, maybe the best nurse that Briggstown had ever seen.

### ###

22-D

"By now, you're probably wondering what in the hell is going on, and if you'll ever know what's going on before your time here runs out." Lifting the rag from the antiseptic, Dr. Bendu encircled it with his lithe fingers, each decorated with an outgrown nail, and squeezed the brownish fluid back into the clay basin. He smiled down at his experiment, dabbing at the raw edges of her peeled scalp, stroking the dome of her exposed skull. Margot's eyes winced at his touch. She shuddered, palpitating around the gag stuffed in her mouth.

Dr. Bendu didn't strike Nate as being a doctor at all, not one of medicine or otherwise. The utter disarray of his laboratory, and the impulsive, almost juvenile spurts by which his synapses fired, Dr. Bendu appeared to be more of a backstreet hustler who'd seized an opportunity to elevate himself to a status above his misled community. The man constantly referred to an old journal of quilled entries that were obviously conceived by a more enlightened mind.

"Have you ever heard of the *Mary Celeste*?"

The name did ring a bell. He couldn't exactly recollect the strange tale, but he recalled the name as being that of a ship that had met with some sort of a noteworthy tragedy at sea. It seemed he'd read an account of the disaster at a pretty young age, maybe in one of those chapbooks of weird tales of science fiction and adventure that he'd enjoyed as a child.

"She was a ghost ship. Perhaps the most famous ghost ship of all. En route from New York to Italy, the entire crew of the *Celeste* mysteriously vanished into thin air in November of eighteen seventy-two. When she was recovered, they found no sign of a struggle. She was fully stocked with provisions, and her cargo was untouched. There was even food sitting uneaten on the table. There was no reason to suspect mutiny, or famine. Everyone aboard her had simply disappeared." Dr. Bendu jabbed a pointed finger in the direction of his workbench. "Fetch me a scalpel, please."

Nate edged over to the cluttered work surface. He felt hollow inside. His legs were wooden, and his mouth was dry. He'd hardly known the girl strapped to the examination table. In fact, he hadn't known her at all. His profile of Margot was one force-fed to him by the others in her group, who attested she was some sort of a murderer, a selfish thief of human life who could not be trusted, but that didn't make it any easier to participate in whatever deranged experiment this witchman had a mind to conduct.

"It's pink. Yes, that's the one."

Nate's quivering hand lifted a device that appeared to have once been a child's toothbrush. A red-haired mermaid smiled up from the pink handle. In place of the bristles, which had been melted away, was a rusty, razor blade. Rapid breaths filled and emptied his lungs. His lips were numb. Turning robotically on his heel, unable to look away from the terrible instrument, he extended his arm, and Dr. Bendu snatched it from his hand.

"Captain Benjamin Spooner Briggs was in command of that vessel. I kind of like his name. Don't you?" Dr. Bendu sloshed the homemade scalpel in the basin of filthy antiseptic. "His wife and infant daughter had come along with him on that particular voyage, in addition to a crew of mostly Germans. Arian Martens and Gottlieb Goodschaad. You don't get much more German than that, do you?"

Nate heard a sound escape his throat, as Dr. Bendu dropped the corner of the razor blade onto Margot's sternum, and neatly flayed her belly open to the naval in one decisive stroke. Knots of gray intestines bulged through the hot, new fissure. He stepped back, smiling patiently, arms folded around his chest, until her screams waned into a low mewling around the wadded rag.

"What really happened to Captain Briggs and his crew will forever remain a mystery back there, on the other side, but here in Briggstown we have the rest of the tale." Bendu tossed the scalpel into the basin, and lifted his precious journal from a nearby shelf. He clutched the thing to his chest, closed his eyes, and inhaled whatever aroma the old book still exuded. "They came here, obviously, in the company of a vector. Now, this is important because it may provide us with the starting point of a timeline in a series of similar events, of which you and I are all too familiar."

As Dr. Bendu leafed through the hoary volume of notes, Nate's gaze drifted over to meet the tearful eyes of Margot. In a glance she seemed to plead to him, to beseech him to intervene. Only fringes of her hair remained in a bloody fray above her ears. The balance of perhaps her finest attribute was just a red dome, rising from her brow like an otherworldly polyp. Nate had to look away, or he was going to be sick.

"Briggs writes that he dined on the eve of November sixth, the night before the fateful voyage, with one Captain David Morehouse of the British registered *Dei Gratia*. It was at that last supper that Captain Morehouse mentioned an ongoing manhunt around the distribution reservoir of the Old Croton Aqueduct, wherein authorities hoped to apprehend a scoundrel attempting to poison the water supply of New York City with what was believed at the time to be cholera." Dr. Bendu slammed the book shut with force enough to make Margot's exposed innards jiggle. "Fast-forward around twenty days, and the claims proved quite accurate, as a stowaway was discovered in the hold of the *Mary Celeste* who showed all the signs and symptoms of that deadly malady, which was the most feared disease of the nineteenth century. To save the lives of his wife and daughter, no doubt, Captain Briggs and his crew decided to abandon ship. They took only the navigational equipment and a small supply of rations aboard the yawl as they attempted to make their escape."

Dr. Bendu placed a hand on Margot's shoulder, allowing his pearly claws to drag up her throat as he passed behind her, and made his way to another shelf. From this alcove hacked into the volcanic pumice wall, he removed a large, wooden compass. He smiled fondly at the instrument, brushing dust from its glass covering, before returning it to its place. "They did not make it, Nate. Know why?"

Nate shook his head, and swallowed dryly.

Dr. Bendu seemed to find his lack of insight amusing. He allowed a nasal chuckle, while drifting toward the far end of his workbench. Before him rested a cylinder of polished metal, fluted with neon green tubes not unlike bubble levels, or miniature sight glasses. From the endcap protruded a pair of crooked wires with tabbed ends, like an insect's antennae. "They didn't make it because the vector leapt over the bulwarks, and swam after them. Captain Brigg's last memory from the world he left behind were the hands of the vector slamming down on the yawl's transom, followed by a blinding flash of green light."

Nate's eyes widened. In Dawn's final moments, that's all she could talk about, a flash of greenish light just before the plane came apart in the sky. He'd evidently been too engrossed in the hijacking to notice whatever phenomenon had made such a marked impression on his wife, but he recalled that in her opinion, the flash held profound significance.

"Vectors. What are they? Let's look at the evidence, Nate. They are people, yes? They are people carrying some sort of a deadly disease, as well as a highly-advanced, technological implant." Dr. Bendu lifted the strange contraption from the workbench, and held it out for Nate to see. "There have been many vectors sent through space and time, each carrying one or more types of implants, and each was delivered to a heavily populated location. Africa, Japan, France, Italy, and New York City. All of these places have been targeted more than once with diseases that you've not yet heard of, all bioengineered specifically against the human animal. AIDS, SARS, swine flu, bird flu, cholera ... and Ebola, Nate, thank you very much. All of these diseases were painstakingly designed, tested, aimed and fired at the heart of humanity. We are under attack, Nate! Starting to get it, now? We've been under attack for more than a hundred years. Our governments know about it, but they have no clue as to how to stop it. That's where we come in.

"After more than a century of reverse engineering scrap implants here in Briggstown, we finally have in our hands a semi-functional device. This particular implant was recovered by a team of U.S. Navy SEALS after a commercial airliner carrying a vector had to be shot down just off the American east coast in nineteen ninety-six. The event caused quite an international flap, and a subsequent cover-up, as you can well imagine, but the TWA Flight 800 tragedy did provide Briggstown with a team of formidable warriors, a stock of modern weapons, and most especially—*this.*"

Dr. Bendu cradled the implant in his arms, as though it were the infant messiah. He lovingly fawned at the device for a spell, before stepping softly across the laboratory to present the thing to Nate, clutching it protectively to his bosom. "We've learned so much from this particular artifact, yes. We determined that each implant is equipped with a heart monitor," Dr. Bendu said, gently strumming the protruding wires, "and three separate relays with programmable timers. After many years of painstaking research, we've discovered how to activate them. This is where it gets interesting."

Nate watched Dr. Bendu slink around the back of the room. Margot thrashed her head to keep an eye on him, as he passed behind her. Standing directly behind her, in her only blind spot, he peered suddenly over her scalped head in a demented game of peek-a-boo. He placed a clawed hand atop her skull, and drummed his polished fingertips upon the bone.

*Click-click-click-click. Click-click-click-click.*

"The first relay beams the vectors through time and space to their highly-populated target location. After an exposure time of approximately two weeks, the second relay is activated, beaming the vectors—along with everyone and everything within twenty meters—back in time to the Garden of Eden, which is obviously a geographical location that is deemed un-survivable by whomever or *what*-ever is bent on our destruction. Once the heart monitor detects a dead vector, the third and final relay is then activated, beaming the technology back—we must presume—to wherever it originally came from."

Letting his claws slide down her skull with a terrible scrape, Dr. Bendu edged around the examination table to Margot's side. He patted the strange cylinder lovingly, still cradling it in his arms as he might a child of monumental destiny. "Why?" He turned to Nate. "That is the question. Is it not? Why would anybody do this to humankind?"

Nate shrugged, and gave a halfhearted nod.

"Come on. Take a guess. We're all scientists here." Dr. Bendu grinned at Margot, and nodded.

"If all you've said is true," Nate replied, clearing his throat, "then it would seem obvious that someone out there is trying to wipe us all out."

"No shit." Dr. Bendu bent an antennae with a single claw, and let it spring to waggle to and fro. "Is that the best you can do as my lab assistant, or do I need to start accepting applications?"

"Well, the only reason an enemy would have to wipe out an extant population of a single intelligent species would be for the purpose of eventual colonization."

"Very good. That's the alien theory, but there's no reason to presume an extraterrestrial threat. There is another. Try again."

Nate felt panicked under the deranged scrutiny of the so-called doctor, whose salacious grin belied any real hope that he wanted Nate to succeed. In fact, he sensed that Dr. Bendu wanted him to fail. If he wasn't deemed intelligent enough to make the cut as his own version of Igor, then a slot would probably open for him on Margot's examination table. "People," Nate said. "People from the future."

"Why? Why? Why would people from the future attack the past?"

"You have to imagine a situation in which resources have become so limited, the population has grown to a size a thousand-times the world's carrying capacity, when societies have completely unraveled, when the streams and the air have become so polluted that they're toxic, when anarchy rules ... in a desperate situation like that, it's not like the ruling body can just go out and start culling the population at hand. There are too many, and the damage is already done."

"Yessss," Dr. Bendu said, eyes widening.

"But, if the technology was available, in hopes of making for a brighter future for humankind, you could send someone back to cull the population before it ever got out of control."

"Yes!" Dr. Bendu shouted, smacking his clawed hand down onto Margot's thigh. He whisked it away, extended an accusatory finger at Nate, and began marching toward him across the room. "You are right, exactly! That is what I believe is happening. This is a war, Nate. It's a war between the ages. Our own children, Nate—our own children's-children's-children—have gone back in time to assassinate their own ancestors, knowing full well that a great many of them will be erased from existence as a result. That seems a big risk they are taking, yes? However, we must presume that their circumstances have become so dire that the risk of slashing their own population by a wide margin is worth it. Just imagine that, Nate."

"I did."

"Yes, well ... welcome to Briggstown, anyway. I guess you'll make a fine addition to my laboratory."

"Thank you, Dr. Bendu."

"Think nothing of it." He turned, and strode back over to Margot's side, strumming the antennae like a wandering minstrel with some ill-conceived, musical instrument. "This brings us to our mission, here in Briggstown. The same mission embraced a century ago by our loving founder and benefactor, Captain Benjamin Spooner Briggs. I love that name. I could say it all day long. The mission, Nate, is to quit lying down and taking it. We will launch the first counterstrike in our war between the ages, and let our great-grandchildren know that we are not an expendable populace of vermin to be exterminated at their desire. We've received their messages loud and clear, and tomorrow, we're sending one back!"

Dr. Bendu extended his arms, and dropped the device straight down onto Margot's bulging guts. Working his arms in to the elbows, he ignored her chilling screams as he thrust the strange canister up under her sternum, seating the device somewhere between her lungs. He cranked his head around in Nate's direction. "Needle and thread, please?"

Nate stumbled over his own feet in an effort to hastily reach the workbench. There, he spotted a spool of dingy fiber, and what looked like a hooked talon. He seized these articles, and brought them over to Dr. Bendu's side.

"You may stitch her up if you don't mind, Mr. Nate. I must prepare her injection." Dr. Bendu withdrew his arms from Margot's glistening viscera, and wiped his hands on the chaps of his loins. The pair of antennae were still sticking up from the open wound, and waggling in the air. "You see, we have deadly diseases here, too, just like anywhere else, and tomorrow, we're going to send a prehistoric cocktail of diseased blood into the future. On that device, the third relay was damaged. It thinks that the vector is still alive. Well, tomorrow we're simply going to short-out her heart monitor, and send Miss Margot here on a fantastic voyage through space and time. Does that sound like fun?" Dr. Bendu grinned at Margot, hitching his eyebrows.

Margot emitted a feeble bleat.

"Oh! Thank you for reminding me, Miss Margot. I'd hate for you to go zooming off into the future only to die of a silly infection within a day or two." Dr. Bendu scooped handfuls of dirty anesthetic from the basin, and slopped it into the wound. Particles of dirt and leaves clung to her intestines. "That's better."

"Dr. Bendu!" A shout peeled from outside, down on the plaza.

"What now?" Dr. Bendu tramped up to the windowsill, and glared down at whoever was yelling. "What do you want? I'm involved in science."

"Nurseworms!" the voice shouted. "We've got nurseworms in Briggstown!"

# CHAPTER TWELVE

21-F

He decided not to sleep. He tended the fire, and remained awake all through the night until the Bad Faces were filing out into the pre-dawn gloom. The night had passed quickly. Peanut's mind was overactive with the imaginings of a deranged future in Briggstown, where his daily trials of blood and fire would be rewarded nightly with Tara Riley, his jungle princess. These dramatic dreams kept a luster in his eyes all through the night, until dawn's silver edge found him emotionally spent and bedraggled, staring down into the coals through puffy, red-rimmed eyes.

Briggstown was at last revealed to him when they left the barracks. Contained within the looming walls that rimmed a vast crater was in fact a fishing village built around the shores of a mountain lake. Already, the fishermen's canoes plied the still waters as they paddled out to check their trotlines and traps. The dwellings and stores were excavations in the crater rim, where an ancient network of lava tubes served as connective tunnels between caverns chipped right into the pumice stone, stacked one upon another in the sheer walls of porous stone, with the uppermost being accessible only by ladders. Here and there, recovered relics from a faraway world sprawled out of context where they'd been left like abstract sculptures open to interpretation. Automobiles, partial and whole, were parked in the shadows of building remnants. The corner of an apartment complex, a prison cell, and a Red Cross medical tent provided portentous snapshots into those final moments before vectors and their captors fell together from Eden's skies. It was haunting, in a way. Every scrap had been recovered, and carried back up the mountain to be painstakingly reassembled on Briggstown's flagstone shores. Peanut understood the importance of preserving those moments, and they'd done a fine job in doing so. One day, he hoped to see the tail end of their airliner reassembled, every seat locked back into its proper place, to serve as a memorial for every life lost affected in that terrible instant when half a commercial airplane had slipped between moments.

Peanut inhaled a bouquet of baking bread, smoldering wood, and the greenish aroma of algae coming off of the lake. For the very first time since he'd swam to Eden's shores, he felt a sense of sanctuary. Briggstown felt like it might be a place that he could call home. He hoped that Tara would eventually feel the same way, because this was it. This was where they were going to stay. They'd start a family of their own here, and watch their children frolic along the shores of a private mountain lake. God, he wished Alex could've made it this far with him. He was the only thing missing, the only thing preventing his new life in Briggstown from being perfect. However, there was a thought, and Peanut didn't dare think it too loudly, that perhaps everything happens the way it does for a reason. There was only one Tara Riley, after all.

They passed through the rolling gates single-file, and they marched in silence into the jungle, in the direction of the sea. Following a narrow footpath that looked to have been used for over a century, they wound through the forest in a steady descent that took them behind a waterfall. The cascading tonnage produced a deafening roar, as water was hammered into mist against the rocks, half a mile below. Life was heard more often than seen, crashing off through the trees with an expressed fear of man that was evidently learned, because it could not have been instinctual.

By the time dawn's rays gilded the eastern horizon, they'd reached an overlooking outcrop with a commanding view of what had so recently been a long strip of sandy beach. That pale hem between worlds was gone, drowned beneath a hungry sea that had swollen over the barrier reef to crash into the jungle's edge. Saw-toothed monsters rolled between waves. The sea thrust in and out of the forest, smashing itself to foam against the trunks of palms. The play of electricity within the thunderheads to the west was something ominous to behold. Quite a storm was brewing.

"Do you think the herd will come through today?" Peanut asked Gavin, or whoever might be listening, but no one replied. His eyes wandered through the knot of warriors, taking a mental inventory of bows, hatchets, spears and modern firearms. Every man on the outcrop was armed with at least one weapon. "How am I supposed to help you guys hunt when nobody even gave me a weapon?"

"How's that our responsibility?" Gavin replied, without turning his head. "You think somebody gave me my weapons? Think somebody gave him his?"

"You guys took my pocketknife. I can't even sharpen a stick."

"Why'd you let us take it?" Gavin glared over his shoulder. "What kind of a warrior lets himself be manhandled like a little bitch? You want a weapon in your hand so that you'll be ready when it's time to be tested, but what you don't realize is that you've already been tested, and you failed. You're being tested right now."

"I don't get it."

"Course you don't, because you're not a warrior. That was obvious from the minute you stepped into the yard."

Peanut felt the bottom drop out of his stomach. He felt his Tara fantasy being swept suddenly away. "What do mean I'm not a warrior?"

"Look at us, punk, then look at you," T-Lo said. "Who the hell you think you are, thinking you one of us? Shit's embarrassing. We're warriors, kid. Don't you see that? *Warriors*. You don't decide to become that shit. You either is, or you ain't. Me and my boys was warriors before we ever got here. Gangsters, son. Soldiers of the street. We all got brought straight here from a jail cell when they threw a vector in the tank with us. You know what I'm saying? Straight from a cell to Hell. Gavin and his boys? You don't even want to know, son. Navy SEALS, all of them. Warriors, son. We're the realest. It's all we know. You just a little punk-ass buster trying to get it where you don't fit in."

"I wasn't trying to get in. They voted me into your group. Sandy and Dr. Bendu did." Peanut felt hot tears threatening to moisten his eyes, but he fought them back. "They chose me. They told me to join you guys, so I did."

"That's even worse, kid. See?" Gavin replied. "This wasn't even a life you chose. Your mama chose it for you. Mama shoved you through the door to keep her baby out of the brine tub, but that ain't going to make a whole heap of difference by sundown."

"She wasn't my mom." Peanut searched their faces for some sign of reassurance that he'd misunderstood what Gavin had just said. He had to have misspoken, but none of the warriors would even look in his direction. Their eyes remained focused on the sea. Those heaps of blackened bones by their campfires weren't from animals. Not all of them. He knew that now. Peanut didn't know what exactly he'd presumed about their origin, if he'd even gone so far as to make any presumptions at all. He'd denied what was right in front of him from the moment he stepped into their barracks. Preoccupied with insecurities, hopes of fitting in, fantasies with Tara Riley, he'd chosen to ignore the flesh-eating ogres and trolls that were feasting on human flesh, all around him.

"Don't even think about running off," Gavin said. "It'll be worse if we have to chase you down."

Peanut's heart throbbed dryly inside his chest. His lips and face felt numb, cold. Surely they didn't really intend to butcher and eat him. "I've got good potential," he replied, his quavering voice cracking.

Gavin shook his head. "No, you don't."

"I mean it. I can—" Peanut faltered. He couldn't think of anything to say. It's not that they were right … maybe they were, maybe he didn't have any chance of ever belonging with a bunch of savages like them, but he suddenly felt ashamed. He was ashamed of having desired to become a monster like them, and ashamed he wasn't worth more in their eyes than flesh to fill their bellies. He didn't know which he'd choose anymore, if given the choice. Filled with the worst hopelessness and dread he'd ever known, Peanut gazed down at the rolling forms of black reptiles in the surf. There remained one other choice.

"You had Atari yet in seventy-one?" Dre asked.

"What?"

"Atari. You had it?"

Peanut shook his head, eyeing Dre with a sickened disbelief. They intended to butcher and eat him, but before they dragged him off to the cutting slab, these cannibals wanted to milk him of every last drop of humiliation. A few of the guys chuckled, covering their mouths with the backs of their hands. Peanut never would've imagined that he'd one day develop an inferiority complex over the decade in which he was born, but around the Bad Faces, he not only felt emasculated and useless, but he also felt like he was some kind of a relic, a circus freak from another era.

"He ain't had Atari? You old school, Cuz. You an old playback from wayback."

"How about *Star Wars*, dude? You ever heard of *Star Wars*?"

"No." Peanut stared down into the hungry sea. The churning waves were ready to receive him with their cold and deadly embrace.

"Damn, son. You left just when the shit was fixing to get good. I feel sorry for your punk-ass."

"You the oldest dude here, except for the founders, and they all dead."

T-Lo's gang rolled and hooted, slapping fives. They were right. Just like the Africans, Peanut was an outsider in their midst, but the barrier between them wasn't language, it was time. So much had evidently happened between the seventies and the decades beyond that it seemed an impossible leap from his era to the next. Dread began to percolate into anger. There was nothing wrong with the time from which he hailed. In the seventies, at least people were genuine. They cared. They didn't sit around dogging on each other. They weren't obsessed with little trinkets of technology in their pocket. That was why Tara Riley was something sacred, who deserved to be protected from people like these. Peanut rose to his feet at the edge of the precipice.

"What the hell you doing, son?" T-Lo scowled up at him. "Better sit your punk ass down."

He couldn't take them all, but he could take one of them with him. He would take the worst one, the one he couldn't bear to imagine being with Tara in his stead. Peanut seized the leather thong around T-Lo's throat.

"Hold up," T-Lo shouted, leaping to his feet. "You lost your damned mind?"

It came barreling out of the underbrush with a guttural roar, slamming into T-Lo's flank with a flash of bared teeth. The leather thong snapped like a rotten string in Peanut's hand, as T-Lo was wrenched off the outcrop and flung into the brambles. He shrieked, as flesh tore from his bones before his body had even struck the ground. Warriors rolled and scrambled. Weapons clattered against the rocks. Peanut heard the snap of Gavin's automatic rifle bolt, even as he snatched a dropped spear, and lunged at T-Lo's attacker.

Prattling gunfire shredded leaves all around him, as he thrust the spear in and out of the killer's ribs. Beneath the snarling form, T-Lo thrashed in a fountain of its blood. In and out, Peanut plunged the red shaft into the spine, in and out, folding the madman's paralyzed legs beneath him. The psychopath rolled into the vegetation with most of T-Lo's throat still clenched between his teeth. Peanut leapt over the mortally injured warrior, and pursued his attacker as he scrambled for deeper cover, dragging his intestines behind him. Entangled in briars, he could only bare reddened teeth and growl.

Peanut didn't pity him, and he no longer pitied himself. He was still clenching T-Lo's feathered necklace between his palm and the spear's gory shaft, as he edged into the spiny brambles. The talisman belonged to him. He was just as certain of that fact as he was sure that its previous owner was already dead. Peanut raised his spear with both hands, and with a savage war cry, he reamed out the U.S. Marine's eye.

### 

22-D

"What happened in here?" Dr. Bendu shouted, staggering from one smoldering heap of flesh and bones to the next. "Meyer!"

"Nurseworms," the barber surgeon replied, his throat bulging with an involuntary gulp. "The patients were all contaminated, and my new assistant was bitten." He shifted his weight from one flat foot to the other. "They had to be destroyed."

"Destroyed?" Dr. Bendu whispered, leering at Meyer through a haze of burning flesh. "As long as you've been here, as long as you've known me, the sole purpose of the existence of Briggstown has never been unclear."

Meyer took a step backwards for every step that Dr. Bendu advanced toward him. Meyer's outward palms rose into a defensive gesture, gently tamping at the air. The cadence of his breathing hastened. Each drawn breath was sharpened by the constricting walls of his throat. Nate almost felt sorry for the guy.

"A hundred-year tradition in the study of local diseases in an effort to strike back against those who condemned us to Hell, and when you came face to face with the rarest and most deadly malady ever recorded in this realm—you burned it?"

"You make it sound so bad, Doctor, but they were spreading much too quickly," Meyer replied, still easing backward until his heel struck the cavern wall with a resounding clack. "Lest we forget the lessons learned by Captain Briggs in his final hours, we'd all have been infected. Every one of us. They'd have erased our civilization by the day's end."

"You don't get it, do you?" Dr. Bendu crept nearer. "That, Sir, is precisely what makes nurseworms the perfect weapon for our purposes, and you destroyed it. Nate?"

"Yes?"

"Hold him."

Nate strode up to the cowering form against the wall. He wasn't exactly sure how to hold a shuddering man who was making no effort to escape. Nate tapped his shoulder, as if to excuse passage behind him, and when Meyer leaned forward, Nate took him gently by the bends in his elbows. It felt rather awkward, not to mention unnecessary.

"Please," Meyer whined, "I was only thinking for the safety of our community."

"That is exactly why you failed us, Meyer. We don't matter. None of us do. Don't you understand that?" Dr. Bendu placed his palm against Meyer's chubby cheek, and gave it a pat. "Everyone here is already dead."

The blade appeared with the speed of a striking viper. Before Nate realized what was happening, before Meyer could cry out, Dr. Bendu had stabbed him three times through the heart. As his murderer casually wiped the blood from his knife, Meyer emitted a bubbling wail. He appeared to deny that he was a dead man still standing, and rather, a child stunned by a sudden spanking. Nate didn't want to hold onto him any longer, but he felt guilty letting him go, knowing that he was soon going to fall.

"I think you like it a little too much. That's what has always concerned me about you, to be perfectly honest. I think you might be a bit of a pervert." Dr. Bendu lectured the barber surgeon as he crumpled to his knees, spattering the cave floor with his blood. He began to crawl away. "You think I haven't noticed? Hmm? How many patients come in here, and how many actually leave? This room is less a hospital than an execution chamber. I've always feared that something may be wrong with your mind."

Meyer stopped crawling once he'd made it beneath a workbench. Teetering on his hands and knees, his breaths rattled horribly in his throat. His head swayed from side to side. Falling droplets drizzled the stone beneath his chest.

"Come, Nate. Let's see what there is to salvage of this killer worm, if anything at all." Dr. Bendu turned, as Meyer collapsed, his back heaving with snores of death that practically shook the cave.

Nate felt the need to wipe his hands on the sides of his pants. Even though his palms weren't bloody, they felt unclean for having held Meyer while Dr. Bendu stabbed him. He tried to ignore the dying man's rattling honks, as he followed the witchman from one burned corpse to the next. They all looked about the same, charred and grimacing in lakes of rendered fat, burned to the extent that their genders were indiscernible.

"I hope perhaps their core temperatures remained stable, even while the surface of their flesh burned away," Bendu said, as he knelt beside one of the victims. His blade went to work, carving a circular incision around a corpse's eye.

Nate covered his mouth, as Dr. Bendu eased his fingers down into the incisions, and lifted out the steaming glob. He shook his head, and flung the roasted eyeball off into the shadows, where it bounced wetly around the cave floor. Next, he plunged the blade into the cadaver's bloated gut. A geyser of steam spewed from the wound, around the blade.

"I cannot believe this terrible misfortune," he whispered, rising to his feet, and moving to the bedside of another cadaver. Again, the blade sank into the crisped flesh around the orbit, and began sawing a circular path around the organ. Gently, he pushed his fingertips into the socket, hooked them around the backside of the eyeball, and lifted. A small amount of steam accompanied a sucking noise as the translucent orb pulled free of its housing. Dr. Bendu sliced through the connective cordage, on the backside. He held the eyeball up to the glow of an oil lamp, turning his treasure back and forth between his nails. His eyes widened, and a barely perceptible smile curled the corners of his lips.

### 

21-F

Fiery hailstones perforated the bellies of thunderheads, and streaked down from the sky. Moon Kiss had arrived on the far side of the world, and the annual tempests to which Gavin had alluded were already preceding the lunar spectacle that spawned them. Lightning pulsed hotly through the scum of swirling clouds, and the ocean below them groaned with godlike resonance. Offshore, breakers slammed the barrier reef with spectacular explosions. White jettisons leapt to catch electric bolts in a game of elemental tag. Below the outcrop, muddy tides rushed up into the jungle, scouring filth and debris from the jungle floor, wagging the sodden boughs and snapping trunks in devastating display of the sea's greater might.

Identified as the same U.S. Marine who unwittingly fired the first shot in what was to be a secret war between the castaways and Briggstown, the wild man was summarily decapitated. His devilish head was mounted atop Peanut's killing pike. A dozen cupped hands plunged into the twin streams of his gushing blood, washing Peanut's face and hair, stamping crimson handprints all over his body. The talisman of rex feathers once worn by T-Lo was secured around his neck. Bloody hands seized his waist, his thighs, and raised him like a child of the lightning. To a chorus of howling, and thunder's deep rumble, he was initiated into their guild.

###

23-A

Peering from beneath her hood at the preparations in the plaza, Tara dabbed her scabbed lips with the lip of her tongue. Her lips were so badly split from the blows she'd received that she was barely able to speak, and smiling was as an act she might not ever perform again. Her body would heal. It hardly seemed possible, but she knew that it eventually would. Her mind, however, bore a different sort of wound that would forever fester. Tara added another stave of hardwood to the kiln.

It was Margot out there, bound to the stake. She knew it was her, even though the young model was hardly recognizable without her flow of golden hair. The rain turned pink as it drizzled over her red cap of exposed meat. An angry, red cleft was hemmed from her naval to her sternum. God only knew what they'd done to her, and what they intended to do. The scene on the plaza looked like a stage for the burning of a confessed witch. Kneeling in a puddle on the flagstones with her elbows pinioned behind the pole, Margot swung her buzzard's head to wail at those who passed her by, but no one paused in their daily habits to pay her mind. It appeared as though horrific sights in Briggstown were rather commonplace, where a hardened populace had been desensitized by their repeated exposure to brutality.

Throwing back her head, Margot beseeched the heavens with the squalls of an ignored child. Thunder replied, shunning her with its titanic rumble. The doomed girl slumped to one side, and hung sobbing from her bonds. In a way, she was a condemned witch. At least, that was the evil guise that fate demanded she wore in her final hours. Briggstown was nothing if not swift in its judgement, and merciless in the deliverance of its penalties for transgressions, be they real or perceived.

The warriors who'd fallen upon she and Margot made a point of justifying what would be lengthy and repeated assaults as a form of justice served on the behalf of their murdered brother, who was allegedly shot down in cold blood by one of the castaways. The toll of vengeance that was then exacted on them was one that they could barely afford. The jungle secreted everything that happened to them, every hour of it, until they emerged through the curtains of vegetation forever twisted as those vines, and utterly defiled. No one asked. No one who looked upon what remained of them questioned what had happened. No one cared. It was as though their ordeal in the jungle was nothing more than a nightmare that was hardly worth retelling, when everyone in Briggstown had suffered a similar dream.

A few heads turned as Margot was approached by a pair of men carrying tools, and a collection of nameless fitments. The one in the lead Tara recognized as the local scientist and inventor, Dr. Bendu. A wraithlike entity, he appeared to glide over puddled flagstones through the downpour, his clawed fingers moiling over one of those rectangular telephones that seemed to fascinate everyone in the village. His assistant followed him closely with a tattered umbrella positioned over his master's head, protecting the little piece of technology from the elements. Dr. Bendu knelt before Margot, his cloak clinging to his dark skin, as he connected the device to a set of wires that protruded through the stitches in her chest. When the wiring was complete, Dr. Bendu wrapped the telephone in clear plastic, and with the same material, strapped it to Margot's chest.

Tara lowered her hood. She blinked her swollen eyes in disbelief, and covered her mouth, when she realized that the mad scientist's lab assistant was none other than Nate. Abandoning her station at the pottery kiln, Tara bolted out across the plaza, and into the storm.

"Nate?" she said, gaping up into the eyes of the man hovering over Dr. Bendu with the black umbrella. "What are you doing?"

"You should probably go," Nate replied. The inner-light that once shined from within his fatherly eyes was gone, extinguished by whatever horrors had been repeatedly thrust upon them.

"Where is Sandy?"

The musculature of Nate's face gave an involuntary twitch. "You should probably go."

Dr. Bendu grinned up from the umbrella's shadow. His serrated teeth caught every flash of lightning. Seemingly from out of nowhere, a gleaming dagger appeared in his hand. "The eye," he said, extending a clawed hand at Nate's chest.

Probing his bulging shirt pocket with evident disgust, Nate produced a jiggling globe of translucent flesh, festooned with dangling bits of tissue. As he placed the horrid trophy in the center of Bendu's palm, Tara found herself the focus of one of Sandy's green eyes.

Dr. Bendu sliced an incision across the iris, and he laid his knife on the ground. Holding the pierced organ as though it were a shot of liquid gold, he ordered Nate to tilt back Margot's head. Through the tiny slit in the eyeball, probing snouts emerged. Writhing, dabbing, a mass of living vesicles peered around at the outside world.

"Pry open her mouth," Dr. Bendu crooned as Nate wrenched back Margot's screaming head. "Use my blade to coax her open if you need to. We can't afford to waste a single worm."

"Oh my God," Tara whispered, clasping her split lips with both hands. It hurt so bad to grimace, but she could not stop from shaking her head in denial. How could they have fallen so fast, and so far, from the decent people they'd been just a day ago?

The device wrapped in plastic, wired and strapped to Margot's chest, was now discernible as some sort of an electric timer. The countdown showed less than ten minutes remaining on the screen. She staggered back one step, and then another. When Dr. Bendu tipped the squirming organ over Margot's gaping mouth, and squeezed, Tara spun, and ran away. She couldn't bear to witness anything more in this place, this living hell whose demons corrupted every soul who passed through its rolling gates.

"Tara, wait!"

She glanced back over her shoulder. He was coming, running after her through the rain. Nate didn't even look like the same person to her. Something fundamental about him had changed. She didn't trust the thing that he'd become. After all she'd been through, she didn't know if she could ever trust another man again.

"Tara, let me explain!"

She felt his hand clamp down on her shoulder. Her scream reopened every split on her lips, and her tongue warmed with the metallic salts of blood. She fought, but he wouldn't let go. He was pulling her close. It felt as though what had happened to her back in the jungle was about to happen all over again, right here in front of everyone, and she knew that no one would stop him. No one would care. "Get away from me! Get away!"


### 

21-F

*Lost in a Roman ... wilderness of pain.*
*And all the children are insane.*
*All the children are insane.*
*Waiting for the summer rain, yeah.*

Peanut's eyes brightened to the familiar timbre of Jim Morrison's voice reverberating through the green chaos. They'd started the music. Could it be evening already? Had the most glorious day of his entire life really flown by so quickly? Tipping an offered wineskin that seemed to keep coming back around, Peanut swallowed, and slipped in the greasy mud. Cursing, he fell. Laughing, he rolled. He loved the feel of the mud, and the blood, and the rain. Lifting his hand to his forehead, he streaked his gory face with blackened fingertips. He imagined his demonic appearance, and the image that filled his mind pleased him in the darkest sort of way. At last, he'd been reborn.

*The killer awoke before dawn.*
*He put his boots on.*
*He took a face from the ancient gallery,*
*And he walked on down the hall.*

"Get up, Peanut."

"I told you, don't you call me Peanut anymore. Name's Matthew."

Red hands seized his upper arms, and hoisted him back to his feet. Their support was all he needed. He was one them, a Bad Face. Back home, he was nothing. He was just a naïve kid, a slave obeying orders, a little robot conforming to the social programming that robbed a boy of all wildness in his soul. Not here. In the Garden of Eden, he was free to be the creature that God had designed him to be. Here, he was the Lizard King, and he could do anything.

*He went into the room where his sister lived,*
*And then he ...*
*Paid a visit to his brother,*
*And then he ...*
*He walked on down the hall,*
*And he came to a door.*
*And he looked inside.*

"Open the gates!" Peanut bellowed over the tempest at the sentry perched high on Briggstown's tower. Tonight, he was going to make Tara Riley his wife. Tara Riley, the girl of his dreams since the seventh grade, she was really going to be his, and only his. No other man would be permitted to look at her. He'd keep her safe. He was her hero. If anything that walked or crawled upon this world ever threatened her, there would be Hell to pay.

The gates trundled woodenly along their tracks. Beyond, a crowd had gathered on the plaza. At its center, a battered and bleeding young woman struggled in the arms of a man he recognized, a man he knew all too well. The girl fell into the mud beneath him. She emitted a primal scream as he flipped her onto her back, and seized her by her thin shoulders, shaking her, shouting in her face.

*Father?*
*Yes, son?*
*I want to kill you.*

His vision seemed to constrict inward, darkening all peripheral detail but the man in the center, the man on top of his bride. There would never be another like him. Not one. Not another man in the village of Briggstown would ever dare touch Tara Riley once they'd all beheld the gruesome example that would be made of this one. Knuckles tightening around his spear's bloodstained shaft, Matthew leveled its lancet point at Nate's chest, and he charged.

# CHAPTER 13

23-A

"Watch the timer!" Dr. Bendu shouted, pointing at the device rigged to Margot's chest. "The ultimate moment in the War of Ages approaches, when the ancestors teach their great-grandchildren a painful lesson. We will show our descendants that we will not tolerate their misbehavior. We handed them our world on a silver platter, and they ran it into the ground. Is that our fault?"

"No!" the crowd replied.

"Should we pay for their mistakes?"

"No!"

"They lack the gall to cull their own for what they've done to the world in their time, so we'll do the culling for them! We'll show them how it's done in real time!"

Courting moons waltzed over distant reefs of vegetation, spinning between the jungle dancefloor, and a billowing canopy of clouds. The space between them visibly shrank as their gravities attracted, drawing them nearer, nearer. Lifting her veil of moon dust, the larger celestial body descended upon its mate with an almost predatory lust. They wanted this. Another year's worth of yearning for one another was released as the heavens moaned, the world trembled, and spumes of meteors seeded the earth. A burning wad plunged down into Briggstown's crater lake, birthing a great phantom of steam. Another slammed into the rim, collapsing a section of the wall. Logs toppled, tumbling over dwellings in a fiery cavalcade.

*Kill, kill, kill, kill, kill, kill …*

"I need you to listen to me!" Nate said, placing his palms on either side of Tara's bloodied face. "No one is going to hurt you."

Tara shrieked, wrenching his hands away.

"All of this you're seeing ... it had to happen this way. There was never any choice in the matter. This was the whole purpose, right here, right now!"

"You're insane! Just like all the rest of them! You've gone totally insane!"

*The is the end,*
*Beautiful friend,*
*This is the end,*
*My only friend, the end.*

"Ten ... nine ... eight ... seven ..."

As the crowd began to chant, he appeared, red as brimstone and glistening. Tara caught just the flash of his eyes, the striated patterns, and the reek of blood that glistened on his skin. Nate never even saw the devil come hurtling out of the darkness, coming straight for his soul. She watched Nate's eyes fill with mystery and wonder, as both of his lungs collapsed with a hollow pop.

"... six ... five ... four ... three ..."

Meteors streaked the skies beyond that plunging shaft. It drew back, and it reamed him, again and again and again, until the solidity of Nate's ribcage sucked wetly with every thrust. She could feel its lethal energy through his corpse, its mechanical action, as the spear plunged repeatedly through one side of him, and out the other.

" ... two ... one ..."

### 

## 28-D

The sound of the music that he'd been following came to an end with a thunderous explosion. The concussion shook the very ground beneath his feet, and made a few of the monsters trailing him rear their heads to snort in surprise. Hart took a moment to press his ear against the shackled man's chest. He nearly panicked when at first he didn't hear a beat at all, but after a moment his ear detected the weak pulse of his dying friend. Still there. For the moment, he was there.

Whimpering, he cradled his friend close to his chest, and resumed plodding in the direction of the explosion. The monsters followed him, as always, loyal if not to him, then to whatever bitter end their reptilian brains intuited he'd usher them. Hart couldn't remember why he'd been following music through the jungle, but he suspected that a better version of himself had once known, and had good reason for propelling him in that direction. There were clues, like those letters painted in blood upon his chest. These glyphs seemed important, like hints as to the man he'd once been, or perhaps the significance of this final mission in life. Words held no meaning anymore, but he still recognized the letters. Hart wondered how long it would be before he lost that ability, as well.

"HEL," they read.

Trees snapped and crashed to the forest floor, all around him. The monsters were right on his heels, champing along in their demonic parade. He could smell the sour reek of death emanating from the shuffling folds of dank feathers, and he could hear their basal groans, the clattering of dagger teeth. These were perfect killers, voracious consumers of flesh, but they treated him as their master, following him like a pack of enormous, stray dogs that had nothing better to do than to tag along behind him with the hope of being rewarded a treat.

The muted ambiance of the jungle lifted, as he clambered up a burning ridge line over a vast clearing around the shores of a hidden lake. Burning logs were strewn everywhere, amongst the remnants of some bygone civilization. Small fires flickering throughout the wide depression burned as brightly as those fleets of meteors that streaked the sky. Twisted human bodies were strewn over what resembled a small battlefield, where every combatant had simultaneously fallen along concentric valences, as though they'd all been pulverized by shockwaves originating at the epicenter of some tremendous blast.

It looked wrong to him. All of this was wrong. Hart gazed across the open graveyard. Whatever had happened here was not just a random accident. By the manner in which the bodies were scattered, Hart was certain that a crowd of spectators had gathered here to watch some sort of a great stunt. A vestigial part of his hijacked mind still remembered how stunts, no matter how well planned and controlled, could often go horribly awry.

Shaggy beasts thundered around him, and into the feast. Flesh was all they wanted. Just flesh. All that these creatures really cared about was filling their mouths with flesh, and he'd led them right to the banquet. All of this was for them. It was not for him, and it was certainly not for his dying friend. It didn't seem fair. All of his efforts, his hopes, and his dreams along that road over which he'd long struggled, in the end would amount to nothing more than a feast of flesh. For the scavengers, life was a fair and perfect circle. Not so, for the billions departed with unrealized dreams, gutted to a shell of their innocent selves by a lifetime of cruel twists. For them, the only reward was to fill the vultures' bulging guts with their pounds of unloved flesh. Life never promised to be fair, and it never was. Life was nothing more than a window with a view, better for some than for others.

Hart lowered his head to his only friend's chest, as the lesser moon was rent asunder by the lust of the larger. Emitting a lugubrious death moan, it departed life with great wedges of moon-flesh that calved its celestial bones, and glittering fountains of its essence that sprayed across the heavens. Meteors gushed from its open chest, pouring down upon the earth like blood rain. Hart closed his eyes as the moon carcass fell, darkening the world below in the shadow of a shared demise. All eyes that could see beheld the end, as necks turtled to the imminent promise for the death of one savage age, and the birth of another.

The beats within the shackled man's chest became irregular, like the footsteps of an elderly man who'd suddenly stumbled, and began to fall. Hart hugged his friend close, weeping. He wouldn't leave him. He'd never let him go. They'd depart this world together, and if it pleased their worm-infested gods, they'd walk together through gilded gates into a brighter age, and a second chance to fulfil their destiny.

The heartbeat stopped. An internal relay clicked. Every man and beast within twenty meters departed their doomed world together, in a flash of blinding green light.

## < THE END >

 SEVERED**PRESS**

# CHECK OUT OTHER GREAT DINOSAUR THRILLERS

## THE VALLEY
by **Rick Jones**

In a dystopian future, a self-contained valley in Argentina serves as the 'far arena' for those convicted of a crime. Inside the Valley: carnivorous dinosaurs generated from preserved DNA. The goal: cross the Valley to get to the Gates of Freedom. The chance of survival: no one has ever completed the journey. Convicted of crimes with little or no merit, Ben Peyton and others must battle their way across fields filled with the world's deadliest apex predators in order to reach salvation. All the while the journey is caught on cameras and broadcast to the world as a reality show, the deaths and killings real, the macabre appetite of the audience needing to be satiated as Ben Peyton leads his team to escape not only from a legal system that's more interested in entertainment than in justice, but also from the predators of the Valley.

## JURASSIC DEAD
by **Rick Chesler & David Sakmyster**

An Antarctic research team hoping to study microbial organisms in an underground lake discovers something far more amazing: perfectly preserved dinosaur corpses. After one thaws and wakes ravenously hungry, it becomes apparent that death, like life, will find a way.

Environmental activist Alex Ramirez, son of the expedition's paleontologist, came to Antarctica to defend the organisms from extinction, but soon learns that it is the human race that needs protecting.

# CHECK OUT OTHER GREAT DINOSAUR THRILLERS

www.ingramcontent.com/pod-product-compliance
Lightning Source LLC
Chambersburg PA
CBHW032001170626
46807CB00006B/2584